GORGEOUS SCARS

ASPEN GOLD SERIES 14

M.A. JEWELL

Cover & interior design by Cat & Doxie Author Services

Photo Credits:

rabbit7c_dep/Depositphotos

Kamchatka/Depsoitphotos

Subbotina/Depositphoto

Gorgeous Scars is dedicated to the people who plan extra time to bathe and dress—or even require help to do so—before they go to work or attend a child's baseball game. You inspire me. Every day.

ACKNOWLEDGMENTS

Always first on my list of people to thank is my husband, Jim. He is there for me every single day, picking up my household-duty slack and cheering me on to boot. Those heroes we write, who seem too good to be true, do exist in real life. Love him to death.

Neurosurgeon Dr. Les Hellbusch, respiratory therapist Celina Weaver, RT, and telesitter coordinator Joseph E. Hall BSN, RN, provided their expertise to help me keep the healthcare parts of this story credible. Thanks Les, Celine, & Joseph!

Thank you to fashion model and industry insider, Scott Duquette who graciously answered endless questions about modeling and shared many of his personal experiences. I am forever grateful.

My personal editor, Ann Pullum, came through again to make this book better than it was, just as she does each time. Thank you, Ann.

A big shout out to the Coordinating Faculty members of the American Hippotherapy Association, Inc., Joann Benjamin PT, HPCS (Hippotherapy Clinical Specialist), Pippa Hodge, PT, HPCS, Carol Huegel, PT, HPCS, Mary Helen Chaplin, PT, M.S., HCPS, and their Member Services Coordinator, Adria Peterson who pulled it all together.

These women came together from all over the world via video conference to educate me on hippotherapy. "It's more than a pony ride," they said. No truer words. The videos they shared astounded me.

Finally, a huge THANK YOU to my BFFs in the Friday Nite Critique group. Cheryl StJohn, Lizzie Starr, Debra Hines, Sherri Shackelford, Donna Kaye, and Bernadette Jones—these gals waded in knee-deep to make this story better and they helped me keep the Aspen Gold world together.

Thanks to these fine folks, *Gorgeous Scars* is a better story. No doubt, I screwed up a couple things along the way, but that's on me. I hope you enjoy the read.

M.A. Jewell

PROLOGUE

A fog unwrapped itself from her mind, and she sensed that she had risen from these same depths countless times before. Something held her eyelids closed, and sparks of color flitted across the dark nothingness. Finally, a piecemeal awareness intruded. Maybe she had fallen asleep.

She recalled sipping wine—a robust red. Instead of the merlot's savory notes, the taste of plastic filled her palate. Swallowing against a hard tube in her mouth, a baffling hesitation kept her from biting down. She explored the tube with her lips, and the motion tugged on painful cracks at the corners of her mouth, making her wince.

Soft footsteps approached. "Good morning, Harper. You might remember me, I'm Angela." The woman's low-toned voice was at once soothing—and her name both familiar and new. "I'm your nurse again, today. We're getting to know each other pretty well."

After the disconcerting din, Angela's lilting chuckle and casual manner took the edge off Harper's anxiety. She wished she could see her to put a face with the voice. Belatedly, she processed the nurse's comment. My name is

Harper. *Harper Inez.* Recapturing a sliver of herself gave her a tiny sense of relief.

Beeps and whooshes of air kept individual tempos in the unseen space, echoing as though the room needed carpeting. Harper grappled for images to match the soundtrack, and a TV medical series came to mind.

A familiar click near her head signaled a pending surge of air. While she pondered how she could possibly know this, the anticipated breath filled her chest. Finally giving in to temptation, she bit down hard, flattening the malleable tube between her teeth. In answer, a discordant chirp joined the symphony.

Nearby, music with the energetic lyrics of *let's go broncos* broke out and then abruptly cut off. "Hi, Dr. Hellbusch." Angela sounded cheerful. "Yes, I got the message and stopped the Propofol … She's perking up, so come on down. Oh, by the way, we moved her to room four last night … See you in a few."

With another mechanical breath, a distracting niggle in Harper's windpipe escalated to a strangling panic. She gagged from deep in her gut, her abs cramping as though she worked a ten-minute plank. A series of excited new chirps echoed in the room.

When she reached for whatever clogged her throat, soft cloth circling her wrists trapped her hands at her sides. Locked in a living nightmare and unable to yell for help, she tugged weakly at her restraints.

"Harper, I'm sorry, sweetie. Your sedation's just wearing off, and you still have that nasty breathing tube." With her unruffled manner, a choking patient might be Angela's routine. "I'm right here, and your oxygen levels are good, I promise."

Her reassurances did nothing to tamp down Harper's panic. The nurse pressed her shoulder back into the mattress with a firm, gentle hand. Then something cool and slender brushed against Harper's arm, stealing her flighty attention. Angela kept her hand steadfastly in place. Within seconds, the suffocating sensation disappeared, and in the very same instant, she relaxed her hold.

"That's better," she murmured, almost to herself. "We're letting you wake up for Dr. Hellbusch's visit. If he thinks the brain swelling is down, we might take you off the ventilator."

Mention of a swollen brain grabbed Harper's unruly focus, and she turned her head toward the nurse.

"You had some bad luck." Angela paused, tugging a sheet back into place. "Someone attacked you, and you're in the New York City General ICU. But don't worry, hun, you're doing great. I know this is a repeat, but I doubt you remember yesterday's chat."

Footsteps too heavy to be Angela's underscored the nurse's voice.

"Oh and here's Ensign," she said. The name rang familiar in a good way, but Harper could not recall anything about him.

"Good morning, Angela." Amid the frightful confusion, the recognizable baritone drew her like a beacon in a stormy night. *Ensign.*

"Excellent timing, Mr. Wells. Harper's what we call *arousable*—really groggy—but she's awake enough to be aware of your visit," Angela said. "And bonus, Dr. Hellbusch is on his way, too."

Ensign Wells—Harper's fiancé.

"Hi there, sweet thing. Can you hear me?" he asked. Long slender fingers felt at home in Harper's hand, and she squeezed back.

"Mr. Wells, pleasant topics are good for Harper. She won't remember anything, but your voice will ground her in the moment."

"I understand," he replied.

A gloved hand rested on Harper's forehead. "Let's get this tape off of your lovely peepers, and then we need to do something about those dry lips."

Angela gingerly removed sticky strips from Harper's brow and cheeks and then plucked tiny pads from her eyelids. With a tsk-tsk, the nurse smoothed a salve over her chapped lips—petroleum jelly, from the scent. The small comfort made Harper groan in relief, but no sound emerged —only a hiss of air through the tube.

"Even though you'll be tempted, Mr. Wells, please don't untie her restraints. Unplanned extubations make me look bad," Angela warned.

"Okay. Glad you said something." He chuckled. "Have they mentioned when she might be able to speak with the detectives?"

"Not to me, but we'll know more after the doctor stops in." While Angela chatted, she wiped Harper's face with a warm damp cloth. "That's better. The protective eye oint-ment will clear in a few minutes. If you open your eyes, you can get a look at your man."

Harper blinked against the goo clouding her vision. Tall and blond, Ensign gazed down at her with killer blue eyes. She would marry him in an April wedding. Maybe a giddy bride-to-be feeling would hit her later. Next to him, a plastic bag of clear fluid hung from an IV pole—no three IV poles. Against her will, her lids drooped, shuttering the world.

"Everyone misses you. Your shark agent calls every other day." His laugh sounded forced. "I told her not to worry. The Argentine Empress of the runway is as beautiful as ever. When your hair grows back, it will hide any scars from the bullet wounds."

Brain swelling—bullet wounds. She had been shot. However, as with the nurse's name, this breaking news had an eerie *déjà vu* quality. A distant echo of a gunshot rang in her ears. The elusive memory lacked substance, floating away as crepe paper caught in a breeze.

Ensign caressed her face, and his fingers grazed what had to be stubble on her scalp. They had shaved her trademark long dark locks—right before her wedding. Being bald should fill her with rage or grief, but an odd distance blunted the wound—as though another woman had lost her hair.

"I'm sorry, Harper." Ensign lifted her hand and pressed a kiss to her fingers. "You'll get well, and we'll get married as soon as you're ready."

He probably wanted to postpone the wedding until her hair grew back. When she could speak, she would remind him that she knew the best hair gurus in the fashion industry.

"Look at me, sweet thing," he said.

Unaware she had drifted off again, Harper opened her eyes, unable to truly focus on him.

His brows shot up. "Wow, you really are awake. That's such a relief after watching you sleep for nearly two weeks."

With a sluggish mental effort, she counted days. They had missed their wedding. She accepted this realization with a curious indifference. Maybe the drugs had put her emotions to sleep right along with her body.

Ensign leaned down, and his lips brushed the shell of her ear. "Do you remember what happened?"

Waiting for her to respond, the worry filling his gaze intensified. He speared his fingers through his hair. She tried to shake her head.

"I wish I'd caught the bastard, but I had to get you help. You don't remember a short guy with a ski mask coming in the balcony door?"

Fatigue weighed her down, and she gave the smallest shake of her head. She would get the story later.

Heavy footsteps approached the bed. "Good morning, Miss Inez. I'm Les Hellbusch—your neurosurgeon. Can you open your eyes?"

Harper complied and tried to bring the tall man into focus. Even half-asleep, her internal fashion censor approved of how the black suit set off his silver hair. A nurse in scrubs stood next to him. Angela—maybe.

Ensign rose and the two men exchanged a casual hand-shake. "Hi, Les. Glad I caught you during your rounds."

"Yes, convenient." Almost dismissive, Dr. Hellbusch tapped his phone and studied the display. "Angie, I'll be out of the OR around three. Could we get Harper's mother and sister on the phone say—around three-thirty?"

The nurse nodded and moved to a small counter to jot a note. "They were here earlier. I'll give them a call."

Harper let her eyes close while they talked over her.

With quick movements, the doctor untied the wrist restraint nearest him, and an instant later, Ensign released her other hand. "Les, the nurse said you might stop the medically induced coma today."

"Maybe. We'll see. I'd like to let her wake up. But not until she's ready." Hellbusch's voice filled the room. "Harper, look at me again, please."

With a monumental effort, she raised her eyelids, and a light flashed in one eye and then the other. He asked her to squeeze his hands and to perform a few other simple tasks. Uncertain she had actually followed his directions, his intense scrutiny troubled her. She pinched her brows together.

"You look so worried." His smile softened his angular features. "Don't be. Your facial muscles have normal func-tion. Your left arm and leg are a little weak, but the deficit is minimal. Overall, better than expected."

She was *deficient*? Wondering why her body parts were

lacking, and how that could be better than expected, she sought out Ensign for answers.

He took her hand. "Hear that, Harper? You're going to be fine."

With a brief scowl at him, Dr. Hellbusch gave a heavy sigh. "It's too soon for firm predictions." He returned his focus to her. "However, I believe you'll function independently. We'll talk more about rehab—"

"Can she stay awake today?" Ensign interrupted, sounding almost frantic. "The detectives want to speak with her."

Naturally, he wanted to track down her attacker, and his worry struck her as sweet. While she wondered what *independent function* meant, her eyes closed again.

"As I said before, we want the brain to rest, so the NYPD will have to wait." The surgeon sounded mildly irritated. "We've kept her asleep so the neural cells can use their energy to heal. There're no do-overs."

"Understood," Ensign replied. On his best days, he had an impatient streak. However, even after the mild rebuke, he had stayed surprisingly pleasant—as though he needed something.

"My concern is that during the few minutes she's been conscious, the pressure inside her head has increased," Dr. Hellbusch said. "Enough that we need to restart the Propofol —the sedation."

"Okay, I'll let them know," Ensign replied.

"We'll check her again in a couple days."

Harper understood what they said, but with a distinct lack of interest. She was content for others to make any decisions.

Ensign squeezed her hand. "We won't take any chances with your mind."

What if she didn't wake up? Beeps chirped fast above her

head, likely synced to her pounding heart. The brief worry flitted away. The next time they woke her, she might remember more. For now, oblivion didn't sound too bad. Another wave of unnatural fatigue crested over her body.

"Okay. That's what we'll do." Hellbusch's voice sounded hollow and a million miles away. "Angela, we'll wake her up again on Wednesday—keep talking to her."

Angela chuckled. "Talking is my best thing, you know that."

"Text if you need anything," he said.

Heavy footsteps faded from the room.

"Mr. Wells, why don't you tell your girl goodnight? When I restart the drip, she'll drift off pretty fast."

Ensign pressed his lips to Harper's forehead. "I'll be right here when you wake up. Next time, it will be for good, to come home."

Home sounded wonderful—maybe. At least it should. A sense of foreboding blossomed into an irrational fear. Her reaction seemed unusual, but she supposed going back into a coma would give anyone the creeps.

Angela pulled an IV pole closer and tapped a keypad on an attached blue box, eliciting more beeps. She squeezed Harper's shoulder. "I think two days will be forever for your fiancé, but for you, it will seem like a minute."

Against her will, Harper's head listed to the side, and her eyelids lowered. The sounds in the room grew louder with an echoing quality, and the fog rolled back in.

Ensign clasped her hand. "I'll stay for a while."

Angela placed ointment in her eyes, one after the other, giving Harper a winking view of the nurse before she taped soft pads over both.

"There we go—peepers all nice and safe." While she spoke, the nurse tucked a pillow behind Harper's back, and ignored aches eased into comfort. "Sir, every time you visit talk to Harper as much as you can, even if you say the same thing over and over."

"I will." Hearing Ensign's voice while she drifted off reassured Harper like nothing else could.

"When you say something, watch her heart rate change on the monitor. I'll be back in a few to check on her." Angela's soft-soled footsteps receded from the ICU suite.

Ensign released Harper's hand, leaving her skin cool without his touch. He paced the room, and she marveled how she could even recognize his footsteps. A moment later, familiar tones sounded near the head of the bed. She must have drifted off. Now, someone adjusted the ventilator.

Odd that she could recognize these beeps amid all the others. Possibly, like now, she'd had other moments of awareness while too sluggish to move. Rollers on the sliding glass door sounded, and the room fell silent—save for the mechanical orchestra that had become her world.

After a moment, she realized Ensign had left, too, and he had not said goodbye. Or maybe he had, and she had already forgotten. Regardless, a sense of abandonment set in, and a miserable tear leaked from the corner of her eye. With her morose frame of mind, she welcomed the blankness of the coma and wondered when the medication would take her away.

A lengthy pause followed the ventilator's click, and the machine pushed in a breath. Pressure built in her chest that had nothing to do with sadness. She tried to force an exhale, but her muscles lacked the needed strength, and the incoming air kept coming. Her ribs resisted the onslaught, and the sharp pain increased, making her think they would crack. Her panic soared.

An unfamiliar tone blared from the ventilator, and its sharp pitch lent it more urgency. An instant later, frantic chimes sounded outside her room.

"I need help in twelve," a woman hollered.

"Jody, with me—Terry, grab the crash cart so we have it." The terse staff voices sounded over pounding footsteps outside the room, and heavy rolling wheels joined the fray.

"Attention-attention …" A calm, feminine voice came over the intercom. "Rapid response—ICU room twelve." The operator repeated her life-saving announcement in the same retail-recording tone.

Thoughts of her mother and sister ran through Harper's mind, and she thanked God the nurses were coming.

As some of the air left her body, unbelievably, the ventilator clicked again. The pressure built anew, and Harper imagined her lungs as two balloons stretched to translucent. The tension mounted further in her chest, and she wondered if a priest had already given her the last rites.

The clatter beyond her suite faded into the distance. The nurses were not running toward Harper, they were running *away*.

CHAPTER ONE

"Folks, up next is this year's top winning tie-down roper—Landon Macek. Boy-howdy, does he have a nice lead, too. Let's give this cowboy a Greeley Stampede welcome."

In the early evening shadow of the arena grandstand, Landon gripped his piggin' string between his teeth and cued Rocket into the starting box. He ignored the crowd noise and the hometown announcer Jake, who manned the mic every Fourth of July rodeo. Landon tugged the rope tied to his saddle horn again.

"The bovine babies are winning this go-round. It'd sure be nice if Macek and his superhorse could get a loop on one."

The crowd applauded. Except for two adolescent girls standing behind the right front rail, holding an animal rights sign between them. The high-school-aged kids held up their poster and booed.

Rocket wouldn't let a little flapping paper mess with his head, but not all horses had his good sense. Security should pack them out of the arena before someone got hurt.

After turning his mount within the three-sided box,

Landon backed into position. He eyed the orange flag hanging from the barrier string that crossed the opening to the arena. Breaking that vertical plane before the calf got its head start would ruin his run with a ten-second penalty.

Rocket's ears pricked forward like a dog on point, and he snugged his tensed rump into the back corner of the starting box. A black calf shifted inside a metal chute to their left. Landon dipped his chin, signaling the gateman. The chute door banged open, and the little dogie blasted out at lightning speed.

Rocket gathered his hindquarters under him, and at Landon's nudge, he exploded into the arena. The savvy horse ignored the flailing poster to their right, but the startled baby cow hooked a sharp left. Rocket gamely pivoted after the calf, slipping in the loose arena dirt. Swinging his loop overhead, Landon planted his weight into his outside stirrup, and as his mount righted himself, he tossed his rope, easily snaring the calf.

In perfect sync, Rocket slid to a stop, and Landon swung to the ground before the horse came to a halt. He sprinted alongside the rope and flanked the roughly two-hundred-pound calf to the ground. The stunned dogie didn't fight as many did. Landon pulled his piggin' string from his teeth, gathered the calf's legs—wrap, wrap, hooey knot—and threw his arms out to his sides, signaling the clock to stop.

Before satisfaction over the run could set in, the rope tied to his saddle dropped slack to the arena floor, wrenching Landon's attention. Belatedly, Rocket took an odd hop backwards, tugging it tight. The horse set his right front hoof on the ground, immediately lifting it again. The go-round forgotten, Landon strode to the big chestnut, mindful not to spook him.

Unflappable Rocket kept the calf in his sights, waiting for his rider to remount. Even injured, the horse stayed on task.

An animal like him came along once in a career—if a guy was real lucky. Landon loved him like no other horse he'd ever owned.

With a comforting hand on the gelding's shoulder, he waved for a chute helper to release his calf, disqualifying their ride. He wouldn't get aboard his injured partner to make the run count.

While Landon removed a protective boot from the horse's right front leg, the arena fell silent. He fingered a puffy spot on the back of the leg about an inch below the knee. The gelding flinched, snatching his hoof from the ground.

The bulge expanded while Landon stood by, helplessly. He removed his Stetson to wipe his brow and dropped his head. This was bad.

The PA system shrieked, and Jake cleared his throat into the mic. "Folks, for the safety of all of our stock, as well as our competitors, please refrain from waving objects during the events." Unfortunately, his poignant announcement came too late for Rocket. "I see our on-site veterinarian has left her seat. Some of you might know this horse's story, but while we have a moment …"

Landon shot a glare at the girls, but security had already escorted them and their sign up the stairs to the exit. He wanted to rage at the pair, but in truth, he was angry with himself. He could have said something to a rodeo official before his run—or even withdrawn from the event.

"… good roping horses can run into tens of thousands of dollars—even over a hundred. This here cowboy needed a cheap horse that he could make into a champion…" Jake droned on, killing time while Landon examined Rocket's leg again. The skin stretched tight over the growing lump, making the short hairs stand up at an angle.

The vet couldn't get there soon enough. Landon loosened

the horse's cinch, signaling to the gelding that his work for the day was done. No stretchers for injured horses. Landon coiled his lariat and then led his wounded teammate at a snail's pace toward the arena gate.

"… that chestnut pony out there earned Landon over two-hundred thousand dollars so far this year. You do the math. I reckon over half of that is limping out of the arena. Give ol' Rocket a hand and wish him a speedy recovery."

Without looking back, Landon acknowledged the crowd's condolences with a wave of his hat. Rocket would recover—and have a home for life, no matter what. As they entered the alley behind the arena, the gelding's head bobbed each time he put weight on his injured leg. The possibility of retiring his horse tightened Landon's throat. Without Rocket, the world championship disappeared. Dreams died hard.

There was still a chance he was wrong. He wasn't a veterinarian. Maybe the horse had only banged a hind hoof into his cannon bone. That's why ropers used sport boots in the first place. Maybe the lump was simply a bad, swelled-up bruise. Holding fast to the sliver of hope that he could still make the finals in Vegas, he swallowed his self-pity.

A pint-sized woman in jeans and a girlie cowboy hat rounded the stock pens, and at sight of him, she strode forward to give him a much-needed hug. "I'm so sorry, Landon." His good buddy's wife, veterinarian Jessica Lambert, stepped back and scanned a few curious chute helpers keeping their distance. "I'll get my truck and meet you at Rocket's stall."

"Glad you're here, Doc." He used her formal title, more or less, grateful fate had made her tonight's rodeo veterinarian. Since her husband team-roped, she often signed up for a few extra bucks. "Barn C."

"Yeah, I saw your rig. I won't be long." She turned and headed down the aisle with a crisp, no-nonsense stride.

Landon suspected that the woman didn't weigh a full hundred pounds, yet she'd surprised many with how well she handled the cattle and horses, as well as the cantankerous bulls.

Twilight gave the quiet backyard grounds a lonely feeling, and he took an easy pace between the zipped-up food tents and professional gear booths. Gauging by the uneven cadence of Rocket's gait, the horse was plenty lame. Tiny muscles over his brown eyes tensed, and he side-eyed the shadows along their path. Rocket's leg pained him.

"Sorry, buddy. I'd have it be me, if I could," Landon said, a sense of helplessness eating at him.

As they approached the barn, discordant braying greeted them. Rocket responded with a high-pitched whinny, sounding stressed. Tonight, Landon was especially glad he'd indulged the horse's need for Buck. The little burro would calm the injured horse in the unfamiliar box stall.

Landon paused at his trailer and stripped Rocket down to a halter before leading him into the stable. Buck's vocals increased until the stall door opened and the inseparable pasture pals could rub noses. The big gelding's chest rumbled with a murmured nicker. Happy to see his friend, the burro swished his tail up and down or sideways with each quiet squeak from his throat.

Landon rubbed one long velvety ear and kissed it. Rocket wasn't the only one in need of a friend.

"Landon?" Jess's voice carried down the corridor between the stalls.

Anxious about his horse's injury, Landon stepped out into the concrete alley and waved. "Down here."

The little bit of woman had an equipment bag slung over one shoulder and toted a white five-gallon bucket that made her tilt to the side. He rushed to take the heavy pail, noting the crushed ice inside. "I got this. Thanks for coming."

She set her duffle on the edge of the concrete aisle before treading into the stall's sawdust bedding. The quarter horse ignored her, tugging alfalfa from a metal hayrack on the wall while the more inquisitive Buck nuzzled her pockets. He was accustomed to treats from strangers.

Scratching both of his ears, she smiled. "*You're* the little guy I hear so much about. This is a serious visit, but I'll bring something special tomorrow."

Though eager for the vet's diagnosis, Landon had to observe some social pleasantries. "This is Rocket's roomie, Buck."

The vet gave him a wry smile. "Colt says the other calf ropers plot to burro-nap him. You know, to throw Rocket off his game."

Her husband had told Landon the same. With his horse on the injured reserve list, Landon's laugh was bittersweet. "Yeah, they'd threatened a couple times. Lookin' like they don't need to bother."

"At least for now." Jess gestured to the munching horse. "I need to see him move."

Pulling the animal from his dinner, Landon clipped a lead rope to his halter. Rocket's hooves clopped along the cement as Landon led him past a few stalls and returned to stop in front of her. She ran her fingers down both of the horse's forelegs before focusing on the injury. "All because of a couple ding-dong teenagers."

Furious all over again, Landon puffed a breath through pursed lips. "Yep. I've got a few things to say to those girls, but they're too young to hear them."

During the exam, Buck poked his nose out over the top board of the stall, making quiet braying noises. Landon marveled at how animals sensed anxiety. He swore that the little donkey had told Rocket it would be okay.

Jess picked up the horse's right front hoof, bending his

knee, and then pressed fingers over his lower leg again. The horse flinched and tugged against her hold.

Releasing him with a pat on his shoulder, her grim expression put a rock in the pit of Landon's stomach.

"He's bowed a tendon—at least I'm pretty sure. We need an ultrasound to know exactly what we're dealing with," Jess told him with all kinds of sympathy in her tone.

Not a bruise. At sight of the swollen lump, Landon had feared as much, but the official diagnosis didn't go down any easier. Even without a break in the skin, he had almost convinced himself that Rocket had clipped his leg when he'd stumbled.

Returning Rocket to the box stall, he swallowed, trying to find his voice. "What's next?"

She followed him in, dropping her bag in the corner, and waved at the bucket next to it. "Tonight—ice. Then at least two weeks of *strict* stall rest."

Absorbing the news, Landon tangled his fingers into his horse's coarse mane, working hard to keep his composure. "I've heard they can recover pretty good from bowed tendons. How long?"

Pulling an icepack leg wrap from her duffle, she hesitated. "Not in time for this year. Six to nine months, maybe? I'm sorry."

The news got better and better. He nodded.

Jess scooped ice into pockets of the wrap and then applied it to Rocket's injured leg with Velcro tabs. "Do you have another mount?"

Landon snorted. "Back home in California—not much help, even if he was here. Bandit's a solid horse, but he's not athletic enough for the big leagues." He draped an arm over Rocket's withers. "This boy gave me my shot. He's the key."

"I still can't believe you claimed him at the racetrack."

"Yeah." Chuckling, Landon recalled his late nights with

his laptop. "I bet I watched over a hundred races to find him, too."

"What caught your eye?"

"Price—I needed cheap. Rocket had never even taken the show spot in a race. He stunk up the track."

The vet tried to smother her guffaw with a hand. "Oh, that's terrible."

Recalling videos of Rocket, he warmed to his subject. "Yeah, it was. But no one beat him out of the gate. He'd blast off, and after four or five strides, he'd slow down and find a comfy spot near the back of the pack."

She nodded. "You only need a few strides to catch a calf."

"That's right. But I think he needed a better reason to run. Plus, he's got a little working cow horse on his daddy's side. After he figured out we were catching calves, when I missed one, he'd get mad and shake his head to let me know."

"Colt says the best roping horses are like that." She placed a hand on Landon's forearm. "He can be that horse again. Let me make some calls in the morning. *Someone* in Greeley has an ultrasound."

"Okay. You mentioned stall rest. What about trailering him to California?"

As though he'd asked to jump the horse off a cliff, Jess shook her head, swinging her ponytail. "No way." She tapped a finger on her lips. "It's pricey, but you could fly him home."

"Oh, man. That'd be thousands. Plus, I don't think we could catch a flight tomorrow." Landon shook his head. "I've got to have him out of the barn before noon. What about a few hours to Spencer? I planned to stop at a friend's for a couple days before Cheyenne."

"Maybe. Let's see what the ultrasound shows before you make any plans."

Landon's mind raced, worrying about Rocket and trying to think of a way to get back on the circuit. He had a big lead

on the second place roper, Bart Jenkins. A couple missed
rodeos wouldn't knock him out of the running.

❦

The next morning, Landon stirred cream into his coffee,
seated at a booth in a familiar greasy spoon. The food was
good, if not healthy, and a short walk to a cheap hotel near
the rodeo grounds kept the place in business. Red-padded
chrome chairs and Formica tables gave the cafe a fifties feel.
Other contestants, mostly men and a couple gals made up the
dozen or so customers.

"The number two, please. Over-easy. Bacon," he said and
handed his menu to a gum-chewing waitress. The slight
motion made his booth creak. Dolly, according to her
nametag, appeared a few years past his twenty-nine.

She tucked the laminated sheet under her arm. "We love
when the Stampede comes to town." She perused the few
cowboys scattered in the dining area before focusing on him,
a smile curving her lips. "Nothing like a man in a Stetson."

Other than polite nods, Landon hadn't engaged anyone—
he was still in a mood over Rocket and their lost championship. No buckle-bunny would draw his attention. He
offered a manufactured smile. "A few of them are single."

The woman's flirtatious grin evaporated. "I'll get your
order in."

She marched off with her ponytail swaying. He hadn't
lied outright, he'd only misled her into thinking he was
hitched. One-night-stands were not his thing, but she'd find
someone interested.

Jenkins across the way had a few women strung along the
circuit and would likely be glad to add another. As though
the other calf roper felt Landon's eyes on him, he lifted his
chin in greeting. Landon nodded in return.

While he waited for breakfast, he snatched an abandoned newspaper from the table next to him. Wanting to find out who'd won last night, he thumbed for the sports section, and a photo of Harper Inez above the fold caught his eye. The Argentine Empress was the hottest thing in print. Maybe they'd made an arrest in her home invasion shooting.

The *Fiancé's Story Questioned* title hinted at the same speculation they'd put out for weeks. Not much substance in the article—lots of "no comments on an active investigation" peppered the text. Inez's publicist confirmed the couple had separated—unrelated to the shooting, of course. However, the fiancé Ensign Wells had retained a criminal attorney, and that said something. Who could look into those gorgeous obsidian eyes and pull a trigger?

According to the paper, detectives had interviewed her shortly before she left the hospital a few weeks prior. Landon had followed her career for several years now, and the news she'd been discharged relieved him. It was funny how a person could care about a celebrity—a complete stranger.

Earlier gossip rags—his guilty pleasure—had reported that she wanted to branch out into acting. He'd hoped to see her on the big screen one day. Now, they speculated about possible enemies, lengthy rehab, and if she'd ever work again.

He thought Rocket's injury was a bad break. At least no one had tried to kill him. The biggest crime he had to worry about was a burro-napping. Maybe he should quit sulking over his lost shot at the finals.

Two pairs of brown cowboy boots appeared in Landon's peripheral vision. He'd been so engrossed in the article; he hadn't heard the men approach.

His good friend and team-roper Colt Lambert touched the rim of his brown leather hat. "Mornin'."

He sipped from a large to-go coffee. Standing next to Colt, the taller, gregarious redhead Bart Jenkins extended a hand. "You had me beat last night, Macek. I'm sure sorry about Rocket. Winning that way felt pretty lame."

Laying the paper down, Landon rose and shook hands with both men. "Thanks. I appreciate it."

He retook his seat, waving an invitation for them to join him.

"I've got to get on the road, but thanks." Jenkins shifted his weight, clearly uncomfortable about something. "Look, Macek, winnin' won't mean much without you in the lineup. You're welcome to use my extra mare at Laramie. She's no Rocket, but she's respectable."

With a glance at Jenkins, Colt raised a brow.

Surprised to his bones by his number-one competitor, Landon tried to gauge Jenkins's sincerity. Regardless, he did not intend to take help from his main rival. "She's a good girl. I've seen her work. That's mighty generous, Bart. To be honest, I have to take care of my horse before I worry about the next rodeo. I'm going to meet Doc Jess after breakfast."

Jenkins nodded. "Just say the word." As though searching for a new focus, he tapped a finger on Harper Inez's image. "What idiot would shoot a prime bit o' filly like that? What a dirt bag."

Landon had to agree. Her spread in the *Sports Illustrated* swimsuit edition had been a knockout. However, her bottomless dark eyes had captured his attention long before her lithe figure. "I haven't read the whole thing, but it didn't sound like they've got much on him."

Jenkins snorted. "It's always the husband or boyfriend, you know that."

Breakfast arrived, and while an ambitious Dolly chatted up Jenkins, she nearly overfilled Landon's chipped mug.

Unusually quiet during the encounter, jabber-mouth Colt sent Landon a furtive grin. "Well, I'm headed out. Landon, Jess said Rocket's her first stop this morning. I hope to see you in Laramie. Bart, you too—if'n you can tear yourself away."

Jenkins gave Colt a nod. "I'll be right behind you." Beaming at Dolly, he held out his phone. "Darlin', before I leave, would you tap that little number of yours right here?"

That's how it's done. Jenkin's gaze flitted to her nametag before he saved the contact. Landon pressed his lips together against a laugh. The other roper strode out, and Dolly seemed to recall she had an order up. Landon's toast was cold, but the other parts of the meal had survived the wait.

The rest of the Inez article didn't have any new information and he flipped to the sports section. The locals always made sure to give the rodeo good press. He and Rocket got a heartbreak mention in the corner with a shot of them leaving the arena.

Colt slid into the opposite booth, surprising him. "Hey, Landon."

"Thought you left. What's up?"

Setting his hat on the bench next to him, he apparently planned to stay for a few minutes. He speared fingers through his wavy brown hair. "I didn't want to say anything in front of Bart, but do you remember ol' Davey Bingham?"

"Sure. Tie-down champ four, no five, years back? He's retired, right?"

"Yeah, for a while now." One corner of Colt's mouth lifted, and he leaned in as though sharing national secrets. "A few weeks ago, he gave a ropin' clinic in Sioux Falls, and I helped with the team ropers. Anyway, he asked me to keep an eye out for a buyer for his horse, Opie."

Landon remembered the plain-Jane sorrel gelding. His heart rate sped up before his brain kicked in. He snorted. "And you think I can afford a ready-made world-champion roping horse?"

"At least you know Opie can get the job done." Colt's

grin signaled an incoming jibe. "You could always take Blowhard Bart up on his offer—use *his* mare to limp in to Vegas."

"Did I miss the pig flying overhead?" Landon deadpanned.

His friend barked a laugh and then rested his elbows on the table, growing serious. "Truth is, you know guys on the circuit help each other. Any one of us could have a lame horse tomorrow. Plus, I think Jenkins was dead serious. Just surprised the hell out of me."

"Yeah, me, too. But I can't help it—winning with a handout from that guy takes the shine right off the trophy buckle."

Colt frowned. "You ever heard the sayin' *pride goeth before a fall?*"

Landon wanted to win with the horse he'd trained—Rocket. That way, no one could say someone gave him the championship, or that he had bought his way into it with someone else's horse. A pure win.

On the other hand, Landon had a clear lead. No one walked away from a world championship. "I'll think about it. Did he say how much he wanted for him?"

"He wouldn't tell me, so don't expect a bargain. At least start out trying to buy the horse. He's twelve now, and I reckon he's been eating grass for a few years." Colt shrugged. "But I was thinkin', maybe you could work a lease. Beings you're on track to win the world and all, Bingham might go for somethin' short term. People do stuff like that all the time."

Others did. Landon had never warmed to the idea of being responsible for someone else's animal—especially a high-dollar one. What happened if Opie got sick or hurt? *Like a bowed tendon.*

Still, he admitted the notion had possibilities. "I could

offer to tune the horse up and get him out in front of folks. That way, a real buyer could fall in love with him."

A toothy grin split Colt's face. "Now, your grit's showin'. Keep on thinking that a-way. You'll get yourself a big-ass ol' gold buckle for Christmas."

If he brokered a horse sale, he could land a fat commission, but a lease wouldn't earn him a dime. By mentioning the lease deal, he might've given up around ten thousand dollars. Friends like that were hard to come by.

Landon reached out with a fist bump. "Thanks buddy. I appreciate the lead."

This could work. He only needed a temporary mount through December. Besides getting him to the finals, having a horse in the fall would give him a good start on the new regular season beginning in October. If he did well at the National Finals Rodeo in Vegas, he might even buy Opie. A text pinged Landon's cell.

Colt pointed his phone at the sound. "That's Bingham's contact info. Let me know how it goes."

After draining his coffee, Landon tossed enough cash on the table to pay for breakfast and maybe buy Dolly's forgiveness for his lack of interest. They strode out to the tiny parking lot, and the morning sun glinted off the hood of Landon's Ram 3500. The mountain air was still cool but before long, the July heat would take the day. The two men parted ways, and Landon drove to the rodeo grounds to meet Colt's wife.

Rigs leaving the lot for the next stop on the circuit gave him a pang. He should be loaded and gone right along with them.

Jess was waiting for him in Rocket's stall, feeding carrots to Buck. "Good morning."

"Back at you. You're early."

She joined him in the ally and latched the stall door

behind her. "The leg's a little more swollen. Rocket's icing now. I spoke with a Greeley vet a few minutes ago—Halverson. He can do an ultrasound, but he doesn't have room for an overnight patient. He recommended a new place a few hours from here."

A greenhorn vet wouldn't do, not for Rocket. Landon frowned. "I—"

Jess shoved a ripped scrap of paper at him and smiled, seeming to guess his concern. "He said the place is new, but the guy is an experienced equine specialist—and that's what you need. If you're going with him, I'll make the referral."

"Okay… what about the ultrasound?" Landon hadn't slept a wink worrying about his horse. With the increased swelling, maybe Rocket had hurt his leg worse than Jess thought.

"Halverson was willing. But since you have to travel anyway, he recommended that the specialist do the study—then the images will give him the current status of the injury."

Landon released an uneasy breath. "In other words, in case Rocket's leg gets worse during the ride."

"Yep. There's no way to sugar coat it." She checked her phone and then quickly handed him a few bandage rolls from her duffle. "I'm sorry, but one of the broncs got spooked and cut himself when they were loading. Use those instead of a shipping boot on that leg. Standard wrap."

They said a quick goodbye, and she left Landon alone in the aisle with two curious equine noses poking out through the rails. He dumped oats in their feed bins, making his critters very happy. With ten minutes to kill before removing the icepack, Landon dialed his friend, Ryder Barlow.

A couple years back, the Hollywood master of horse had hired Landon as a consultant for a cattle-drive scene. They'd hit it off pretty good and kept in touch even after the horse trainer had returned home to Spencer, Colorado.

The call connected. "Hi, Landon. You getting close?"

The sound of a familiar voice made Landon smile. "Not yet. I'm leaving Greeley in about thirty. I ran into some bad luck yesterday ..."

After he'd updated his friend, proud of his matter-of-fact tone, Landon sighed. "Before I call this guy ..." He unfolded the scrap of paper. Same name as the town—an odd coincidence. "Jackson Spencer, do you know anything about him?"

Ryder chuckled with a sudden lack of sympathy, confusing Landon. "Yeah, I do. He's my cousin—and my business partner. Damn good vet, too."

Relieved by the recommendation, Landon put the phone on speaker to remove Rocket's ice pack. "Wait—partner? You *own* the vet hospital?"

"You don't have that much time, but relax." He could hear the smile in Ryder's voice. "I've got your back. Whatever you need, buddy. We'll figure this out. Step one—get here."

"Thanks, man. I owe you."

Having one decision made gave Landon a mental boost. After tethering Rocket outside to dry off in the warm sun, Landon loaded his equipment into the tack compartment of his gooseneck horse trailer. The sun was rising and so was the temperature. He opened two of his truck's four doors and took a seat before calling the vet. Eleven a.m. He'd make the exit deadline.

"Jackson here."

Expecting a receptionist or answering service, Landon double-checked the number. "Uh, yeah, Doctor Spencer?"

"Set it right there ... Yes, please ... Thanks." The man on the line cleared his throat. "That's me. Jackson Spencer. Sorry about that, a delivery just arrived. How can I help you?"

Landon introduced himself.

"Oh, you're Doctor Lambert's referral. It sounds like Rocket's injury is more heartbreaking than most. I'm sorry."

"That's rodeo. But thanks. Do you think you can help him?"

"Yes, and we'll do everything we can to get him back to his previous level of function." The vet paused, and the *no guarantees* part of his statement sunk in. "Our place is very new. In fact, we're still adding hardware to the stalls, but we have any equipment he'll need—underwater treadmill for one. Tell me exactly what happened."

Doctor Spencer listened mostly in silence, interjecting a question here and there for details.

Landon got the sense he truly cared about Rocket's future. "Besides stall rest, what happens after the ultrasound?"

"We won't know for certain until we get the images, but from the level of swelling you describe, he could need surgery to remove excess fluid from the injury site."

Jess hadn't mentioned surgery. The only thing he knew about horses and anesthesia was to avoid it at all costs. Horses didn't tolerate going to sleep like other animals. Landon had trouble finding his voice. "Uh… I'd rather not."

"I understand. Surgical intervention is always a last resort. We'll table that until we know more." Jackson quickly changed the subject, offering his address for GPS navigation. "I submitted our location a couple weeks ago, so it should be in their system."

Still distracted by the possibility of surgery, Landon numbly entered the info into his phone. "Got it."

Things had gone from bad to worse. The perceptive vet had even picked up on his apprehension—like a damned burro. Rocket was a horse, not Landon's kid. He needed to get a grip.

"Drive real slow, especially on the mountain switchbacks," Jackson said. "Call me when you're a few miles out, and I'll meet you here."

"Will do. Thanks, doc." Landon disconnected and rested back against the seat. A sawdust scented breeze coursed through the cab. Two rigs drove past and the drivers waved. *Surgery.*

CHAPTER TWO

A man's face floated on a disturbed oily pool, and his features wavered in the dark, his dead eyes holding only evil. Paralyzed in her dream state, Harper couldn't move or breathe. She was going to die. Someone screamed and grabbed her shoulders, jarring her from the horror.

"Sis, you're home, safe. Wake up!" Juanita hollered in Spanish, sitting right next to her.

Desperate for air, Harper gasped and opened her eyes, surprised to find herself upright in bed. She focused on the sheets wadded in her fists. "Stop yelling at me. I'm awake."

"You were screaming." Her sister's sable eyes held concern, and she kept her voice calm. Juanita leaned in, and her jet tresses shifted forward. "Are you with me?"

Shocked, Harper met her gaze. "*I* was screaming?"

Her sister nodded before curling her into her arms. "You're okay."

The same nightmare had tormented her countless times, and Harper wondered if the dreams would ever stop. Every time she woke paralyzed by fear, she couldn't help but believe the dream had an elusive meaning that escaped her grasp.

Feeling cowardly for allowing a dream to terrify her, she offered a weak smile. "I'm good, now. Thanks."

Untangling herself from the silky top sheet, she sat on the side of the bed, knuckling her eyes. Ever the protective big sister, Juanita patted her thigh before leaving the bedroom. A moment later, cupboards opened and closed in the kitchen.

The detectives said Harper's fiancé had tried to kill her. Even in the worst of quarrels, Ensign had never shown a hint of violence. If the NYPD had actual evidence, then she could make sense of their suspicions. To pick up a gun and shoot her? She didn't buy it. Or maybe she couldn't buy it. Denial was a powerful defense tool.

Rumpled bedding on the other side of the king-sized bed brought Harper's grim reality rushing back. Ensign hadn't slept there for weeks. Shortly after his first interview with the homicide detectives, he'd left their Soho condo— following legal advice. His attorney had notified her attorney via email. *An expensive legalese Dear Jane.*

In hindsight, Ensign had left in spirit a few years ago. He hadn't loved her for a long time. She'd simply been too blind to see the truth. Part of her felt the fool. Another part ached for what could have been. At least she hadn't married him.

On the first day home from the rehab center, walking into the empty condo had wrenched her heart out. That night, Juanita had simply crawled into bed with her, and they'd fallen asleep holding hands. She'd taken leave from her hospital social worker job and stayed. Harper still didn't want her to go home—not yet anyway.

Her phone said six a.m. Time to get moving. Since she loathed using a cane, she'd left hers in the living room. She tottered to the suite's bathroom using a dresser and wall for support. An involuntary spasm in her left arm made her pause and massage the muscles. She would have to take her spasticity medication first thing. Thank heavens it worked.

"I'm going to shower. Is there a Starbucks drive-through on the way to the medical building?" she called towards the hallway.

"If you gotta have the good stuff, we can stop, but a pot is already brewing. Limo will be here at seven-fifteen." Her protective sister likely wanted to minimize exposure to the public—and any assassins lying in wait.

"Homebrew is fine."

On cue, gurgles sounded from the kitchen followed by a peeping noise. Harper wanted to deactivate the alerts on all of her appliances—her phone—and everything. She had no recall of the ICU, except the never-ending alarms and the sense of doom they'd triggered. Even weeks later, an unexpected beep spiked her heart rate.

Avoiding the mirror, she brushed her teeth before stepping into shower heaven. With three tiled walls, and a fourth made of glass, the enclosure easily allowed two to shower together. Rain sluiced over her from a square shower system above, and six body sprays on the walls usually pampered a person to distraction. Not anymore.

When she'd purchased the condominium, Ensign had lobbied hard for this upgrade. He'd been so right and had frequently reminded her of his brilliance—usually while they'd played in the water. Harper tamped down the memories and the sadness that followed. At some point, she'd find a new place without the echoes of a love betrayed.

Gently shampooing her almost nonexistent hair, she glided her fingers over a two-inch-wide depression in her head. She traced the bony edges under her scalp and paused over the yielding skin in the middle.

"Like a baby's soft spot," Dr. Hellbusch had said.

Skull *defect*—neurological *deficit.* The insulting medical terms were painfully descriptive. Since the shooting, she'd felt defective—and deficient.

The surgeon would eventually reconstruct her skull, and her gait should improve with rehab. But how to fix the broken part inside? She met with a psychologist weekly but so far, she couldn't tell if the counseling helped.

The NYPD detective could be wrong about Ensign. According to them, they had motive—a four million dollar life insurance policy and half the New York City condo—but no real evidence. Their money theory had holes in it, too. Ensign had way more to gain if he'd married her first. Things didn't add up.

One problem at a time. Moving under the water, she rinsed, resigned to living with a hole in her head for the next six months.

Juanita knocked on the open door. "Hey, Tyson called. His son cut his chin, and he's taking him in to the ER for stitches."

Harper's driver-bodyguard never cancelled. On the other hand, in the past, she'd only needed him for big events, not every stinking day. "Oh, man. Poor little T.J. Did Ty say anything about back up?"

Stepping into the tiled bathroom, Juanita shook her head. "I doubt he had time to find anyone. I think it just happened. The kid nearly blew out my eardrum over the phone— not a temper-tantrum cry. Plus, Tyson sounded crazy-frantic."

"Jeesh, I hope the squirt's okay. I'll call Ty later."

"Should I reschedule?"

Harper turned off the water, and stepping out of the shower, she grabbed a towel from a warming rack. She dried off while they chatted. "I can't hide my entire life. Let's go."

"Okay, I'll call a cab."

A white orthotic helmet glared back at Harper from the

vanity counter. Raising a halting hand, she caught Juanita. "Will you drive me?" So much for not hiding. "Please?"

Juanita's brows shot up. "After strutting butt-ugly couture in front of zoom lenses, you're worried about that motorcycle gang hat?"

Furious tears stung Harper's eyes, and she parted her lips, hoping words would come. The helmet and the cane were necessary, and she needed to get over her ridiculous pride. She was livid with herself.

With kind eyes, Juanita clasped her hand, giving it a gentle squeeze. "I'm sorry—bad humor. We should wait for Tyson, anyway. You know Dr. Hellbusch—*Les*—will make time for you whenever you want." She smirked with her tease. "Who knew brain surgeons actually answered their own phones?"

Les had been a godsend. And if a little celebrity-awe was involved, hey Harper couldn't help that. "I'd rather not wait on Ty. This appointment is important. I need to talk to Les about that awful rehab place—today. They promised privacy and didn't deliver. Did you tell me you cancelled those appointments?"

"Oh yeah, I was all over that." Juanita rolled her eyes. "So is your attorney. If one photo shows up *anywhere,* you'll own their little operation."

Warmth for her sister made Harper smile. "Thanks for handling the drama. I couldn't deal."

The previous week, she'd attended her initial therapy assessment, ready to get moving on recovery. After the consultation, she and the therapist had worked in an open gym with other clients and staff. All was fine—until a guy wearing facility polo snapped a photo of her with his cell phone.

"Always my pleasure to put assholes in their place,"

Juanita said over her shoulder on her way out. "By the way, I told Les about it, too. Can you say *pissed?*"

The mirror loomed large, and Harper needed to get ready. Girding her psyche for the daily body-image assault, she looked herself square in the eye. In the midst of dark hair a little over an inch long, a tightly curved scar dominated the right side of her head and circled the area of missing skull.

At least the scar had flattened some and lost its pink tone. However, rebellious hair along the edges of the ridged line spiked up. A touch confirmed hair stood up around a bullet-sized pockmark below her crown. The entrance wound. The coward had shot her from behind.

She should be happy to be alive. However, facing her reflection and dealing with uncooperative body parts had worn her out. Worse, she wasn't close to the finish line.

No tears. She refused to waste energy on what she couldn't change. Her scars. Ensign. However, she controlled her reactions and choices. By God, she would do it. Each day, the view in the mirror became less unsettling. Further, few enjoyed her blessings. She had wealth, but more importantly, she had family. Juanita. Mamá.

With a burgeoning determination, she vowed to reclaim her life, and the decision filled her with energy. She memorized the hopeful sense of expectation, planning to draw on the feeling later, when the challenges of reality weighed her down.

No matter what the tabloids said, she was more than a pretty face. As she pulled out a small suitcase of makeup and flipped on the lights circling a high mag mirror, the irony of her thought made her snort.

Mostly, her makeup routine was unchanged. However, a blind spot in her left eye made it awkward to apply mascara on that side. She was getting it, though.

She studied the plastic helmet resting on the vanity

counter, fighting off the resentment. *Protecting brain tissue is important.* With a sigh, she pulled the snug-fitting orthotic on and clipped the strap under her jaw. Bad-hair day solved.

"Tick-tock." Juanita hollered from the other room. "Hellbusch's office is about forty minutes away."

"Hey, cut me a break. I've got more work to do than usual," Harper shouted back.

A few minutes later, she exited her bedroom wearing store-brand cropped pants and a sleeveless cotton blouse with sensible slip-on flats. Nothing blended into a doctor's waiting room like a mega-mart outfit. She followed the coffee scent down the hall into the sunlit, open-style apartment.

As she reached for her cane propped against the sofa, the living room's glass wall raised the hair on her arms. The expanse of windows had always invited people to take in the scenic view of the park across the street, herself included. However, since her return from inpatient rehab, her home's most stunning feature gave her the creeps. She needed to sell or call in a Feng Shui consultant—or maybe a shaman to burn a bushel basket of sage.

Shaking off the willies, Harper grabbed her purse from the kitchen island and joined her sister at the elevator. A private lift would top the must-have list for her next condo. At a glimpse of her reflection, she gave the entryway's circular mirror her back.

Juanita politely carried their coffee mugs and pushed the down button with a knuckle. "Let's get going."

The trip from the second level to the underground garage took less than a minute. The boogieman would need a helicopter to get into Harper's next place. She planned to buy in the nosebleed section. The heavy doors split open, and she followed her sister past a row of garages.

Number thirty-eight made her pause. She hooked her

cane over her arm and tapped in the code—her wedding day that never happened. Zero-four-one-five. April fifteenth.

Juanita halted a few steps beyond her, wheeling around. "What're you doing? We're going to be late."

"Relax, I'll only be a second."

The garage door rose with a high-end hum. *Empty.* Harper had expected this, but a part of her had hoped Ensign would wait—offer to return such an expensive gift—be the classy guy she'd believed he was.

Behind her, Juanita gasped and then materialized at her side. "That pig took the McLaren?"

"The car was a gift," Harper replied. She'd given Ensign the car of his dreams out of love. If he *had* left the convertible, or offered to, Harper admitted that she might have told him to keep it. No doubt, her therapist would have a few thousand things to say about that.

"Oh, bull. Titled property worth a quarter mil is jointly owned—or it should be, anyway."

"You keep forgetting—we weren't married yet."

"You would've been common law anywhere but New York. Why do you give people such expensive gifts ..." Juanita's rant stalled, and she turned a stricken expression on Harper. "I changed the garage entrance PIN when I changed the condo elevator access. How did he get in here—and *when?*"

"I've got no idea. The car was still here when we got home last week." Too numbed by repeated disappointment to react, Harper punched the code again, and the sectioned door lowered. "Tyson can follow up with the building security. Let's go."

"Les said he's very pleased with my progress. Finally, I feel a little encouraged," Harper said to her sister who sat across from her at the kitchen island. "Plus, he really came through on the rehab. Privacy *and* security."

With empty Chinese takeout containers decorating her white granite counter— evidence of their carb splurge—she sat on a stool, scanning a color pamphlet for Stick Pony, a new hippotherapy facility in Spencer, Colorado that hadn't opened yet.

"That's great, sis." Her tone less than enthusiastic, Juanita squinted at the brochure. "The red DRAFT stamp on the cover isn't reassuring."

"I can't have everything. They're new, but they're empty." Setting the pamphlet aside, Harper couldn't argue the point. "I think Les put some effort into this. He said something about the grandson of a friend. Or maybe he said patient. I'm not sure. But this camp is a creative solution to my privacy issues."

Juanita nibbled at her fried rice, intermittently tapping her keyboard. "I get that horses are fun to ride, but it seems a stretch that riding would help you walk."

Nothing about horseback riding had shown up in Harper's earlier research, either. However, that was before this morning's appointment. "I guess something about maintaining your seat aboard a horse strengthens your overall balance and other brain functions, too."

Juanita offered a droll stare. "This would be a lot easier if you had waited for me to go into your appointment with you. I missed a bunch of important stuff."

After she'd abandoned her job and flown in from Chicago, it wasn't fair to keep things from her. Nevertheless, Harper wasn't ready to share the extent of her *deficits*. "I'm sorry. Next time, sweetie."

"Whatever." At least her sister didn't press the issue. "I

know you want a place to yourself, but if this horse therapy doesn't help you, it's not worth avoiding a few photographers."

"What if the next one takes a video?" Even saying it made Harper shudder. "If I can't make myself go to the clinic, I won't get better, either."

Les had compared the small town of Spencer to Aspen, where celebrities were commonplace and politely ignored. But even better than that, the camp owner had offered a soft opening solely for Harper. Private care. He'd stapled a green sticky note with his personal number to the pamphlet.

Even though she'd silenced her phone, it vibrated a third time, and without looking, she ghosted her very persistent agent Joni—again.

"You have to talk to her sometime," Juanita said.

"I don't want to discuss a movie deal that's already gone sour."

Harper considered Joni more friend than agent, but the disappointment of losing the acting debut stung, and she didn't want to waste energy on a painful conversation. She should invite her out to Spencer. Joni was the only member of her New York tribe who'd visited her in the hospital. Later, she'd even delivered a dietary supplement care package to rehab.

The girls from the agency had sent flowers. It was nice to hear from them, but few called and no one visited. They'd always shown up for a trip to the club, though. Maybe if the hospital had had an open bar, they would have stopped in. Harper squelched the bitter thought, refocusing on her recovery.

She raised the Stick Pony pamphlet. "They're willing to recruit a temp therapist who specializes in brain injury." Recalling the brief conference call with the camp's owner, she regretted ghosting her agent. "Maybe I *should've* talked to

Joni. The owner hinted he'd appreciate an endorsement later."

With her elbows on the counter, Juanita pointed her empty fork at Harper. "I definitely should've been there."

"Thanks for looking out for me." Harper scowled at her latest fashion accessory. "If they help me lose that flipping cane, I'll rep them for free."

The hippotherapy rabbit hole was deep, and eventually Harper yawned. Two hours had gone by, and the condo was empty. She vaguely recalled Juanita mentioning the gym downstairs. Packing up her leftover noodles, she vowed to eat bran for the next two days.

The intercom to the lobby chimed. Another alarm to wish away. "Yes, Edward?"

"Ms. Inez, a Detective Roarke Hennessy is here. He says it's important."

Harper went on high alert. Nothing stressed her more than a discussion of the shooting. "Thanks, please send him up."

She grabbed her phone and sent Juanita an SOS text. A minute later, the entryway elevator doors opened, revealing a familiar man with auburn hair wearing a lightweight gray suit. The detective greeted Harper with a nod.

The grim set of his jaw did little to harden his freckled, choirboy features. "Good afternoon, Miss Inez. I tried to call. Phone working?"

Already waiting for him in the foyer, she pulled her cell from her hip pocket. One glance at the call history made her groan. "Oh Detective, I'm so sorry. I'd thought you were someone else. Please, come on in." She led him into the living room, gesturing for him to take a seat. "Your regular? The pot is sort-of fresh."

One corner of his mouth rose. "Motor oil, if you've got it."

Apparently, she was forgiven. Returning a smile, she

detoured to the kitchen. "What brings you all the way out here?"

The detective set his phone on the coffee table. As before, he'd record their chat. "I wondered if you'd remembered anything new."

"If that's all, you might not need a full cup." This definitely could've been handled on the phone. Harper would check the incoming names from now on. However, maybe her night-mares held a clue. *Eyes* would hardly be of help. If she recalled more, she'd tell him. She shook her head. "I don't have anything to add. Sorry."

"I'll ask again, later. Sometimes, things come back in pieces." He paced to the panoramic window and surveyed the park across the street. "There's more. We might have some new evidence on Ensign."

Fixed with inexplicable anxiety, Harper froze. She couldn't make herself respond.

The detective's eyes softened. "Do you remember a nurse named Angela?"

Recovering her composure, she finished filling two white square-rimmed mugs and then claimed a chair adjacent to Hennessy, who now sat on the sofa. "Maybe. A nurse's voice comes to mind. I transferred to a different unit before my memory really kicked in. Why?"

"A while back, she contacted the D.A.'s office. Said she'd noticed some *irregularities* with Ensign's visits."

Harper's heart pounded. "And…"

"Ventilator malfunctions. One occurred during a medical emergency with another patient. Angela described it as a near miss."

The room turned like a slow motion merry-go-round.

CHAPTER THREE

*S*itting in his truck outside of the empty Stick Pony barn, Landon waited on a shipment of a couple horses. He set his tawny straw Stetson on the dash. Helping out with Ryder's fledgling business kept him out of trouble, and since he'd stayed twelve days longer than the two he'd planned, Landon wanted to earn his keep.

He pushed the driver's door open to allow some air into the cab and then passed the time skimming his inbox. A quick check of the tie-down roper standings showed Jenkins gaining on him. If Landon could cut a deal on Bingham's horse, he could stop Jenkins's in his tracks.

He opened a message from the Greeley Stampede, wondering what they needed. They'd forwarded him something from a fan.

Dear Mr. Macek,

Rachael and I are so sorry for Rocket's injury. We both love animals and the last thing we wanted was to hurt him. He's such a beautiful horse, you must be heartbroken.

We hope you will forgive us.
Annie & Rachael

The girls had written the note shortly after the Greeley rodeo, but the Stampede organizers had forwarded it yesterday. A message across the top from the secretary vouched for the girls' sincerity, and below, Annie and Rachael had inserted a picture of them holding a giant get-well card for Rocket.

The communication shocked Landon, and he read it again. He was surprised how a simple *I'm sorry* soothed a raw spot that had been festering inside him. Did he forgive them?

The horse's surgery had gone well, and his gait had improved significantly. After a couple weeks of stall rest and double bunking with Buck, Rocket had graduated to the underwater treadmill. Landon had to admit that while losing a fancy truck and a ton of prize money rankled, his horse's needless pain had grieved him more.

Holding grudges wasn't his style. He tapped a short reply.

Dear Annie & Rachael,
Thanks for the get-well card. Rocket's a trooper and recovering well. Apology accepted.
Take care,
Landon and Rocket

A familiar Chevy Blazer pulled in next to him with Ryder behind the wheel. Landon donned his hat and stepped out to greet him. The men exchanged a fist bump, and then Landon leaned against the Ram's tailgate. "I didn't expect to run in to you, here."

"This first patient's a big deal—she's pretty famous—I can't afford a screw up." Ryder's Adam's apple bobbed. "I wanted to see the new therapy horses firsthand. There's a lot riding on them. No pun intended."

Glancing at his phone, Landon double-checked the time. "The driver's name is Jeb. He texted a few minutes ago. They'll be here in about fifteen."

"Good timing then." Ryder relaxed his big frame against his SUV. "Any news on Bingham's roping horse?"

"Yeah, last night. He's stuck on getting ninety-five for him, and my low-ball offer ruffled his feathers. He's thinking over a lease deal."

"I'm rooting for you, Landon. While you're waiting to hear, I was hoping for more of your help."

"Sure thing. Say the word."

Ryder smiled. "I need things to go smooth for this VIP. Thing is, I'm in a bind with construction projects and certifications. How'd you feel about being a real employee? For as long as you're here—I understand if you get the horse, you're gone."

Caught off guard, Landon tipped his Stetson back on his head. "What did you have in mind?"

"Stay onsite, manage the stock and train them up so they're greenhorn safe. Cut the ones that aren't. The staff quarters up in the main office building aren't too bad, either. Private room and bath with a small, shared kitchen. A therapist and her assistant will be here next week. They'll take a couple rooms, too."

Landon had already worried about overstaying his welcome with his newlywed friend. "My partner runs our training stable during the rodeo season, so if you're really in need, I'm available. But I can go on home and come back for Rocket later. Doc Spencer's everything you said. I don't need to hover around like a mama nanny goat."

Scuffing a boot against the gravel, Ryder smirked. "You think I'm trying to get rid of you?"

Landon grinned. "A smart man would. Your little Vianna is a pretty special girl. Probably be nice to get your privacy back."

"She is that, but I'd never chase you out. I really do need someone to manage the stock. Ten head show up next week. I'd planned on training them myself, but that's not happening."

After some mild negotiation, Landon reached out to shake on the deal. "I can stay for a few more weeks, get you over the hump." Thoughts of a mystery celebrity sharpened his curiosity. "You gonna tell me who this VIP is?"

"I can't. Which reminds me…non-disclosures." Ryder returned to the Blazer and dug around inside, emerging with a folder. He shut the door and rejoined Landon. "…everyone at Stick Pony has to sign one. Her treatment starts a week from Monday, so I need to get these taken care of."

Using the side of his truck for a desk, Landon reviewed the document, searching for hints on the VIP, disappointed not to find a celebrity name pending a signature. While the text addressed all manner of disclosures, the contract referred to all camp patients. Amused by his own curiosity, he handed the signed contract to Ryder. "Wow, you're serious about her privacy."

"Yeah, her presence here is strictly under wraps." Ryder slid the document into the folder and then put it in his vehicle. "Thanks, I'll email you a copy."

A Ford truck pulling a two-horse trailer rumbled up the gravel drive, and Landon walked out into the lot, using hand signals to direct the driver to a spot near the barn. The truck came to a full stop, and a stocky man with a sweat-stained cowboy hat and a tanned left arm emerged.

The men shook hands and made introductions. Jeb gave Landon a big smile. "You didn't make it far from Greeley. I was watching on the rodeo channel. How's the horse?"

Not many people recognized him, and Jeb had caught him off guard. Landon didn't really want to share his business with a guy he didn't know. "He's better. It'll be slow going."

A rodeo fan noticing him now and then was flattering, but if this happened all day and everywhere he went, he might want a non-disclosure agreement, too. The horses in the trailer moved around, jostling the rig.

Probably anxious to get moving, Ryder waved at the trailer. "Let's get our cargo unloaded."

Landon opened the back doors of the trailer and stared at the shortest rattail he'd ever seen on a horse. Spindly strands of white hair didn't reach the gelding's hocks or even cover the skin of his tail. He shared a look with Ryder who shrugged.

Landon stepped in the side door and untied a pretty-headed bay mare. As he backed her out, he gave the appaloosa's splotchy roan pattern a double take. Ryder hopped in from the back and grabbed the appy. They led the horses into the shade of a big aspen and tethered both animals to the barn's hitching post. The gelding got uglier out in the open.

Ryder and Landon stared at the odd-colored horse in silence. Large patches of white splattered his dull orange roan coat. Instead of full brown eyes, crescents of white bracketed his irises, giving the horse a startled appearance.

Jeb closed up the trailer and joined them with a snort. "That there's one unsightly critter. What in blazes do you boys intend to do with him?"

Suddenly protective of the homely gelding, Landon removed his hat and slapped it against his thigh. "He's a highly trained therapy horse. Thanks for getting him here in one piece."

Jeb took the hint, and they said quick goodbyes. Before

the man's rig was down the lane, Landon rubbed the back of his neck. "That *is* some awful color, and he's long-headed, to boot. But the rest of him isn't bad. Decent shoulder, and short-coupled."

Ryder walked around the gelding, studying him. "Yeah, he's sort of athletic."

"Tell me the truth. What's it cost to rent a grand steed like this?"

"His name's Pongo." He scuffed a boot on the new gravel. "I had to find a specialized therapist with a horse right away, so my back was against the wall. You might get a better deal on that world champion roping horse."

❧

The following Monday morning, Landon reported to the Aspen Gold Lodge offices where Ryder introduced him to the head of security, Deke Ward. Middle-aged, with white hair and a trimmed beard, Ward stood a few inches shorter than Landon, though his imposing physique made him seem larger. Landon got the impression the older man could hold his own in a fight.

"Our client's staying at Aspen Gold while she's in therapy," Ryder said. "As the head of Lodge security, Deke needs to clear everyone working at Stick Pony."

Ward scrutinized Landon with cagey brown eyes and then handed him a couple stapled forms. "Thanks for stopping in. Fill out the questionnaire and sign the release, and we'll do the rest."

Apparently, they took their security seriously. After Landon put his life story onto paper and authorized a criminal background check, Ryder took him on a tour of his grandfather's lavish resort. Aside from the guest suites, some of the Spencer clan had living quarters onsite. The Lodge grounds boasted water sports, riding stables, snowmobiling, and a host of other activities.

When they circled back to the main building, Landon welcomed a break for lunch on Ryder's dime. However, when they entered the supposedly casual Sun Room restaurant, he felt a little out of place. Cheerful yellow linen and fresh-cut flowers decorating the tables gave the place an understated formal vibe.

"Want to eat outside?" Ryder asked, gesturing to a bank of windows showing patio seating that appeared more laid back.

Landon quickly agreed, and the hostess seated them near an outside bar. After a few minutes, he appreciated a subtle, relaxed atmosphere.

Customers wore anything from ripped blue jeans to uppity casual, and no one seemed in a hurry. Sunhats and visors were popular, too. Like the other men and women on the sun-drenched terrace, Landon left his hat in place out of necessity.

In a homey balance to the formal linen, servers addressed many of the customers by name. A group nearby apologized to their server for occupying their table for so long. He could see where the peaceful view of Twin Owl Lake off the patio would lure people into hanging around.

"We've got another coming." Ryder spoke to a petite Asian server he called Aom.

With a nod, she disappeared.

He returned his attention to Landon. "This is awesome that you're stepping in. I've got contractor meetings most of tomorrow, and they're ready to hang drywall in the camper cabins." He paused while Aom set three glasses of water on the table. "Thanks to you, my sixteen hour day has dropped to twelve."

"I saw the big rig bring in materials for the barn." Landon

upended his glass, taking a deep swallow. The stakes marking the Stick Pony building site laid out a large facility. "How many stalls?"

"Twenty boxes with heated automatic waterers. The crew should get the stable framed this week." Ryder's jaw tensed. "The arena section will go up next."

"Nice." Landon could tell his friend was stressing over the multiple construction projects. A change of topic seemed like a good idea. He gestured at the gardens and lake. "This is some kind of place your grandfather built."

"Yeah, he's almost a legend around here."

Landon propped one leg across the other. "I can see why."

The Aspen Lodge empire stretched far in the region, and his Hollywood friend's connections had stunned Landon. While in California, Ryder hadn't given any hint of his wealthy roots. He had lived modestly like nearly everyone else and never even mentioned the Spencer clan.

Jackson Spencer strode to their table, greeting them with a good-natured smile. He slapped Ryder on the back before taking a seat. The veterinarian had taken good care of Rocket, and he and Landon had hit it off.

Aom materialized, and Jackson waved off a menu. "I'll take the ribeye sandwich and a bucket of imports for the table please."

"Same for me," Ryder said. "But I'll drink his beer."

The men laughed, and Landon closed his menu. "They know somethin' I don't. Ribeye sandwich it is."

With a smile, Aom placed the menus into the crook of her arm. "It's our bestseller."

A minute later, she returned with a miniature stainless steel washtub holding assorted iced bottles of ale and then stood at the ready with a bottle opener.

Ryder grabbed a dark brew and held out a hand, waving his fingers for the church key. "I'll take that."

At Jackson's waved invitation, Landon selected a light ale with a long German name. "How's Rocket doing today? I haven't checked on him yet."

They passed the opener around the table, and Jackson took a swallow of his beer before responding. "Phoebe says he's warming to the treadmill."

"Your new vet tech seems to know her stuff," Landon said.

"She does," the vet said. "And she wants to steal your donkey. Buck has her wrapped around his tiny hoof."

The damn burro had done it again. Landon laughed. "He does that to everyone."

Jackson's gaze skated to the side and back. "Depending on next Tuesday's ultrasound, we might let Rocket jog short distances. We'll see."

Wondering what had caught the vet's attention, Landon tracked his line of sight. A few tables away, a tall, slender woman wearing a medical helmet set her purse on an empty chair before methodically taking a seat.

Stretchy jeans hugged a taut rear end and legs that went on forever. Nothing got Landon's interest like lots of leg. From his limited view, she appeared young and athletic, making the cane she carried seem out of place.

The helmet conjured up a variety of injuries, and he wondered what had happened. A striking woman a few inches shorter with long dark hair accompanied her. Both women had flawless bronzed skin and chatted in Spanish. His high school language classes failed him, and he only recognized a couple words.

The second woman tugged at his memory, which made absolutely no sense. He didn't know anyone who'd show up at this hotsy-totsy place. Landon returned to the conversation about his horse. "That sounds great. I appreciate everything you're doing for him."

"Well when you get back to kicking ass on the rodeo circuit, spread the word for me." Jackson tilted his beer towards him. "There aren't enough local horses to keep me in business. I need a national network."

The promise of Rocket's recovery gave Landon a sense of ease he'd been missing. The horse would heal up, and he had a realistic shot at a world championship next season. "You got it."

Ryder checked out the new guests, too, but snapped back to their conversation. "The therapy horses arrived...."

Without realizing his eyes had strayed again, the willowy woman's gaze collided with Landon's. The most beautiful black eyes in the world shone back at him. *Harper Inez*. How in the world had he not recognized her to begin with?

His heart pounded, and he had no hope of keeping the shock from his expression. With an iron will, he turned back to the vet, trying to recover his composure.

Ryder gave him a knowing smile, and Landon's imagination took off. He doubted that he could even speak to Harper Inez without imagining that iconic red-bikini beach shot in *Sports Illustrated*. He needed to rein himself in and relax. A stable hand wouldn't have any direct contact with the celebrity patient. He'd have to be content saddling her horse.

Raising his brows, Jackson's line of sight shifted beyond Landon in the model's direction. "You two are quicker than me—I didn't recognize her. The other head turner must be family. Looks just like her."

According to Ryder, celebrities were standard issue at the Lodge. However, given his reaction, the supermodel had even impressed him. He cleared his throat and raised his beer. "To Vianna."

Laughing, Jackson did the same. "Here's to Kate." He jutted his chin at Landon. "But I think we should start an office pool."

Joining in the humor and indulging in a small what-if fantasy, Landon clinked his bottle to theirs. "Out of my league, boys. But I'll gladly crash and burn trying."

CHAPTER FOUR

While Juanita settled herself at the table, Harper propped her cane against one of the empty chairs, hoping the tablecloth would act as camouflage. "I swear people are staring at me." Even though they spoke Spanish, she still lowered her voice for privacy. "And not in a good way."

"A few noticed us." Juanita whispered back. "But you always attract attention."

"This is different. It's like I've got a giant wart on my nose, and when people see it, they quick turn away not to be rude."

"Come on. If you see someone with an amputated leg or a tragic scar, do you think *that person's a freak?*"

"I know, I know." Harper shook her head at her sister's reminder of their previous conversation. "I wonder what they went through and question if I could deal if I was in their shoes — and I *don't* want to hurt their feelings by noticing that they're a little different."

"Exactly. Like you, other people look away to protect *your* feelings." Why did Juanita have to be so smart?

"I wish it didn't feel so creepy to *be* that person."

Maybe if the smoking cowboy in the Stetson hadn't looked so shocked, Harper could have ignored everyone else. Worse, Mr. Stetson had recognized her. A flare of certain knowledge had shone in his hazel eyes before he'd nearly broken his neck turning away.

Following her sister's advice, she tried to reframe the event, considering that recognition alone may have caused the rubberneck reaction.

When the server stopped by, Harper ordered a grilled chicken salad with oil and vinegar on the side, declining the table bread. Even though Juanita didn't need to be rail thin, she did the same.

Unfortunately, the rehab facility food had added ten pounds to Harper's frame. She'd whittled that down to five, and she hoped to have it all off by the end of August—four more weeks of starvation. One day she'd gain ten pounds on purpose.

A server delivered three yummy-looking sandwiches to the cowboy's table. Harper wondered what it felt like to be full for longer than thirty minutes. She turned away from the sight, but the savory beef scent tortured her.

"This resort seems pretty nice," she said, hoping to distract herself.

Juanita agreed.

A tall, uncoordinated girl of about thirteen, sporting short shorts, knees, and elbows, ambled cautiously to their table. Blushing scarlet, she turned back towards her friends, and curtains of auburn hair swung with the motion. Two smiling teen girls seated near the railing mimed encouragement, waving her on. After tucking a ginger lock behind her ear, she fisted her hands at her sides and resumed her approach.

With her last hesitant steps, she beamed at Harper, and

clear plastic encasing her teeth brought ancient silver braces to mind.

"Hello Miss Inez. I'm sorry about what happened to you," the girl said.

"Thank you, I appreciate that."

"I want to be a model like you one day." She fidgeted with a cocktail napkin in one hand and a pen in the other and then thrust them at Harper. "Could I get your autograph, please?"

After the earlier stares had made her feel like a freak, an autograph request brought Harper a welcome sense of normalcy. She smiled and took the napkin. "What's your name, sweetie?"

"Chelse. C-H-E-L-S-E."

A bartender wearing a gray vest abruptly left his post and strode into the dining area. With an apology in his eyes for Harper, he drew up alongside the girl, reaching for the napkin. "Miss, I'm sorry, but the management doesn't allow autograph requests on Lodge property."

Gold lettering on the man's nametag identified him as Victor, the Sun Room's assistant manager. Still holding the pen, Harper kept her hand poised over the napkin. Privacy was why she'd come to Aspen Lodge in the first place. But how could she deny a young girl who looked to her as a role model?

She laid the pen possessively on the folded paper square. "Thank you, Victor. We want to follow the rules."

"I'm sorry." Chelse's lower lip quivered. "I-I didn't mean to be rude."

Harper offered her most reassuring smile. "Oh, Chelse, you weren't. A guy shoving three glossies under my nose is rude." She clasped Chelse's hand. "But I bet it's not against the rules for you to join us for lunch."

The girl beamed, and Victor laughed, obviously relieved.

"No rules against eating. In fact, let's make that lunch on the house."

Grinning, Juanita patted the chair next to her and introduced herself.

"Nice to meet you, Juanita." As Chelse settled onto the empty seat, she gushed her thanks to Harper. "I've read everything about you, Miss Inez. *Model Biz* said you got started by winning a contest. Should I enter one? What did you wear? Why do you think you won?"

Harper laughed. "That's a lot of questions."

Planting both palms on her cheeks, Chelse groaned. "Sorry. I'm so thrilled to meet you, that I'm being a demented fan-girl."

With her own drama taking all of her attention, Harper had forgotten that many young girls admired her. Further, she still had responsibilities as a role model. After her self-conscious moments entering the restaurant, the reminder gave her a boost. "I'm flattered. Thank you."

"Did you always want to be a model?" Chelse asked her.

Juanita's amused smile was no surprise. She knew full well the answer was *no*.

Diet sodas arrived, and Harper sipped, feeling nostalgic as she recalled her modest roots. She'd told the story a million times, but it was new to Chelse.

"I think I was a little older than you, sixteen. A lot of it was luck. I was tall and slender." She nodded at her sister. "Juanita had done my makeup. She wanted to model and talked me into entering the contest with her. She was motivated—and prettier too. But they wanted girls over five-foot-ten."

Chelse took in Juanita with new interest. "Did you model, too?"

"No. I went into social work." Juanita shrugged. "But I've

got no regrets. I like helping people. It's important to have a back-up plan that you're passionate about."

Despite being in the awkward early teen years, the girl had striking green eyes with good cheekbones and great hair. Modeling was a brutal business, but Chelse might have a shot.

While the two chatted, Harper took the moment and signed a good luck note on the napkin. Her alias hadn't changed much of anything. So far, only the resort employees had accepted her Luciana Rodriguez pseudonym. Keeping the napkin under her palm, she slid it across to Chelse, checking to see who might've witnessed the exchange.

Mr. Stetson's compelling gaze met hers for a charged instant, and he seemed to study her. He'd clearly lost his surprise over her presence, and his confident regard held more than simple curiosity or celebrity awe—she sensed approval.

With a slight curve of his lips, he dipped his chin and touched his fingers to the rim of his hat in a sort-of salute. His penetrating gaze gave her the sense that he saw *her*. Unhurried, he returned his attention to his companions, and an inexplicable pang of loss followed.

⚜

A few days later, after a room service breakfast with Juanita, Harper rode in the back of an Aspen Lodge Acura MDX boasting full security features, all excited for her first hippotherapy session. Maybe she'd erred when she'd encouraged Juanita to go sightseeing instead of coming with her to the camp. The mountain scenery was stunning.

Morning sunlight glimmered on the aspen trees, living up to the travel guide's description. Along with spruce and fir, the rugged forest crept to either side of the road. She lowered her window to enjoy the vivid colors, and the gray glass stopped mid motion. She tapped the button again. "Fletcher, is something wrong with the window?"

The huge bodyguard behind the wheel met her gaze in the rearview mirror, wearing aviator shades. She hated not seeing a person's eyes.

As though reading her mind, he raised his sunglasses and settled them into his short dark hair. "I'm sorry, Miss Rodriguez." The tinted glass whirred back up. He'd over-ridden her controls. "The glass is bulletproof, so we need to leave the windows closed."

With his warning, the glorious mountainside turned into a sniper's haven of high ground and cover options. She inched toward the center of the leather bench, until her seat belt held her in place. An instant later, a wall of rock filled the near side of the road.

Outside the opposite car window, a guardrail occupied the entire shoulder, offering meager protection from a drop-off with no bottom in sight. Rifles weren't the only murder weapons to consider.

An involuntary shudder pulsed through her. "Thanks. I didn't think."

Living in fear sucked the life out of her—and pissed her off. Maybe she should have brought Ty along, but he'd consulted with the detective and the Lodge's security. They'd all agreed that the risk was low. The NYPD had men watching Ensign, so if he left the area, Detective Hennessey would notify Lodge security.

The detective had even said that Colorado might be safer than SoHo. If she let the pros do their jobs, she could afford to relax a little. Soon, she'd enjoy the scenery up close at the Stick Pony facility. Maybe one day she could enjoy the mountains on horseback.

After a short drive, the Acura pulled into a gravel drive

with pasture on one side and a sprawling single-story building with a log-cabin façade on the other. Fletcher parked in front of a temporary lawn sign reading "Office".

With shades back in place, he stepped out onto the gravel and then ushered her out of the vehicle. To her surprise, one of Mr. Stetson's lunch companions emerged from the log cabin's front door. A short, athletic woman in a baseball cap followed him on the cement sidewalk.

The man from the Sun Room restaurant strode forward with a nod at Fletcher, offering her a handshake in greeting. "Welcome, Miss Rodriguez. I'm Ryder Barlow. We've spoken on the phone a few times."

"Thank you, I recognize your voice. If I'd known that was you at lunch the other day, I'd have said hello." Hopeful that Mr. Stetson with the kind eyes would be nearby, Harper searched the grounds, mildly disappointed not to find him.

Fletcher kept a discreet distance near the limo, intermittently scanning the area. Unlike Ty's routine suit jacket, he wore blue jeans with a leather vest that kept his weapon from plain sight. He'd added a cowboy hat to his aviators and blended in well enough.

Ryder gestured to the small thirtyish woman at his side. "This is Callie Emerson, the hippotherapy specialist I mentioned. She brought her best mounts along, too."

"Good to meet you." Harper's gaze shifted to the therapist's cap, which boasted a picture of a horse with a speckled rump. "You're an appaloosa girl—me too."

Callie lifted a hand for a high-five. "Spots rock."

While they laughed, Ryder smirked, and she retaliated by slapping his shoulder. Obviously *not* a spot fan. People either loved appies or hated them.

Harper focused on the therapist. "Thank you for interrupting your life to help with my rehab."

The petite blonde grinned. "You're welcome. It's rough

duty out here." She waved at the majestic Rockies on the northern horizon. "But I'll manage."

"Your resume is impressive. A doctorate in physical therapy—plus hippotherapy certification?" asked Harper.

"Yes, ma'am. Horses and therapy go together like—well, you'll see." Callie beamed her enthusiasm. Her energy was contagious. "Shall we lose the appy hater and get you started?"

Ryder fought a grin, clearly amused by the tiny bundle of energy. "I've got a meeting, ladies, so I won't detain you."

While she led Harper inside the office building, Fletcher stationed himself outside the front door. Callie gave him a second look as they passed by. After the door closed behind them, the therapist fanned herself. "Wowsa, where did you get him?"

"He came with my room at the Lodge," Harper deadpanned.

Callie's lips parted. "That's totally unfair. All I got was a kitchenette."

The women shared a chuckle. They passed through an unoccupied reception area to a suite of computer stations, and Callie waved at a desk holding a cardboard box. "My corner office."

Their laughter echoed in the spartan interior with empty walls. Callie dug inside the box and retrieved a clipboard and pen before waving Harper into a gym. They strode toward a low padded table with more real estate than a California king-sized bed.

Callie settled cross-legged on the edge of the table and gestured for Harper to join her. "Have a seat. I reviewed your history, but I need to do my own assessments, too."

"I understand." Harper scanned the empty space meant for multiple patients. "I can't tell you what it means to me to have privacy."

"I'm glad we were able to work it out. But you do need traditional therapy, too. I'll make a referral later today."

The therapist took a history, jotting notes on a paper worksheet, and then observed Harper walk and perform other tasks. The questions, the exam, all brought back memories of the picture-taking creep in New York. Harper wanted to avoid a repeat at all costs. "Could I do the regular therapy here?"

Callie frowned. "To be honest, it wouldn't be the best choice. You'll progress faster in an established, fully equipped department. However, I think I've got a good alternative. Come with me."

Harper tried to hide her disappointment. "Okay."

They returned to Callie's corner office, and she handed Harper two business cards. "I wrote my cell on the back. She gestured to the other card. "I checked this guy out. Ask for Chad Emmett. A friend of mine worked with him and says he's top notch."

Imagining cell phones pointed at her, Harper bit her lower lip. "I don't know —"

"Dr. Hellbusch told me about the wanna-be paparazzi in New York. That therapist who took your picture will need to find a new line of work. Healthcare is fierce about privacy anywhere, but especially in the Spencer area."

With the humiliating photo op fresh in her mind, Harper had more doubt than faith. She looked the therapist in the eye. "I hope that's true."

Concern filled Callie's gaze. "I'm sorry that man violated your privacy. He was a disgusting excuse for a professional. But believe me, that kind of behavior is *not* the norm."

Her sincerity touched Harper, and she wanted to believe her. "Thanks for understanding."

Callie nodded. The silence between them said more than words. After a beat, she dug in her office box, pulling out a folder. She set a form on the table in front of Harper. "Speaking of privacy, I need your authorization to send Chad your New York records and my notes."

Eager to begin, Harper signed the release. "Will we actually work with a horse today?"

"Indeed, we will." Callie's cheerful smile reappeared. "How about now?"

The woman was infectious, and Harper chuckled. "I've wasted three weeks doing nothing since that photograph incident. I'm more than ready."

"One more thing." The therapist opened a credenza above her desk and pulled out a box. She removed a shiny blue helmet from Styrofoam packing and handed it to Harper. "This is why I needed your hat size. Unfortunately, your orthotic isn't rated for a fall from a horse."

Though Callie specialized in brain injury rehab, and had likely seen many anomalies, Harper was uncertain how she felt about exposing her cranial defect. Hesitant, she released her chinstrap and pushed her helmet off. "Okay."

While Callie put the riding helmet on and off, adjusting the straps, she didn't seem the least put off by the ugly scar or the skull depression. Her matter-of-fact manner put Harper at ease.

She slid a finger under the strap. "That's good. When can you have your reconstruction surgery?"

Harper snorted. "November, and it can't come soon enough."

Callie smiled and grabbed her clipboard. "That's what everyone says. Come on, let's get moving." She tapped her phone and put it to her ear as they left the office. "Hi, Tad. We're on the way to the arena now. I think Pongo will work."

After declining a ride in a golf cart, Harper paced alongside her, and they followed a level sidewalk past a small barn built on a rise. Part of the arena fence came into view, and beyond an adjacent gravel lot, workmen and trucks occupied a large graded area. Ever-present Fletcher trailed them by a few polite yards. The paved walkway appeared out of place in the rustic barnyard setting—a stone path would have been more attractive.

However, even a few steps over the gravel drive had made her rely heavily on her cane. Clearly, uneven ground posed a barrier to all but fully abled people. The network of sidewalks was imperative for campers using mobility aids and wheelchairs.

Harper's breath came faster, and she concentrated on following the sidewalk. The arena was farther than it had appeared. The next time someone offered a ride, she would accept.

Callie had pulled her blond ponytail through the back of her cap, and it bounced with each stride she took. She pointed at a sorrel appaloosa tied to an arena post. "I think you'll like Pongo. He's as steady as they come. And he has spots. You've ridden before?"

"A couple years of 4-H stuff." Thanks to a well-off friend's invitation, Harper used a borrowed horse for a couple summers during middle school. Two of the best summers ever. She sucked in another breath. "Nothing serious."

The therapist halted. "I suspect you're used to being in excellent physical condition." The corners of her eyes tightened, and she suddenly appeared very much the concerned professional. "Don't let this temporary low exercise tolerance concern you. The Rockies' altitude makes even elite runners and cyclists work hard."

Realizing that the thin mountain air played a part in her diminished stamina relieved Harper—a little. "Thanks for the breather. I'm deconditioned for sure, but I've lost my cardio endurance and muscle definition, too."

"You've got more to overcome than most athletes who

come here to train. But your fitness level *will* return. Muscle tone will take more work," Callie said.

By lumping Harper in with the bicyclists and marathoners, Callie seemed to appreciate how hard models worked off camera. Few did. A professional's certainty brightened Harper's lagging spirits, and she felt an instant connection to the therapist.

"You sound optimistic," Harper said.

"Because I am." Callie spoke with easy confidence. "Bedbound patients lose strength at a staggering rate. They say that for each day of bedrest, it takes a week to recover what is lost."

No wonder Harper felt like a wet noodle all the time. "That's impressive. In a bad way."

Callie restarted their walk. "If you're up to it, easy treadmill work on your off-therapy days will speed up reconditioning." She raised a brow. "But don't get nuts like you're training for a five-K."

"My regular four-mile run is probably out of the question."

Callie laughed. "For now, anyway."

"I don't know if it's worth …" Harper took a couple breaths. The daunting battle to regain a camera-ready body weighed her down. "…trying to go back to work."

Callie slowed their pace, and her gaze held sympathy. "It's early, but I've done this a few times. Based on your initial assessment, I think you'll regain most of your baseline function."

The confidence in the therapist's tone emboldened Harper. No one had offered recovery specifics, and even when she'd asked, they'd been vague. Summoning her courage, she lifted her cane between them. "And this? Do you think I'll need it forever?"

The woman pushed tendrils of hair from her face and

pursed her lips. From across the yard, nail guns snapped a two-beat tattoo in an expectant drumroll.

Harper's throat tightened while she waited for Callie's verdict. She was lucky to be alive—blessed—everyone said so. But in truth, she was cursed with a *defective* and *deficient* body. And a damaged heart. Some days she was angry. Others, she wallowed in depression. Anger seemed healthier.

The cane symbolized all of Harper's emotional and physical challenges, everything that she'd endured since that fateful night.

As though she understood the importance of her opinion, Callie paused, cocking her head a degree. "Right now, I'd say fifty-fifty. Ask me again in a couple weeks."

Not the guarantee Harper had desperately needed. She swallowed hard, willing composure. Modeling was half-acting after all. "You can count on it."

The power tools in the background cut off, and the women traveled the last few yards to the arena in silence. Callie set her clipboard on the top step of a freestanding aluminum ramp. A wiry young man wearing a baseball cap strode toward them from the construction site.

She waved him over and made introductions. "Tad's on break from college. His family trains dressage horses, so he's got a strong equine background. I lucked out. He wants to get into a physical therapy program, so he's shadowing me this summer."

"Nice to meet you," Harper said.

Tad snatched his baseball cap off and worried it between his hands. "Hello. Um, nice to meet you, too, Miss In-Rodriguez." After staring at Harper for a lengthy beat, he blinked and then his cheeks reddened. "Oh, Callie, I almost forgot. The contractors will take their lunch early, so no hammering."

"Good job. Thanks."

"When we're ready for a sidewalker, Landon said to text him," Tad added.

"Okay." Callie tapped on her phone.

"What's a sidewalker?" Harper asked.

"Sort of like a spotter," he said. "While you're in the saddle, I'll drive Pongo from behind, like he's pulling a cart—I'm what they call a *horse handler*. Then Callie and Landon will walk on either side of you. You know, for safety."

They needed three people for her to ride a horse. "Ah, I see."

Callie's phone chirped, pulling her attention. "Landon's up in the little barn. He'll be right down." She waved at the tethered horse. "Harper, why don't you and Pongo get acquainted?"

Harper migrated to the colorful therapy horse to say hello, pulling a baggie of room service crinkle-cut carrots from her pocket. Pongo's saddle had an unusual wide-gripped handle instead of a saddle horn. The gelding nuzzled her hair, pulling her attention.

"I know what you want." She held out a carrot stick, and his velvety lips tickled her palm. The simple contact made her smile. "You're a different sort of appaloosa. Did a sixties artist toss buckets of pain on you?"

A minute later, the hazel-eyed cowboy from the Sun Room restaurant strode toward them. Apparently, he worked at Stick Pony, after all. A lonely whinny erupted from the barn behind him as though the horse worried over his absence.

He was the *sidewalker*. Harper wanted to hide. The thought of the hot cowboy watching her therapy, or maybe even helping her get on a horse, made her want to hobble back to the car. She had nothing to be embarrassed about, and she was more comfortable being out in public, but still…

Wearing the familiar straw hat with a braided leather

band, he offered the same confident half-smile he'd worn at lunch the other day. He didn't pause for Callie to introduce them, offering a hand. "Landon Macek. Nice to meet you … Miss Rodriguez."

A few days' worth of beard stubble gave him a luscious, rugged appearance. Admittedly, Harper had a weak spot for the innately masculine style though she suspected the stable hand had simply skipped his morning shave.

Smiling, she took his hand. "Likewise, Mr. Macek." She couldn't pull her eyes from him. "As much as we'll all work together, the formal titles might get old fast. Call me Luciana?"

"Luciana, then." His lips twitched as though fighting a full-on grin. "Landon suits me fine."

In the restaurant, his eyes had appeared to be brown. However, in the morning sun, up close, a deep green infused the compelling hazel. His captivating gaze enthralled her for an instant, and his smile creeped up on one side. Heat skated to her cheeks.

With parted lips, Callie looked from one to the other. "You-you two know each other?"

"Not really," Harper said, still smiling at him.

"We sort of met." Shrugging, Landon responded simultaneously before glancing at the others and breaking the spell.

Tad gave a lopsided grin.

"Okay, then." Callie laughed. "Since that's cleared up, Miss Rodriguez, let's get you aboard Pongo."

"Really, Callie, please call me Luciana," Harper said, realizing she'd only invited Landon to use the informal address. She nodded at the horse handler. "You, too, Tad."

Following the shorter woman, she walked up the ramp to a platform where Callie buckled a familiar gait belt around Harper's waist. The wide woven-cotton straps were a popular accessory for therapists in rehab. All had worn them either around their waist or as a sash over one shoulder.

At some point, Tad had snapped extra-long reins to Pongo's bit and taken a position behind the horse. The appaloosa seemed to anticipate every move required, and with no direction she could see, the horse stepped sideways towards the ramp.

The horse handler motioned to Landon. "Move in on the right pretty close like we talked about."

Landon's smile dropped away. If Harper had to guess, she made him a little nervous, so she smiled. "I don't weigh that much."

Mischief lit his eyes. "I don't expect you do."

Harper hung her cane on the ramp's handrail and then gave the horse's neck a pat, excited and anxious at the same time about mounting up. She could do this. It had been several years, but as a kid, she'd gotten on a horse countless times.

Standing next to her, Callie gave her a reassuring pat on the shoulder. "I'll hold on to you until you're in the saddle. Don't worry; we've got lots of help here. Go ahead and lift one leg over then lower down."

Landon met her gaze and dipped his chin, as though he had confidence in her. With his unspoken encouragement, Harper gripped the saddle's handle and raised one leg. Before she could adjust, her supporting leg crumpled, and she dropped onto the cantle of the saddle, tumbling forward.

Like lightning, strong hands caught her by the waist and pulled her into the leather seat. She righted herself in the saddle, keenly aware of Landon's warm hands on the skin of her abdomen. As soon as she steadied herself, he politely released her.

Callie straightened with her hands on her hips. "And that is why we have the sidewalker. Good job, Landon."

Self-conscious over her exposed weakness, Harper tugged the rumples from her cotton T-shirt, avoiding eye contact. "Thanks." She patted the horse's neck. "I guess we've got some work to do."

A casual baritone chuckle quelled her unease, and she dared a glance at him. He tipped his hat, giving her that same smile that was somehow more genuine than a big grin. "Don't worry. You'll be riding the trails in no time."

Landon was a good-looking guy, but that was nothing new in her world. Some other intangible quality attracted her. Surprising. With her history, she should have full immunity to all male charm. It had to be the cowboy hat. She returned a cautious smile.

Callie walked down the ramp, and the metal rumbled with each step. Unbothered by the noise, Pongo didn't flick an ear. She drew up next to the animal's head. "Luciana, since you've ridden before, these first sessions may seem pretty lame. But our goal is to rebuild the neuro-pathways that your body uses to walk."

Seeking reassurance this therapy could really help her, Harper wanted to know more. "I found encouraging patient testimonials online, but I don't understand how the improvement actually happens."

Still at Pongo's side, Landon raised the brim of his hat. "You're not alone."

So the tall drink of water wasn't a trained therapist. He must be filling in. Stick Pony didn't officially open for months. They'd recruited Callie, Tad, and her horses ahead of schedule for Harper. Landon probably hadn't asked for the extra duty, either. At least he seemed nice.

Callie included both in her gaze. "All we really have is theory and some study results that say it works, so I'll give you the prevailing wisdom. When you sit in the saddle of a moving horse, the hip motion and balance required is very similar to what you use to walk." She gave Pongo's muzzle a rub. "The nerves and brain synapses are forced to work like they used to. In turn, this makes your gait on land more natural."

The dots connected for Harper, and real hope to improve her gait and balance took root. The Stick Pony Therapy Center could help her reclaim her life. Energized with optimism, she wanted to get started. "That's much clearer than anything I could find online. What do I need to do?"

"For today, relax and enjoy the ride," Callie said with a smile. "But don't be surprised later when you're worn out."

Harper chuckled. "I can do that."

The therapist took charge. "I'll take this side. Landon, you walk on the other with a forearm across Miss Rodriguez's thigh. That way, you'll detect a shift in her balance instantly."

Harper nodded her consent, which seemed a little late since he'd already caught her with both hands.

Callie's gaze settled on the wrangler-turned-therapy-aid. "Pongo follows voice commands extremely well. If you have any concern at all, tell him 'whoa'."

"Got it." Lines appeared in Landon's forehead. "Don't worry, Luciana, I'll keep you safe."

With the artless sincerity in his gaze, she almost believed he could protect her from all of life's perils. She arched a teasing brow. "My knight in shining armor?"

His eyes lit up, and he adjusted his hat. "Nope. It's the cowboy code—protect the womenfolk."

An exaggerated twang of the Old West permeated his speech, and Harper's laugh bubbled up light and effervescent. She had not truly laughed in so long, the easy sense of fun surprised her. In that instant, she glimpsed a real-life future, including happy moments shared with people she cared for. A normal life.

Her rump shifted to the side, and she tugged on the

pommel handle to re-center herself. She'd allowed the cute cowboy to distract her. Since the horse handler drove Pongo from behind, and Harper didn't have reins to guide her mount, the lack of control unnerved her. Too similar to her life. She tightened her fingers around the rawhide handle in a death grip.

Landon paced alongside the animal with his forearm lightly draped across her thigh. As a model, she was accustomed to strangers touching her, sometimes intimately, but she'd always hated it. Instead, she found his presence oddly reassuring. Maybe not so odd. He'd already saved her from one fall.

As though he'd sensed her gaze on him, he offered an encouraging smile, making her think he'd read her insecurities. "You're doing great."

He was a pretty good liar. Her nervous laughter sounded strangled.

After a few wobbly minutes, her hips rolled side to side in time with the gelding's rhythmic four-beat gait. Recalling her 4-H instructions from years ago, she alternated her weight from one stirrup to the other in time with the horse's rear footfalls. Her left leg was definitely weaker.

Callie nodded enthusiastically. "There you go, you got it."

After about forty minutes of walking the length of the arena with wide turns at the ends, their procession returned to the ramp. Fortunately, dismounting was easier, and after a moment to regain her land legs, Harper retrieved her cane to negotiate the descent to the sidewalk.

While Landon held Pongo's lead, Tad removed the longlines, as he'd called them. Callie confirmed the next session with Harper, recommending a recovery day in between.

At a break in the conversation, the cowboy touched the rim of his hat. "Ladies, I'll see you on Wednesday. Pongo's ready for his *siesta*."

Harper hadn't forgotten her horse etiquette or her hippotherapy research. If patients were able, they often cared for their horses. Clearly, he intended to give her a celebrity version of treatment.

She gave him her best smile. "Mr. Macek-Landon, I might be a little slow, but I can still put up my own mount."

"A true horsewoman, if I ever saw one." He handed her the cotton lead rope. "I'll show you around the barn."

"Well, since you two have Pongo taken care of, I'm going up to the office to chart." Callie gestured at Harper. "You did great today. I'm excited to see how your next ride goes."

They said their goodbyes, and the diminutive woman strode off at a crisp walk. Harper longed to do the same—very soon. Pongo pressed his head against her shoulder, almost as if he tried to get her moving. He probably had an itch.

While she rubbed behind his ears where his coat was damp from the bridle, the horse leaned into her touch. "Ready for your nap? Let's go, then."

Seeming to eaves-drop from afar, Fletcher made eye contact with Landon and pointed up a rise to the small barn with the log-cabin siding. No plain metal buildings here. At Landon's thumbs up, the bodyguard strode off toward the stable.

She coiled the lead in her left hand, leaving her right free for her cane. The gentle slope up to the barn stole her wind again, but she muscled through it, huffing each breath until they reached the open stable. A cooling draft from within gave her hope she'd make it the rest of the way.

A few feet inside, a welcoming bench almost ruined her resolve to make it to Pongo's stall. An ajar door next to it opened to a room holding saddles and other gear—the tack room. She could take her time unsaddling the horse here and catch her breath. Only a couple box stalls occupied either side of the aisle, so his had to be close.

A reddish-brown horse stuck its head out of a break in the upper rails and whickered. Pongo returned the greeting, and his throaty whinny made her insides quiver. She'd forgotten how loud a horse could be.

Landon gestured towards the bay. "That's Pongo's girl-friend, Dixie. She's been calling for him most of the morning."

A bead of perspiration trickled from Harper's temple to her chin, and her wet scalp itched under her helmet. She was too fatigued to discuss Pongo's love life. If only she could scrub the living daylights out of her head.

Giving Landon a limp smile, she readied to unsaddle her mount. "Where does Pongo's saddle go?"

He took the lead rope from her. "Do you mind waiting here for a minute?" On the other side of the aisle, he tethered Pongo to a post using a short rope with a metal snap hanging from it. "I need to clip his whiskers. I meant to earlier, but I could see you ladies leaving the office."

"That, sir, is the most contrived pretext I've ever heard." As Harper dropped onto the slatted bench seat, gulping air, she beamed at him. "And I love you for it."

"Busted." His smile almost showed his teeth. "But you were so determined to make the finish line. I didn't want to spoil it for you."

She wiped a stray drip from her forehead with the back of her hand. "I do have a bullheaded streak."

Holding her gaze, Landon loosened the horse's cinch and slid the saddle off with one hand. "I can see that."

As exhausted as she was, she might've toppled over trying to carry it to the saddle rack. He took the gear into the tack room, and after a minute, he emerged with a small electric clipper, setting it on a shelf outside the door. Two bottles of water hung from his fingers, and condensation already clouded the clear plastic. He handed her one.

In grateful surprise, she twisted the cap off and took several swallows. Ice-cold ambrosia.

"Landon, you're a god. Thank you."

He chuckled before taking a few pulls from his own bottle. He waved at the tack room door. "Anytime you're here, help yourself to the fridge."

On the floor next to her bench, a five-gallon bucket of water held a giant floating sponge. In a small kindness to the animal, he must have put the chilly well water out earlier to warm up.

With his free hand, Landon toted the pail to Pongo and set it next to the far wall. He dunked the golden sponge and then, in a practiced motion, sluiced water over the horse's back, focusing on a damp spot shaped like the saddle pad. The appaloosa shook like a colossal dog, and Landon jumped back, his face misted with spray.

Harper smothered a giggle with her hand.

Looking a little embarrassed, he grabbed a utility towel from a stack on the shelf and scowled at the horse. "Thanks a lot, you spotted traitor."

While he dried off, Harper laughed. "I know exactly how Pongo feels. I want to rip this blasted helmet off and shake my head."

Landon waved toward the back of the stable. "There's a full water trough in the lot. When it gets good and hot, I dunk my head. Feel free to indulge. It *is* a barn."

"You tempt me. But my hair is ugly-short under this darn helmet—I'd scare the horses."

"Hair?" Landon doffed his hat, revealing stubble the same dark color as his shadow of beard growth—sparse on top and thicker on the sides. "It's highly overrated."

Harper's long absent laugh returned a second time. "Well,

short makes doing my hair a snap, I'll give you that. But I do kind of miss it."

He repositioned his hat with a practiced hand and grabbed the clippers. "I take a look in the mirror on my way out and say, *screw it*."

She laughed again. "Funny, I've taken to some of that myself."

"Pongo's a little baldy, too." One corner of his mouth rose, and he buzzed off a section of mane behind the horse's ears, clearing a spot for the bridle. "Poor guy's tail is so straggly, I had to put sunscreen on the skin underneath."

Again, his kindness struck her. She suspected many wouldn't have bothered. "I suppose they can burn, too."

"They do. It's a shame—there's no need for it."

The man was totally endearing. Plus, he exuded confidence. When Ensign had suspected his hair was thinning, he'd obsessed over his appearance. One day, she'd caught him with her makeup mirror trying to count hairs in a square inch of his scalp.

Landon was comfortable in his own skin, and didn't appear to be the least intimidated by a supposed celebrity. Maybe she'd been wrong and he hadn't recognized her. "Do you know who I am, Landon?"

He repositioned his hat and the almost smile returned along with unmistakable heat in his gaze. "Ma'am, I'd recognize those eyes anywhere."

A thrill shuddered through her, and after everything she'd been through, she marveled that she still had the ability to respond to a man.

CHAPTER FIVE

*H*arper's lush lips parted on a sigh, firing Landon's imagination. Before the ungentlemanly visions sent him reeling, he brushed the loose hair from Pongo's neck.

She beamed a brilliant smile he hadn't earned, revealing perfectly white teeth against her flawless sun-kissed complexion. "Thank you. My self-image is a little bruised right now. I needed a boost." She tugged at her helmet's chin-strap. "My alias seems to be a fail. You recognized me at lunch the other day, didn't you?"

Star-filled galaxies in her black gaze sucked Landon in with a gravitational pull. Photographs in no way did justice to those inky pools, and her missing jet locks only emphasized the real-life impact of Harper Inez. Landon's insides melted.

Like an idiot, he'd told her to go dunk her head. He tried for a casual chuckle. "The dropped jaw gave me away?"

Her laughter almost sounded musical. "Why yes sir, it did."

"For the record, I knew who you were before you'd given

out your autograph." With barn swallows dive-bombing his insides, Landon was surprised his voice worked. "That was right nice of you, too, by the way. You made that little girl's day—probably her year."

Rising from the bench, she crossed the aisle and caressed the horse's muzzle, standing only a few inches shorter than Landon's six-foot-two height. So close. "She actually has some potential. I hope her dreams come true."

The sensation of circling her tiny waist echoed in his palms—and he was ashamed of himself. Technically, he'd been providing care as a professional, but all he could think of was the smooth warmth of her silky skin under his fingers. When she'd lost her balance, there'd been no time to avoid the unintentional contact. Even thinking about it after the fact, he had trouble controlling his reaction.

Landon draped an elbow over Pongo's withers. "I have a confession—I'm a little bit of a fan. But you're not what I expected."

"What's different?" Amusement lit her eyes. "No bikini?"

He blinked, bringing himself under control. "You make a bikini worth looking at, that's for sure." With a low laugh, he delayed his response. He'd actually anticipated she'd be closed off or even haughty. His unfair bias would only hurt her feelings. "I can't really say. I suppose that when you read about someone in the media, you get a notion in your head of what they'd be like in person."

She bit her lower lip before smiling. "And I'm not living up to your expectations?"

Despite her teasing humor, Landon suspected his answer was important to her. "More like you exceed them." Her eyes brightened, giving him the courage to soar with the eagles—or crash to ash. "It's like Harper Inez is still that celebrity I read about last week, and you're a regular person I just met—someone I'd like to know better."

Her smile lit up the space. "Why Mr. Macek—that might be one of the kindest things anyone's ever said to me."

No camera had ever captured that glow. Now was the moment to ask her out. The invitation was in her eyes, and his lips parted. Landon's phone buzzed at his hip, and he fumbled around to ghost the call.

She bit her lip again, clearly amused by him. "That could be important."

The president of the United States couldn't get a minute of his time right now. "Not that important."

Shaking her head, her smile teased him. "Trust me. I've learned the hard way—at least screen."

He retrieved his cell from his pocket. *Bingham.* If they could firm up a deal, Landon could still catch the Houston rodeo. "Sorry, I do need to take this."

Her playful smirk said, *I told you so.* "Okay."

Who takes a call about a horse from an old fart instead of kicking it with Harper Inez? Unbelievable. Landon laughed before connecting. "Macek here."

Her shadow bodyguard still killed time around the alley entry, so he raised a finger at Harper, excusing himself to the tack room. Assorted therapy saddles occupied racks lining the wall, and the scent of oiled leather filled the room. He claimed a chair at a desk in the corner.

After exchanging greetings, Landon got down to business. "Did you have time to look over my proposal?"

"I'm considering it. I've got questions about paragraph eight."

"Hold a sec." After placing the call on speaker, Landon opened the lease contract on his phone and scrolled to section eight, surprised that the lease term required discussion. He needed the horse long enough to finish out the finals. What the hell? "You want to adjust the dates?"

Bingham cleared his throat. "Not the dates, exactly. But I

was thinking, December's pretty far off. I've had lookers. What if I sell the horse thirty days from now?"

"I'm not sure I see your point." Landon played dumb. He didn't like where this was going—at all. "After the finals, I'll trailer Opie to his new home anywhere in the lower forty-eight."

"That's not until December. Four months is a lot of time to rethink an offer. Or what if an early buyer doesn't like Opie's performance and backs out?"

Translation—*what if you lose and make my horse look bad.* Landon bit back a groan. This deal was falling apart. "Go on."

"To make this solid on my end, if I sell the horse, I need the lease to expire. I think they call it a termination clause. I'll make it easy on you. If Opie sells before Vegas, I'll ship him to his new home—unless you can find a way to *buy* him."

Bingham was trying to wheedle him into purchasing the horse. Not at all happy with the man's tactics, Landon tried to keep his irritation out of his voice. "Davey, a termination clause won't work. And as much as I'd like to buy Opie, the truth is, I don't have that much coin in the bank, and a loan isn't an option."

"According to the rodeo standings, you've earned almost two-hundred thousand this season. You didn't spend all of it, did ya?"

"Yeah, and about forty went for gas. Add in some serious vet bills, too." Landon snorted. "If you looked me up, then you know this is my first year with actual earnings."

The question irritated Landon. Bingham knew firsthand the outlandish expenses it took to rodeo. Further, Landon's rodeo bio photo announced his modest sponsorship income with only three smalltime sponsor patches on his shirt. He'd earned the best money of his life this season, but he'd put every spare dime into his training stable. A rodeo career could be one year and done.

He had to think ahead. His partner, Burl Fitzgibbons, had everything he owned tied up in their joint venture. Landon couldn't risk his half of their property for a horse and leave Fitchy hanging like that.

Resolved to his priorities, Landon sighed. "My horse is down until next year. If I go back on the road, I've got to know I can take my game all the way to Vegas."

A charged silence filled the line.

"That's firm?" Bingham's gravelly voice broke the quiet in the tack room.

Landon dropped his forehead onto the heel of his hand. "I don't see any middle ground here."

The season was really over.

Bingham might've said goodbye, Landon didn't hear much until a dial tone sounded. He slid his phone into his pocket and took a moment to recover his bearings.

The lease had been a longshot from the beginning, but he hadn't realized until this moment how much he'd hoped it would work out—how much he'd dreamed of being the world champion. The prize truck and purse money would've been a great boost for the business, but losing out on stuff had never hurt his heart. Leaving the world championship behind put a hole in it.

Last year, he'd ranked in the sixties somewhere—buried. With Rocket, he'd climbed to the top five until he'd finally left Jenkins eating his dust, claiming the number one spot. Something inside Landon needed to prove that he was more than a weekend jackpot roper—that he belonged with the big boys. But the top spot had slipped from his grasp, and he'd have to wait until next season, again.

He took a breath and stepped from the tack room. Harper replaced a sweat scraper to its peg on the wall. She had squeegeed the remaining water from Pongo's coat, surprising Landon. One look at her creased brow, and he knew she'd overheard his conversation with Bingham. "Sorry, I should've shut the door."

Her lips tightened barely short of a frown. "You look like someone stomped on your birthday cake. Want to share?"

Rodeo was his life, but to a jetsetter like Harper Inez, chasing cattle would probably sound like a kid's game. "It's nothing. I tried to lease a horse, and it fell through."

Tucking her chin, her surprise was plain. "People *rent* horses?"

"All the time." He waved at the nearly dry appy. "Pongo's here on lease."

"Okay. I can see contracting for a therapy horse, but why would *you* rent one?"

He removed his hat to wipe his forehead. "In my day job, I'm a calf roper. But I'm afoot at the moment."

She tilted her head. "Why's that?"

With the fresh ball of disappointment in his gut, he almost blurted out his woes, but losing Opie was only a bump in his road. A glance at Harper's helmet put his world into perspective. No one had shot him in the head. He was healthy, Rocket would recover, and Landon could try again next year.

Still, he needed put his mind on something else before he lost what good humor he had left. He waved in the general direction of the vet hospital. "My mount's in rehab across the way. In fact, I need to check on him. Let me put Pongo up, and we can get you and your shadow back to the office."

"My shadow? Oh, Fletcher." She laughed. "He is, isn't he?"

Landon led the gelding to his stall and then detoured to an equipment area in the back where Ryder stored a John Deere Gator. Instead of the classic green, this one was vibrant blue. Landon had double-checked to be sure it was in fact a Gator.

Similar to his at home, the small four-wheel-drive farm

vehicle had a bed to haul feed and other necessities, except this newer, high-end model had four gray seats and a matching soft-top cover. A silver Stick Pony logo looked a lot like a grade schooler had drawn a horse and rider on the rear side panel.

With only a few head onsite, Landon hadn't needed the ATV, but the hill to the barn had used Harper up. He didn't want her to push. In his layman's view, she'd already gotten plenty of rehab. The vehicle fired right up, and he put it in gear before retracing his route to the front of the barn.

As he approached, she rose from the bench, smiling. "This is a nice surprise."

He set the brake and got out to meet her on the passenger side. "I thought we could arrive at the office in style."

"You're such a gentleman."

Accepting his hand, she carefully stepped into the vehicle and claimed a spot on the upholstered bench. She settled her cane against the dash. Relieved she'd abandoned her bull-headed streak, Landon climbed in behind the wheel. They stopped outside the entrance and offered a lift to Fletcher.

The bodyguard hesitated, surveying their surroundings. "Sure, but I'll take the back."

He leapt into the small bed, taking a stance behind the seats with a hand on the roll bar. Apparently, he wanted a three-sixty-five view for the short trip. Wells's pretty-boy tabloid pictures didn't make Landon think coldblooded killer. How big a threat could Harper's ex be?

He didn't know if Ryder allowed ATVs on the sidewalks, so Landon traveled the rougher ground alongside the pavement, taking it slow to minimize the bounce factor.

"What's his name?" Harper raised her voice over the engine noise, catching him lost in his thoughts.

"Whose name?"

"Your horse, silly. He has a name doesn't he?"

"Yep. He does." Landon chuckled. "His papers say something wordy that I can never remember, so I call him Rocket."

"Does that mean he's fast?"

Remembering the first time he'd let the quarter horse run full throttle made him nostalgic. With open road in front of him, the mediocre racehorse had bunched up under Landon like a bronc ready to unload, but instead, all that power had blasted forward.

Recalling his awe, he shook his head. "When he's healthy, he's damn near supersonic."

"He sounds incredible." Harper appeared almost shy, surprising him. "I'd like to see him some time."

Landon met her hesitant gaze, and hints of vulnerability shone in her eyes. The blown horse deal faded from his mind. "The vet's place is on this same property—he and Ryder bought the land together. But I was going to grab a sandwich before stopping in." No finals go-round had ever made his heart pound like this. "Join me?"

Instead of answering right away, she looked over her shoulder at Fletcher.

"No pressure." Landon might've sounded casual, he couldn't tell over the pulse whooshing in his ears. "I understand if it's complicated."

Her smile said yes. "Not complicated. Thank you. I'd enjoy lunch." An impish gleam shone in her gaze. "But since I skipped the water trough, I need to dunk my head under the shower. Mind waiting on me a few minutes?"

Hours. He'd wait hours for a lunch date with Harper Inez. He reminded himself to breathe. "Sure thing. I need to clean up, too. There's a sport's bar and grill in town— the Wild Card, I think. It isn't fancy, but I've heard the food's good."

They pulled in at a reserved spot near the office front door. Fletcher hopped out and strode to an Acura in the lot.

His meticulous inspection of the car's undercarriage again brought to mind the threat level surrounding Harper.

The activity caught her eye, too, but she quickly returned her attention to Landon. "That sounds perfect. Meet me in the Lodge lobby in about an hour?"

Reining in his enthusiasm, Landon conceded that lunch wasn't really a date. However, sandwiches could lead to an evening of drinks and dinner—he might even dance. He finally took an easy breath. She's a regular person, like anyone else. If only a guy could ignore the *world-famous supermodel* part.

CHAPTER SIX

*S*eated on the hotel suite's cream sofa, Juanita's face screwed up in certain condemnation. "For real, Harper? You're going to lunch with a *cowboy* you met this morning?"

She had a point, and Harper smoothed rumples from her scoop-necked t-shirt, feigning nonchalance. "He's nice. Fletcher says he's a friend of Barlow's from Hollywood. Remember, we saw them together. Plus, Ryder said they'd done background checks on everyone."

Juanita's jaw dropped. "And this nice guy happened to leave Hollywood to shovel horse poo in Colorado? I was going to break this to you easy, but you need to see it, *now*." Rifling through a shopping tote at her feet, she pulled out a folded newspaper too thin to be anything but a nasty tabloid. "I was shopping in Old Towne and stopped for a soda. I found this little surprise at the convenience store."

She tossed the folded paper onto the sofa between them as though it was too disgusting for touch. Dread made Harper's heart pound, and she steeled herself for the worst, flipping the menacing newsprint open. A full color shot of her in her helmet glared back at her, captioned, *Not an easy patient to deal with.*

Somehow, the tabloids always got a legal pass for stolen photos and all their other garbage. Her face heated with her fury. "That cheesy therapist got a big golden parachute with his lost job."

Appearing at once contrite, Juanita's gaze misted over. "I'm sorry. Really, I am. But I'm freaked that you're going out with a guy we know nothing about."

Livid and trying to hold it together, Harper waved at the picture. "This was inevitable. Legal threats can't compete with a tabloid's big money. I'm surprised it took this long."

As though trying to erase the event, Juanita folded the paper and tossed it on the coffee table. "That asshole was probably busy managing a bidding war. I love you, and you don't deserve this."

Harper's passionately protective sister was easily as furious as she was. She took a deep breath. "I love you, too. I'll call my attorney later."

"Don't bother. I got him on the phone first thing. The clerk at the Quick Stop is still talking about the potty-mouthed, crazy lady who slapped a tabloid in front of her."

The image pulled a tension-breaking chuckle from Harper. "You didn't."

Juanita's snort devolved into laughter. "You know I did."

She was right about Harper's impulsive decision to go out to lunch, and Harper conceded that she'd been an idiot. But Landon seemed so sweet. He'd said things that made her feel good. Better than good—normal. Like a regular person. Not famous, and not damaged.

She could ask Fletcher to send her regrets. She should. "Fletcher says that their head of security already knows what size underwear Landon buys, but the guy's out of the office today."

"Good, go to lunch tomorrow *after* you have his waist-band measurement. Not today, please."

Despite the tabloid article, or maybe because of it, Harper sensed the defiant resurgence of her bullheaded streak. "I want to do one normal thing. A nice guy asked me to grab a sandwich, and I'm going. Fletcher will tag along—there's no way to lose him. What more do you want?"

Juanita gusted a familiar *I-give-up* sigh and pulled out her phone. "At least we can do the basics. What's his name, again?"

"Landon Macek—and no, I don't know how it's spelled." A warm flush of embarrassment washed over Harper. She could've done a simple internet search, but she'd never had to bother. "I guess I'm out of practice. Even the times I considered leaving Ensign, the thought of trying to meet anyone new made me cringe."

"Online searches are imperative when you're dating. Especially if you're going to lunch with a *nice-guy* stable hand."

With her penchant for online dating, Juanita would know. Harper snorted. The thought of celebrity matchmaking sites made her left eye twitch.

She doubted much had changed since she'd dated. It seemed only jerks and weirdos had enough nerve to ask her out. The whole sordid process disturbed her, and thinking back, she might've even stayed with Ensign partly to avoid it. He was a known quantity—safe. At least he used to be.

Their drift apart had been subtle, insidious. Every time his agent notified him of a lost role, he'd be sullen for a while. Then he'd get better. Looking back, each rejection seemed to chip away at his confidence, and he'd changed over time. At some unknown point, they'd gone from happy to habit. She shook off the grim reverie.

Hoping to appear casual while a couple tense minutes

ticked off, she tried not to show too much interest in Juanita's search. When her sister's brows shot up, panic rocketed through Harper.

"What?" she snapped.

"What kind of a cowboy is he?"

"I don't know." Heart in her throat, Harper leaned over, trying to peer at her sister's phone. "He mentioned roping."

"He was behind me in the restaurant." Juanita flipped the screen toward her, displaying Landon over a downed calf throwing his arms out to his sides. "This him?"

"Give me that." Harper snatched the phone from her grasp.

Juanita leaned in. "Apparently, your Mr. Stetson is—"

"—in *Sports Illustrated*." Stunned, Harper scanned the Cinderella story of this year's rodeo sensation, Landon Macek; all but forgetting Juanita was in the room. "He never said ... only talked about how fast Rocket was before ..."

"You're mumbling. Who's Rocket?"

Brought back to the present, Harper took a breath. "His horse, it was in the story."

Juanita pursed her lips. "Yeah, I might've read it if you'd given me the chance."

"Sorry." Harper returned the phone. She'd soak in the full article later. "That was published in June. Since then, Rocket got hurt. His injury was a much bigger deal than Landon had let on. He was number one. Maybe he can get back in it somehow."

Even as she spoke, Harper knew that wouldn't happen. The deal Landon had tried to make on a new mount had fallen through. When he'd walked out of the tack room with that miserable expression, he'd been devastated, and she hadn't even realized that his dreams had been shattered. She pulled out her phone and tapped to locate the article again.

"That's tragic, for sure." But the good news is, instead of

stalking you and your fly-by-night cowboy at lunch, I'm going to the spa." Juanita shifted next to her, gathering her tote. She almost bounced from the couch. "Don't worry your little head over me. I'm more than happy to go alone."

"That fast? He's okay now?"

Juanita lifted her phone, still showing Landon's picture. "Well, it's clear that he's been too busy to be a hitter on the side."

The pragmatic attitude they'd adopted over Harper's attempted murder struck her anew. She couldn't afford to ignore her new reality. From now on, vetting dates would be an unpleasant fact of life.

The article reassured her about Landon's nice-guy status, but she'd been too comfortable. She'd actually asked to see his horse. The thought sobered her, and she vowed to be more careful. After lunch.

About a half hour later, Harper exited the elevator with Fletcher, scanning the lobby for Landon. She spotted him several feet away sitting on a teal sofa with a booted foot draped across his knee. Beard growth matched his scalp stubble, and the masculine style suited him along with his jeans and a gray short-sleeved shirt. She paused to savor the sight. The bodyguard politely wandered to the front desk to speak with an attendant.

With a baby grand in the background and chandeliers overhead, Landon scanned his phone, appearing relaxed in the formal setting. He shifted and moved his hat from his leg to the seat next to him. When his eyes met hers, the delight in his gaze belied his composed expression. He was happy to see her.

Giving him her best smile, she fluttered fingers at him, ignoring the butterflies doing summersaults in her stomach. She hoped he wouldn't mind the adjustments she'd made to their lunch plans.

He rose and his boot heels struck the lobby's parquet floor as he strode towards her. His athletic grace made her wonder if he'd miss the sexy strut she'd perfected for the runway. She did—or rather the ease of walking a straight line.

She stuffed the pang of self-pity away with all the others that had accumulated. When she stored her cane in the closet for good, she'd have a pity-party blowout to celebrate. Losing the cane was a long-term goal.

Today, she was pleased to wear shorts for the first time since she'd left rehab. The muscles of her weak leg had filled out to the point the disparity between the two was miniscule. More baby steps in her recovery. Enjoying each one kept the negative thoughts at bay.

Landon joined her near the desk, and his attempt at a discreet head to toe scan fell barely short of lecherous. There was no mistaking his approval. "Hello there."

She'd never appeared less sexy in her life, and with one look, he'd made her feel desirable. A slow burn swirled deep in her pelvis. She tracked his broad-shouldered frame down to his boots and back up to meet his hazel gaze. "Hi right back."

Inside, his eyes took on a golden-brown hue, muting the hints of green. A dazzling smile showed his teeth and put delectable hollows in his cheeks. The change from ruggedly handsome to boyish cute jump-started the butterflies in her stomach. "You have dimples."

He ran a hand down his face and scaled back his smile to his signature curve of the lips, giving her the impression that he tried to hide the darling feature. "Sometimes."

The self-conscious moment was endearing, and the flirty banter was heady. It had been years since she'd enjoyed playful words with heated subtext. Landon definitely had piqued her interest.

Looking very official in his gold polo with a blue AG logo, Fletcher joined them, dispelling the moment. He'd changed clothes, too, and Harper wondered where he'd hidden his gun. "Miss Rodriguez, the Sun Room has a table, or they're happy to prepare something to go."

Trying to temper the surprise in Landon's expression, Harper rushed to explain. "I'd wanted to ask you about changing our plans before you got here, but I didn't have your phone number. Security needs more notice to cover me off Lodge property. Will lunch here be okay?"

"Sure, that's fine." He turned a thoughtful gaze on Fletcher, as though realizing the bodyguard was a permanent fixture. "Safety first. We can eat sandwiches anywhere."

"I hoped you'd understand." Harper shifted her gaze to Fletcher. "Maybe we can go into Spencer sometime with more planning."

"Twenty-four hours is generally enough," Fletcher replied. "If you go into town, I need at least one other man along."

The last thing Harper wanted was to be a demanding diva. "That's reasonable." Knowing Landon had a legitimate profession, and that he was super good at it, gave her more courage. "If Rocket can wait for us a little while, how does lunch by the lake sound?"

Landon chuckled. "Rocket's in good hands." Any concerns he might've had over their adjusted plans seemed to vanish. "I'm surprised you went to all this trouble."

"One of the bennies of having a local bodyguard is that they know all the tricks. Fletcher recommended we try one of the Lodge's private picnic sites, and necessity aside, Boulder Raspberry sounds like a lovely place to enjoy lunch."

His dimples almost reappeared with his smile. "Ryder gave me a tour of the Lodge but he didn't take me by any picnic areas."

At a word from Fletcher, a young man behind the desk produced a leather folder. The bodyguard stepped away, and Harper automatically jotted his usual two clubs on the order sheet. If she'd asked for his order, he'd have declined because *he was on duty*.

She and Landon huddled over the menu at the counter while they made their selections—not an easy task, as it turned out. His muscular arm touching hers proved distracting, but she did nothing to make space between them. Three sandwiches and a variety of sides later, they plotted to share the assortment. In the ultimate sin, Harper added a s'mores dessert kit.

Landon slid the order sheet towards the smiling clerk. As they turned from the counter, he offered her his left arm and with his free hand, gently took her cane. "Should we take a seat while we wait?"

After a brief instant of confusion, she linked her arm with his and then realized what he'd done. She was now a woman walking with a man, not a cane. Overwhelmed in a good way, she gave his arm a squeeze. "You're such an old-world gent."

"I try, ma'am."

After they returned to his couch and settled in, she plied him with a couple innocent questions about his horse, hoping he'd divulge his pro-athlete status, but he never gave up the goods. He'd share his life with her in his own time, so she didn't push it. Instead, she politely answered his benign questions about her recovery.

In what seemed like five minutes later, Victor arrived carrying an honest to goodness picnic basket and set it next to Landon. Harper couldn't recall the last time she'd gone on a picnic. According to the ginormous clock on the wall, a full twenty minutes had flown by while they'd waited.

The Sun Room assistant manager smiled at them both.

"It's a beautiful day for a trip to the waterfall. Fortunately, there was a cancellation. Enjoy."

Harper's excitement for the afternoon grew. "Thank you, we will."

"Waterfall?" Landon asked.

Behind him, a man took an innocent picture of his girls at the piano, and Harper dropped her gaze to the floor, waiting until the father took his kidlets to another photo stop. If the dad recognized her and shot a picture of her with Landon, it could turn into a mess. She didn't have the energy to deal with a tabloid story about her and *a new cowboy boyfriend*.

If her brief inattention had offended him, Landon didn't let it show. This first foray back into the single life was a big event for her, and she resolved to forget the tabloids and enjoy their time together. "Yes, Fletcher said that's why Boulder Raspberry is the most popular. It sounds lovely."

"I'm sure it will be." He surveyed the lobby with an arched brow. "Everything around here is over the top."

CHAPTER SEVEN

*H*arper had warmed nicely to holding on to Landon's arm, and even though he'd contrived the whole thing, he reveled in the contact. He sent a thank you up to Grandma Macek.

In her later years, she never went out without Grandpa to lean on, openly admitting that she was simply too vain to use a cane in public. With all the adjustments Harper had endured, Landon could only guess at the emotional price she paid.

He escorted her through the elegant lobby with soaring ceilings and an opulent staircase curving up to an open floor above, well aware that he didn't belong here. With her hand warm on his arm, he tabled his worry over the skyrocketing cost of lunch. No way was Landon allowing her to pay for their picnic. Surely, Victor could access Harper's bill so that he could cover it.

An attendant in a navy Lodge polo opened one of the tall gleaming wood doors for them. Apparently, he was a permanent fixture—he'd greeted Landon earlier. At the hotels

Landon used on the rodeo circuit, he was lucky if the desk clerk looked up from her computer.

Under the portico outside, Fletcher waited behind the wheel of a four-person courtesy vehicle with their basket on the empty seat next to him. After assisting Harper into the rear seat of the cart, Landon skirted around to the other side and slid onto the padded bench, acutely aware of when his thigh touched hers. The electric motor whirred, and the golf cart pulled forward.

They traveled along a ridge, and the view of Twin Owl Lake opened up before them. Childlike awe suffused Harper's expression. "This whole area's gorgeous. See how the lake mirrors the mountains?"

The glorious vista had nothing on the woman beside him. Landon could hardly pull his eyes from her. "I'd like to see the Rockies from horseback while I'm here. We've got the Sierra Nevada nearby in California, but each range has its own magic."

"Yes. That's exactly what it is. Magic." She snapped a couple of pictures with her phone before settling back into her seat, and her dark gaze found him. "You're from California? Me too, originally."

He'd read this before, but somehow it seemed intrusive to mention it. "Really, what part?"

"I was raised in Redding. It's a few hours north of Sacramento. And you?"

"I've got a place down south near Copper City. Do you still have family in California?"

"Mamá lives in Los Angeles, and my sister moved to Chicago. We're spread out, but we stay connected. Sometimes, I have shoots near L.A. Not so often in Chicago, but we make visits happen. In fact, Juanita is here with me now."

"I think I saw your sister. It was hard to miss the resemblance," Landon replied. Harper had done a good job of keeping her family out of the media, so this was all news to him. "Your father?"

With a small frown, she shrugged. "My parents are from Argentina. Papá wanted to go back home, and Mamá didn't, so they split."

"I'm sorry. That must've been hard on everyone."

"Juanita and I were pretty young when it happened. We fly down now and then to see him, but it's a long trip." She straightened in her seat. "Oh, wow."

Landon hadn't noticed anything but Harper. The courtesy cart had pulled into a small parking area at the forest's edge, and Fletcher stopped the vehicle. They disembarked, heading for the picnic area that didn't compare to any public park Landon had ever seen.

A good distance away, a brook tumbled over several feet of large, stacked variegated stones, cascading into a pool. A cobblestone patio on either side of the falls hugged the stream a short distance, and varied colors of shrubs made inroads between mossy boulders at the water's edge.

As they neared, Harper appeared more entranced. She gestured to the trees on the far side of the patio. "Oh, my. Look at that."

Offsetting the verdant theme, tall wildflowers with tiny white petals edged the outside of the patio, holding the forest undergrowth at bay. A leggy tan bird with a black crown perched near the protection of the trees, tugging furiously at a stubborn raspberry.

Scanning the area, he gave a whistle of appreciation. "This sure is something."

Maybe a professional eye could determine if the setting was natural or manmade. Landon suspected a little of both. Since he planned to cover the lunch date, he couldn't help but wonder if their parkland reservation came complimentary with her room. Not likely.

He stepped out of the vehicle and paced around to her side to offer a hand of support while she exited.

Fletcher materialized next to Landon and handed him the picnic basket. "I'll give you two as much privacy as I can, but you'll always be in sight."

No doubt, the man spoke more to Landon than Harper. He had no intention to seduce her over lunch, and in public, no less. A little Tim McGraw and candlelight was more his style. Still, he tried not to read any insult into the subtle warning. "You're doing an important job, and I appreciate that."

Fletcher gave a half-smile. "You'd be surprised how many don't." He turned to Harper. "If you do need me, holler. I won't be far."

"Thanks, Fletcher," Harper said, and as he turned to leave, she raised a hand. "Wait, there's a box lunch in here for you."

He accepted the lunch with a smiling thank you and then strode off to take a seat near the forest's edge. The bodyguard tag-a-long reminded Landon of an oversized-dad chaperone. Next, the guy would show him a gun collection.

Voices came from beyond the trees, and a child's high-pitched laughter carried to them. Even without Fletcher's company, they didn't have privacy. Leaving her cane in the modified golf cart, Harper tucked her hand into the crook of his arm, and her dancing black eyes turned his brains to mush. He was the weakest man on earth.

"Let's check out the waterfall before we eat," she said.

He was starving, but … "Whatever the lady desires."

No truer words. If his attraction was simply lust for a hot-bod celebrity, he could've walked away. But it wasn't. The striking woman in front of him was kind, sweetly vulnerable, and she'd been nothing but decent people to him and everyone around her.

For the millionth time he puzzled how anyone could

think to harm her. Screw the world championship. He was staying in Spencer for as long as he had a shot with this amazing woman.

"Look, there's a table and a fire pit to make our s'mores." She pointed across the pond before glancing around. "But how do we get there?"

Landon jutted his chin downstream where the collection pool overflowed into a miniature rocky torrent. "I think there might be a crossing farther down a piece. It can't be more than a foot deep."

They strolled along a stone path following the winding brook, serenaded by the melody of the rushing water, though the sound wasn't loud enough to hide the rumble of his stomach.

She turned a mocking smirk on him. "Maybe we should eat first?"

"Maybe so." He laughed. "Bears could be around. Food might draw them out, so it would be the safest thing to do."

With widened eyes, her gaze snapped to his, and he realized he'd made her nervous.

"Black bears are in the Rockies, but they'll stay clear of an area like this." He smiled, hoping to reassure her. "So no bears."

She pursed her lips into a pouty bow. "You were teasing me."

He laughed. "More like a lame joke that fell flat on the room. No one gets me."

Her pretty smile held forgiveness. "I'll try harder."

When they rounded a copse of trees, a masonry bridge arching over the miniature rapids seemed to come up out of nowhere.

"Oh, my," she said on a sigh. Harper slowed, squeezing his arm. "Don't you feel like you've been thrown back in time by about two-hundred years?"

The pure wonder in her expression charmed him. "I've been thrown, all right." The woman had made him downright dizzy. "This way, m'lady."

With basket in hand, he escorted her over the paved bridge and then set their lunch on the shaded table beside the fire pit. She sat down, toed off her shoes, and then crossed one long bare leg over the other, fueling his imagination. All that lithe limb. She tucked her foot behind her ankle before innocently lifting the wooden lid to remove their lunch.

The woman was going to kill him. No wonder Fletcher had warned him off. Landon claimed his own seat next to her—and her long legs.

Trying to distract himself, he rubbed the back of his neck and searched around—for anything. The bodyguard ate his sandwich with furtive glances in their direction. Landon wondered if she ever left home without him.

With an impish smile, Harper lifted a giant chocolate bar in one hand and a plastic bag of marshmallows in the other. "I may have dessert first." She set them next to a trigger-style lighter and then played with a telescoping camp fork, extending it. "And look at this. I've never seen one. When we were kids, we stripped bark from skinny tree branches."

One article had mentioned she'd started modeling at seventeen. Campfires might not have been part of her life. "When was the last time you roasted a marshmallow?"

"Oh, gosh. I don't know. Ten years, or more." She cupped her mouth as though telling a secret. "They're not an approved food."

Stunned, Landon's jaw dropped. "For ten years?"

She sighed. "Weigh-ins are pretty serious stuff."

"I just figured you had great genes. You know, blessed with natural beauty."

"Oh, I *am* blessed, just not with a high metabolism. I was super lucky, too. Well, until this." She tapped her helmet.

"Overall, the sacrifices have been worth it. I've got financial security. And so does my family."

"It's got to be nice having enough money to take care of loved ones, but dang. I'd never considered what it might take to be in your line of work." He snatched the lighter from the table. "We need to fix this right now. One roasted marshmallow per decade won't ruin you."

She laughed. "The shooting has changed my attitude about a few things. Like dessert. Eat it first—'cause you never know."

People dealt how they could. Uncertain how to respond to her macabre humor, he simply smiled. "Sounds like a good motto to me."

She handed him a bottle of water. "I think so."

Someone had conveniently stacked wood next to the pit's brick wall. The lodge folks thought of everything. Within minutes, a blaze danced merrily in the metal bowl. While he'd started the fire, she'd opened their artisan bread sandwiches and placed a fourth of each one on her plate. Stubs of bacon and cheese sat off to the side. Since she apparently didn't eat a whole anything, maybe she went for variety.

He took his seat and promptly stuffed a big corner of a pineapple chicken salad on ciabatta into his mouth. She frowned at her plate and then gave the marshmallow bag a wistful look. "Yep, dessert first."

With two of the puffy marshmallows skewered onto the long fork, she pulled her chair to the edge of the brick pit. She sent Landon a mischievous grin before giving the delicacies her full attention. "You have to rotate slow and easy, or they ignite. Papá loved the charred marshmallows. We always gave him the ruined ones."

He rose and pulled the table to the pit, placing the s'mores fixings within arm's reach. "What do you mean *ruined*? The black ones are the best."

She grimaced. "Eeewww." A spark flew from her golden dessert, and she yanked it from the flame for a close inspection. "You're distracting me. This is important stuff here."

He laughed at the mock admonishment. While she methodically rotated her prized dessert, Landon wolfed down the rest of his chicken salad, assuaging the worst of his appetite. She kept one eye on the marshmallows while she sipped from her water bottle.

The scent of the toasting marshmallow turned his mind to dessert, too. "I'm shirking my receiving duties." He put two graham crackers with chocolate squares on a fresh plate and then held a graham topper at the ready in each hand to trap the melted goodness. "Right here, Harper."

She stilled, and he realized he'd forgotten to use her alias. "I meant Luciana. Sorry."

Her smile didn't meet her eyes, making her appear sad, of all things. "It's only important when people are around." With a glance at the chocolate, she brightened, apparently moving on. "Okay, here we go."

After she positioned the toasted marshmallows atop the chocolate and graham cracker bases, Landon executed a perfect trap, and the creamy confections squished out the sides, streaked with melted chocolate. He held up the plate, moving it in enticing circles. "Ten years. You don't want to rush this. Take your time. Pick the best one."

She set her camp fork on the brick ledge, and genuine mirth filled her gaze. The tip of her tongue rested on her upper lip while she studied the two desserts. Plucking her selection from the plate, her musical laughter took flight.

The sound infected Landon, and he chuckled before claiming the remaining s'more. "Okay, we chow down on three. One…two—"

In a preemptive strike, Harper bit the corner of her dessert, and creamy white covered her lips and smudged her nose. She gave a bedroom-worthy groan that Landon yearned to hear again—later.

"You didn't wait for me. I'm crushed," he teased.

She licked her lips, not coming close to clearing the chocolaty marshmallow. With the waterfall and trees behind her, and her dazzling eyes, the sight was adorable. He pulled out his phone and snapped a picture. She didn't have any resemblance to the glamorous Harper Inez in the TV commercials. Instead, she appeared joyful. He turned the phone for her to see.

The delight had evaporated from her expression, replaced with a frown. "We hadn't talked about pictures, but—"

"I should've asked. *No pictures* was probably in that contract thing I signed."

She appeared more sad than irritated. "Probably."

"With that darling dab of marshmallow on your nose, I didn't think." Viewing the image in a moment of painful indecision, he couldn't touch the little trash can. "Before I delete it, at least let me send it to you."

"I'd like that. Pictures are something friends do." Apology shone in her eyes. "But for me, pictures are kind of—"

"—a big deal, I suppose." He'd spoiled the day with a stupid photo.

She nodded before giving him an @TorrensPR email addy. He typed it in, figuring the PR stood for *public relations*.

Apparently, he didn't warrant friend status yet. "I understand."

After he clicked send, his inbox pinged with an auto confirmation response from her publicist. If she wouldn't even trade phone numbers, today's memories would have to sustain him. He doubted they'd make more of them. He deleted the photo while she watched.

"You better eat up," he said, lacking enthusiasm. "Don't want the bears to change their minds."

She laughed, and he suspected she was simply being polite. They finished their lunch, and Landon missed the chemistry that had disappeared like the deleted photo. A shameful part of him wanted to find a way to retrieve the image. For his eyes only. If he never showed it to anyone, there wouldn't be any harm.

The least he could do was make it easy for her to bail out. He checked his phone. "It's getting on towards three o'clock. If you still want to see Rocket, we should put out the fire and head back. I need to catch the vet onsite and get an update."

"Sure."

They packed up their picnic leftovers, and Landon doused the fire using a conveniently placed pail and a dip of stream water. During the awkward return trip over the bridge, an anvil weighed heavy in his chest. Her hand on his arm lost its magical power over him, and the stream's melody even sounded off key. He'd blown it.

All too soon, the courtesy cart came into view, and Fletcher waited for them. Likely, the man already knew something was up. Landon wanted to clear the air while they were still out of earshot. "Look, about the photo. I should have—no excuses. I'm sorry, is all."

She gave him a half-smile that didn't brighten her eyes. "It's my fault. I should've mentioned it before we got all involved in our picnic."

The ride back to the lodge was quiet, silent. Landon lost any enthusiasm for spending more time with Harper. He'd apologized and that was all he could offer.

Fletcher dropped them off at the main entrance, and Harper accepted Landon's hand to step down from the cart. However, she used her cane instead of his arm while walking into the lobby. This wasn't how the day was supposed to end. He'd hoped to steal a kiss somewhere along the way.

With the bodyguard hanging back, Landon returned the

basket to the front desk, wondering how Harper would extricate herself from the rest of their day.

She placed a hand on his forearm, surprising him. "Between this morning's therapy and our short hike to the waterfall, I'm kind of worn out. I'd like to take a raincheck on meeting Rocket. Forgive me?"

Even though he'd expected her to cut their day short, disappointment hit him square in the chest. He managed to smile. "Sure, another time."

CHAPTER EIGHT

*K*eeping Fletcher and his friends hopping, Harper and Juanita had shopped the Old Towne district every few days, finding new treasures each trip. They'd hit the Wild Card happy hour a couple times, and with every excursion, Harper had hoped to accidentally run into Landon. Three weeks and it never happened. At least when Juanita had sprung the news that she had to leave, they'd spent some quality girl time together.

The day had come, and Harper escorted her to the Mountain Jay Airport helipad—a block of concrete set on the edge of a cluster of service buildings. A few yards away, Fletcher hung back in the parking area leaning against the Acura, while she and her sister took seats on a bench bolted to a covered patio.

"Thanks for the private lift to Denver." She gestured at a navy chopper with a gold stripe and Aspen Gold logo waiting on the raised concrete platform. "You didn't need to."

In the time since the shooting, Juanita had used up all of her vacation time while burning through the legally allowed family leave.

"I wanted to," Harper replied. "You still don't have to go. I can employ you."

Juanita chuckled. "I'd piss you off, and you'd fire me in two weeks. Besides, I like my job. Most days, I *matter*."

"You matter to me…"

"Back at you." She met Harper's gaze with love in her eyes. "If you truly needed me, I'd stay. But you've come so far —you're ready."

Harper didn't feel ready. She had grown to rely on her sister. Maybe that was the problem, and Juanita knew it.

A fifty-something pilot with a healthy midsection circled the chopper, jotting on a clipboard. Apparently satisfied with his inspection, he approached with a smile. "Good afternoon, ladies. If you'd come this way, we're ready for takeoff."

He took charge of Juanita's stacked rolling luggage, and they followed him to the bird. The reality of her departure hit home harder than Harper had expected, and she swallowed against a knot in her throat. She squeezed her sister's hand, and Juanita squeezed back.

The pilot slid the helicopter passenger door open, revealing bucket leather seats with glossy wooden consoles. His gaze lit on their joined hands, and the corners of his eyes crinkled with a slight smile. "You girls take your time; we'll make your Denver connection, no problem."

While he stowed the luggage, Harper hugged her sister long and hard.

Juanita kissed her cheek. "I love you. Even when you think you're weak, you're the strongest person I know." She stepped from their embrace. "You'll stop in Chicago on the way to New York?"

"For sure." Harper's emotions ran rampant, and her throat tightened. "You've been my rock. Thanks—well, *thanks* doesn't cover it. Love you, too."

Juanita hooked a horseshoe pillow around her neck and

shouldered her oversized tote before stepping into the craft. The pilot slid the door shut and then mounted a metal step into the cockpit. Reluctant to leave before she took off, Harper reclaimed a seat on the bench and waited.

With a click and a whine, the rotors started slowly, and the soulless machine sounded as lonely as Harper. She wiped her eyes. The engine noise and the downdraft gained strength before the wheels left the pavement. Juanita pressed her hand to the glass, mouthing *I love you*.

Harper blew her a kiss, and her sister's face blurred. Once the chopper disappeared into the horizon, she rose and trudged to the limo.

Alone. She hadn't been on her own in the two months since she'd hobbled out of inpatient rehab, too bullheaded to use a wheelchair. Juanita had stayed with her during her recovery at home, running interference on *everything*. Now, it was time for Harper to function independently, sink or swim.

Fletcher greeted her at the car. She'd almost forgotten him and the time. "Are we late for Stick Pony?"

"Callie said no rush; they're working in the office."

Though surrounded by support personnel, Harper had never felt more adrift. "Thanks."

A stop in the Lodge lobby for take-out coffee followed by the scenic drive to Stick Pony gave Harper time to regain her composure before therapy. Even if fate had tossed a hand grenade into her life, being a full-grown adult, she needed to take charge of rebuilding. Renewed focus and adjusted life goals would help. She knew how to work hard and work smart. All she needed was direction.

Modeling had always been a ten-year plan, and her real estate investments had paid off. Retirement was even an option. Travel, shopping, and having fun was wonderful in moderation. However, an idle lifestyle didn't appeal. Harper wanted to *matter*.

Other than money, modeling had never brought her satisfaction. She'd loved the few charity events Joni had set up over the years. A stellar network of industry contacts could provide support for a variety of endeavors.

Amid the trees ahead, the Stick Pony sign came into view. First things first. Step one—walk without a cane. Two—put her wanna-be assassin in prison.

After saddling Pongo and mounting up with only standby supervision, Harper followed Callie's instructions, concentrating on her center of balance and staying relaxed in the therapy saddle. She gripped the pommel handle with both hands.

This first trot in the arena seemed like a milestone, and she squared her shoulders. Having developed an interest in hippotherapy, her physical therapist from town, Chad Emmett, jogged at Harper's right with a hand on her thigh. She missed Landon for the millionth time and wondered if he'd asked Callie to find a new sidewalker. Likely.

"Okay, let's slow back down," Callie announced, and Tad, who jogged behind them driving the horse, took the slack out of the longlines. Pongo dropped to a walk. She beamed up at Harper. "That was spectacular. How did it feel?"

"I had to think to keep my seat, but I never felt insecure."

"Tomorrow, let's go for a leisurely ride around Stick Pony. I think you're ready for what we call a little therapeutic riding—it means saddle up and have fun."

Going for a real ride sounded like graduating from college or something. "Do I get a diploma?"

Callie laughed. "No, but I bet you have a good time."

Harper had made progress and wanted to let out a whoop, but instead she smiled and patted the horse's neck.

"That sounds wonderful. I bet Pongo is ready to get out of the arena, too."

Her mount pulled up to the ramp, and she dismounted with nothing but standby readiness from Callie. In the last week, her gait had grown stronger, and she'd wanted to share her news with Landon. Somehow, she had to make things right with him.

He'd worked in and around the stable during her sessions, but any time she'd been in the barn, he'd stayed clear. She had really hurt his feelings over the picture. However, after three weeks, possibly his avoidance might be more than fall out from a simple faux pas. Maybe, he just wasn't into her.

Callie excused herself, and she and Chad returned to the office. As usual, Harper declined Tad's offer to put Pongo away, knowing he would keep a discreet eye on her anyway. This time, however, if he hung around, the horse handler would mess up her devious little plan.

"Really, I've got this part down. I don't need supervision to unsaddle my horse." She gestured to Fletcher in the distance, who paced outside the barn. They put a bench there for him, but he never sat for long. "Plus he's watching every minute to make sure I'm safe."

The kid seemed to get the message and laughed. "Okay, you're on your own."

When he finally strode off after Callie and Chad, she heaved a sigh of relief.

With her cane in one hand, she led Pongo along the sidewalk to the small barn and then snapped him to the short rope across from the tack room. Taking an unimpeded breath, she recalled her first grueling trip up the gentle slope only three weeks ago. Today, she didn't even need to take a break on the park bench, and her improved endurance gave her hope for more progress.

She took her sweet time unsaddling and currying the

horse, expecting that Landon would eventually return to the barn. They had only gone out once, but he'd been easy company. He made her laugh—and feel *good*. Too soon, she finished grooming the appaloosa.

With nothing else to occupy her, she took a seat at the tack room desk and waited for a few humbling minutes, killing time on her phone. Finally disgusted with herself, she snatched the treats that she'd saved for Pongo's feedbox and returned to the horse. His ears perked up, and he stretched out his neck, trying to grab the plastic bag with his lips.

Holding out a few carrots in the palm of her hand, she laughed at him. "No reason for you to wait on your snack."

Harper snuck a crinkle-cut carrot for herself, and Pongo munched contentedly. After a few minutes, the bag was empty, and Harper's impatience grew. She'd never waited on a man in her life. "Okay, Pongo. It's you and me buddy."

His shod hooves echoed down the corridor as she led him to his stall. She took him inside and removed his halter, giving him a rub behind his ears. Her phone buzzed at her hip. It was probably Joni, wanting to plot her comeback.

Harper closed the sliding stall door behind her and retrieved her cell from her pocket.

Ensign: I've missed you.

Her phone fell from her hand and clattered against the concrete. She grabbed one of the stall-divider rails for support. The device had landed screen up, and another bubble of text appeared.

Bootheels thudded at a brisk pace behind her, and she whipped around. Landon. *Now* he showed. With brows drawn together and gripping her cane by the shaft, he halted a few feet away.

"Are you okay?" He lifted the cane. "This was in the tack room, and when you cried out, I thought you'd fallen."

"I—?" Maybe she *had* hollered—or screamed. She didn't

remember. As she honed in on her phone, she could barely breathe let alone make herself touch it. Landon drew up beside her while the small screen at her feet flickered with incoming texts.

"No. You're not okay," he murmured.

She swallowed hard, and the knot in her throat didn't budge.

He picked up the vibrating device, and snapping to life, she grabbed for it before he could read the message previews. His wounded gaze halted her. After an awkward beat, he handed her the phone—screen side down.

"Thanks," she whispered.

She turned it over, and facial recognition opened the text thread.

Ensign: I could never hurt you. The boyfriend's always the easy target. Hennessey wants to put a high-pub notch on his belt. You know I didn't do it.

Ensign: I love you. Screw the attorneys. Let's find a quiet place to ride this out and get married.

Ensign: You and me, sweet thing. Call me. I'm waiting. I'll wait forever."

Harper groaned and dropped the phone to her side.

Landon took a step closer. "I don't want to intrude, but you look like you could—well faint or something. Really, are you okay?"

"Yes, I'm fine." Reeling in shock, her voice cracked, and she lifted her cell between them. "Considering that the NYPD's prime suspect wants me to marry him."

Landon's mouth fell open.

Bravado failing, she curled the phone into her chest and squeezed her eyes shut against the world. Marrying Ensign now didn't warrant thought. But even on his worst day, he'd never touched her in anger or seemed remotely capable of murder.

For the millionth time, she asked *why me?* One depraved act had left her with a blind spot and uncooperative body parts—*deficient*. She wanted to rale at God. Now she was supposed to decide if Ensign was guilty or not.

A strong arm supported her against a warm body, bolstering her inner strength. She could figure this out.

"What if the cops are wrong? They don't have any solid evidence, so they haven't even arrested him." She reasoned aloud as though hearing her thoughts would help her navigate the storm. "What if he's innocent and goes to prison for life—and I put him there?"

"Let a jury figure that one out. Your most important job is to stay safe."

Landon's voice jolted her back to her surroundings, and she bowed her head in mortification. Without thinking, she'd announced her innermost fears to a near stranger. A guy who hadn't even spoken to her in three weeks.

Cute dimples and toasted marshmallows had almost made her forget the most recent tabloid assault. That bullet had stolen her life *and* her smarts. Pathological fury mushroomed inside her, and knowing that her brain injury ignited the surge couldn't stop the explosion.

Shrugging from his arm, she turned all of her pent-up rage on him. "There's a valuable story—*Harper Inez to Marry Shooting Suspect*—and then you can buy that-that Opie horse."

Hurt like she'd never seen shone in his eyes, and remorse pressed her anger into submission. In her demented rant, she'd crossed a line that didn't allow return trips. "I …"

His injured expression hardened. "I signed that nondisclosure like everyone else, *Miss Rodriguez*. But my mama raised me better than that. I don't need any damned contract to keep private things private." He hooked her cane onto the stall's low wall with a wooden thud. "And I don't send pictures of my friends to gossip rags, either."

He turned on his heel and strode toward the exit.

Regret pummeled her. Everyone in rehab warned her about mood swings. Yet, each time she'd lost control, she couldn't understand how it happened. One more defect.

After insulting him over the picture, she'd intended to apologize. Instead, she'd been irrationally cruel for no reason —to a man who'd been nothing but kind.

"Landon, I'm sorry," she called, pocketing her phone and grabbing her cane, she struck out after him without a clue what to say. "Please. Wait."

Halting, he regarded her over his shoulder, and the implacable set to his jaw almost made her give up. But he'd worried about a horse getting a sunburn— and he'd known she was self-conscious about using a cane. Landon had made her feel special—until she screwed it up.

"The gossip-mill press is merciless. They speculate about anything that will sell their rags—then call it news. That way they can publish pictures without permission. Some-one's always there to help them do it—*always*." She didn't know him well. Yet his grim features tightened her chest with a loss she didn't understand. "I don't think that's who you are."

His jaw loosened, but carved lines still hardened his features. "No, *Miss Rodriguez*, I'm not that guy."

He resumed his exit without a backward glance.

"My real name *is* Luciana," she called after him.

He halted then with his hands fisted at his beltline, studying the concrete.

"When you say it, sometimes ... I pretend you know the real me. The girl who's *not* a picture taped up in someone's locker." She spoke to his back, almost whispering. Mired in the mess that was her life, she'd lost her ability to see people, and she'd hurt a good man. "Will you forgive me?"

He turned, his reaction shaded by the brim of his hat

before he raised an unreadable expression. Could his kind nature extend to her and all of her shortcomings?

She waved at Pongo. "Us baldies need to stick together."

Landon's lips curved to the half-smile that camouflaged his dimples. "Yes we do."

She smiled so wide that she thought her face would break, and he closed the distance between them. When he offered his arm, she snuggled her hand into the crook of his elbow, and he reached over, giving it a squeeze.

Heavy footfalls sounded from outside the barn, and Fletcher entered, striding toward them. The big man halted, his gaze darting from one to the other and settling on Landon. "What's wrong?"

"Something hit the floor, but she's okay," Landon replied. He glanced at her pocket but said nothing.

She loved that he had kept her business private, allowing her to decide what, if anything, to tell the bodyguard. Harper pulled out her phone, opening the screen, and turned it towards Fletcher.

He scanned the text thread, lines deepening in his grave expression. Without asking, he pocketed the device. "Miss Rodriguez, in the tack room. Macek, stay with her and keep away from the window."

The bodyguard's military tone reignited her dread, and Landon put an arm around her shoulder.

"You think Ensign's in the area?" she asked Fletcher.

He herded them through the tack room door. "Until we get solid information, I have to assume he is, ma'am."

Within minutes, an SUV with reinforcements arrived, and armed men in gold polos escorted Harper and Landon to the vehicle. With military precision, the Acura led them out of the Stick Pony lot.

Sitting in the back seat of the SUV, a shudder ran through Harper. As though he felt the tremor, Landon put his arm around her, tucking her into his body. "Friends take care of each other, in good times and bad."

With his presence, her problems seemed less daunting, and a smidgeon of hope even nudged its way into her heart. This man buoyed her spirit. "Yes we do. Especially, the bad."

Her New York party friends had missed that memo. Mamá and Juanita had stood by her since the shooting, Joni too, in her own way. However, friends from Harper's old life now offered their support from a polite distance, as though the bullet had diminished her value. Her posse had left her in the dust.

Friends trusted each other, too. Trust was risky business. Sometimes, you bet your life on it.

CHAPTER NINE

a few hours after Lodge security hustled them from Stick Pony, Landon relaxed on a white sofa in Harper's suite. Beyond a set of French doors, she showered, getting ready for their dinner date in the Gold Room.

Killing time, he tuned an imposing flat screen on the wall to the rodeo channel. The broadcast cut to a highlight on Jenkins. Landon muted the audio, instantly regretting the quiet.

The sound of running water in the other room fired his imagination, and visions of gleaming rivulets snaking down silky bronze skin tortured him. Desperate for a new focus, a collection of framed photos on the console below the television caught his eye. Harper traveled a great deal, and the fact she brought family photos along touched him.

The largest candid shot pictured two girls, maybe around six and eight, seated with their parents. Both beamed, and the youngest of the pair sported a missing front tooth and her father's onyx eyes—Harper, or rather Luciana.

The little darlings shared their fair-skinned mother's features, and their bronzed complexions were several shades lighter than their father's medium brown. Even as a child, Luciana's obsidian gaze made a striking impression.

On the big screen, Jenkins backed his horse into the box, and Landon rested his elbows on his knees to watch the damage. The cowboy tossed a nice loop and expertly tied his calf, ratcheting ever closer to the world championship. The overall standings flashed on the screen, showing Jenkins and another cowboy closing in on Landon's top spot. His throat tightened up, and he rubbed a hand over his face, trying to shake off the gloom.

The sound of the water intruded again, but this time, he welcomed the distraction. The shower stopped, and a few minutes later, a muffled Spanish conversation came to his ears.

He still couldn't believe he was here. Harper had questioned Landon's decency like no one he could recall, twice. When he'd left her standing in the barn, he'd planned to pack up for California and make certain that he never set eyes on her again. Then the vulnerable plea in those inky pools had called on every protective instinct he possessed, stopping him in his tracks.

Luciana. He'd read nearly everything on Harper Inez and had never run across that tidbit. She'd given him a precious gift—and melted his heart. People who'd loved her from birth called her Luciana. Now he did the same. She needed a friend, and though he'd hoped for more, he'd be there for her.

A folded issue of *The Scandal* sat on a coffee table in front of him, catching his interest. Landon didn't usually bother with that rag—and why would she have a copy? Unease put a rock in his stomach. *They make bank ...* He flipped the news print open to a clearly unauthorized image of Luciana in her helmet, glaring back at the reader.

The caustic article below described Luciana as

demanding because she'd insisted on an empty clinic for her appointments. Naturally, they quoted an anonymous, inside source. Landon snorted. The newsprint in his hands justified her concerns. He hoped their readers caught the irony.

His heart sank for her. No wonder she'd been all twitchy about his impromptu picture. Worse, a guy who'd supposedly loved her had tried to kill her. Why wouldn't she think the worst of everyone?

The bedroom latch snicked open, and Luciana emerged, wearing a sleeveless white blouse with a classy stand-up collar. Mint-green slacks hugged her lengthy legs all the way to her ankles. "Sorry I took so long. I had to call my mother." Her gaze landed on the paper, and her smile dropped away. "I see you found something to read."

Her tone had gone flat, and her shoulders rounded with an unseen weight. All he knew is that he wanted to hold her. He folded the paper and tapped it with a finger. "If I'd known this happened, I'd have understood more—about the picture, I mean."

"Really? Most people think it's part of my job." Luciana tucked one leg under her and settled onto the other end of the sofa. "Like when I stepped into the public eye, I signed up to put their kid through college with a photo."

"I would've tried to understand."

"You probably would have." She gave a sad smile. "Most people don't see how those pictures happen. Once, a guy actually spit at me."

Shocked, Landon's jaw dropped. "What the hell for?"

She snorted. "He wanted an ugly reaction, and he got it, too. Front page."

Heart sinking, Landon recalled a shot of her giving the camera an all-out sneer. Guilt over the countless purchases he'd made at checkout stabbed at him. "Wow, I'm sorry. No one deserves that. If I'd known more." He lifted the tabloid. "If you'd told me about the jerk who took this photo."

"I guess I wanted to be *Luciana* for a few hours." Her solemn expression disappeared as a teasing smile curved her lips. "Besides, you haven't shared all, either. You've never mentioned your public persona, have you Mr. Rodeo Sensation?"

Landon chuckled. "You did check me out. I was afraid you invited any old bum off the street out for a picnic."

Tugging at the hem of her blouse, she grimaced. "Actually, you were so nice, I did trust you too much—" She waved at *The Scandal.* "Until Juanita slapped that in front of me. *She* googled you."

Her admission warmed him, and a smile pulled at his lips. "Handy I had a good run this year, or who knows what you'd've found."

Her phone buzzed on the end table next to her, and she jumped. With a deep breath, she picked it up and scanned the screen. "I've got a meeting in the morning to discuss *updated security precautions.* In Mr. Spencer's office. I think he owns this place."

Something was up with Ensign Wells. The armed escort to the Lodge had seemed overkill for a text, and upon arrival, they'd even stationed a guard outside Luciana's room. Landon was doubly glad he hadn't let her face that three-ringed circus on her own.

"Yeah, Aspen Gold's all his. He's Ryder's grandfather," he said.

"Oh, I didn't know that." As though the phone were too heavy, she dropped her hand to her lap. "I so need this to be over and it's not even close."

He wanted to curl her in his arms and tell her it would be okay, that he'd be there. Instead, he scooted closer and planted his elbows on his knees. "Is there something you're not telling me about Ensign?"

"What do you mean?" Maybe Harper didn't have the energy to put the facts together or simply chose to ignore them.

"The gold-polo cops were armed to the teeth, and I didn't buy their *abundance of caution* line—"

Harper's phone rang, and she started again before viewing the incoming call. Her eyes widened.

CHAPTER TEN

*C*aller ID displayed Roarke Hennessey, and dread
sent Harper's pulse whooshing in her ears.

Landon straightened in his seat. "What is it?"

"NYPD homicide." She opened the call and raised the
phone to her ear. "Hello, detective."

Rising, Landon waved for her attention. "I'll head to the
restaurant and give you a few minutes of privacy," he whispered. "Our reservation is in a few anyway."

Appreciating his sensitivity, she waffled in indecision for
a moment before motioning for him to stay put. While she
exchanged greetings with Hennessey, Landon settled back
into his seat. The cushion dipped next to her, and his nearness gave her a boost of courage.

She grabbed a note pad and pen from the end table
drawer and steeled herself for bad news. "What do you have,
detective?"

"During our last meeting, I'd mentioned an ICU nurse. As
it turns out, there's a video of your hospital room, and—"

"Wait—what?" Harper barely kept her voice below a
shriek. Courtesy of Juanita, she'd already seen horrid images

of her shaved head and swollen face. The tabloids would have a field day with hospital footage. "They *filmed* me?"

"Miss Inez, please calm down."

"Okay. Chilling, but it's not easy—" With her tenuous composure ready to explode, she infused sanity into her tone. "Why would they film a patient in intensive care?"

Graven lines bracketed Landon's frown. Placing a firm hand on her thigh as though he could physically hold her together, he looked ready to jump to her defense.

"That's a good place to start," Hennessey said. "After one of Mr. Wells's visits, our ICU nurse discovered dangerous ventilator settings."

Harper's patience hung on by a thread. "You'd mentioned that before. But they hadn't ruled out mechanical causes." The folded tabloid resting on the table made her stifle a groan. More humiliation might break her. "You still haven't explained why they recorded me."

"The nurse became suspicious, so she placed a camera in your room." He paused, clearly waiting for Harper to connect dots that she couldn't see.

They suspected Ensign had messed with her vent settings, but that made no sense at all. "Ensign doesn't know anything about medicine or ventilators. Nor is he the least mechanically inclined. *I* had to show him how to check the oil in his car."

"I'm really sorry, Miss Inez. It's understandable that you'd want us to be wrong. For your sake, I wish with all my heart that we were." The detective sounded truly miserable.

Trying to decide if she had the stamina to hear more, Harper let dead air hang.

A breathy sigh came from the speaker. "Look, from the tape—and changed ventilator settings— it appears that he'd learned enough to increase the *tidal volume*."

Black edged Harper's vision. Volume. Like something that

could make your lungs explode. A bizarrely familiar sensation tightened her chest.

"Miss Inez, are you there?"

Her lips parted, and it took a Herculean effort to form a word. "Yes."

Hennessey paused. "I'm sorry. Before I laid this out, I should have asked if your sister was with you."

"Juanita had to go home." She found Landon's gaze. "But a friend's here."

"Good. That's good. I'm glad you're not alone. Who's with you?"

This evidence had come out of nowhere, and the logic escaped her. It was time to trust someone. With a glance at Landon, she tapped her phone. "Detective, this is overwhelming, and I'm afraid I won't remember everything. You're on speaker so that my friend Landon Macek can take notes."

She shoved the pad and pen at him, and he started before he nodded, taking the stationary. He draped a booted foot over his knee, propping the pad of paper against his thigh. "Hello, Detective Hennessey."

"Macek? Hi. The Lodge security chief mentioned he'd cleared you. You're in rodeo?"

Narrowing his eyes at the phone in her hand, Landon didn't appear up for chitchat. More likely, he bristled over the detective's knowledge of him. "Yep. On hiatus at the moment."

"Cool. We've caught the rodeo at the Garden a couple times. Help me out here—you signed a nondisclosure, too, didn't you?" Hennessey asked.

Fine muscles along Landon's jaw tightened. Cringing internally at the implied insult, Harper mouthed *I'm sorry*. He clearly wasn't accustomed to being under a microscope.

"Yes, I'll keep everything confidential," Landon said.

"He's a trusted friend," Harper added. The curve of his lips relieved her, and she smiled back. Still worried what the tabloids would do with a leaked recording, she wanted to get back to business. "Detective, I'm a little lost. Why did this video take so long to materialize?"

"Because, as you suspected, hospitals don't tape patients. The recording's from a nanny cam."

Trying to think, Harper pressed a thumb and forefinger to her eyes. "I'm not following."

"Our nurse was afraid for you, but the hospital administration didn't act on her concerns fast enough to suit her," Hennessey replied.

"Are you saying that she hid a camera in my ICU room? Isn't that illegal?"

"Yes—and yes. She'd actually shared her suspicions with us before your discharge. At the time, she knew she'd broken the law and was too afraid to tell us about the recording. But a couple weeks ago, she called, worried because we hadn't made an arrest." Hennessey paused. "I admitted we didn't have enough evidence— so she finally offered up the video."

The invisible dots finally lined up for Harper. "*This* is why you've had Ensign in your crosshairs?"

Hennessey's sigh came from the speaker. "Yes."

Ensign's text and the video had to be connected. She mustered her courage to face more ugly truths. "Does *Ensign* know you have this evidence?"

"Yes, we'd used it as leverage for a confession but no luck," he replied, his voice resigned. "We've got a team watching the nurse—just to be safe."

Grateful for that, Harper bowed her head. The kind, steady voice in the fog. "Angela…"

"Yes, Angela." Hennessey sighed. "Here's the rub, if the D.A. can use the nanny-cam vid in court, meaning if it's admissible, the nursing board might have grounds to pull her license. At the least, she'll lose her job."

Angela had put everything on the line to protect Harper. No one had ever gone to the mat for her like this—certainly not a stranger. And she had barely recalled the ICU nurse's name. "That seems wholly unfair."

"I agree. You can see why we kept the video, and our source, on the down-low, even from you."

Angst over the illegal camera evaporated, and if Angela came under fire, Harper resolved to help her in any way possible. "You did the right thing, detective."

"I appreciate that," he said. "Angela's committed. This has been very difficult for her."

Harper wasn't the only victim here, and she ached for the woman who'd tried to protect her. "I can imagine." Harper's voice cracked, and she snatched a tissue from the end table to dab her eyes. "Tell her... tell Angela thank you."

He cleared his throat and then cleared it again. Maybe Hennessey's job hadn't hardened him as much as she'd initially thought.

For months, Ensign's guilt or innocence had plagued Harper. Unbelievably, doubt intruded once more. What if he had simply been curious about the equipment? The head games had to stop.

"Detective, this might sound strange, but I need to see the video. Is that allowed?" she asked.

"It is ..." Hennessey paused. "You think you're up to it?"

Landon frowned and reached for her hand, curling his fingers around hers, warm and solid. Tiny lines bracketed his hazel eyes, and his gaze drew her in. She detected nothing but worry for a friend—no deceit, no avarice. This man would honor her trust.

She held his gaze. "Yes, I believe I am."

"Okay, I'll text a link to securely access the video." The

detective's voice severed her moment of connection with Landon. "Your personal identification of him will give us extra insurance for an arrest."

"The recording isn't enough?"

"Honestly, I've been so occupied with updating the Lodge security and the local sheriff I haven't had a chance to get the D.A.'s final opinion on admissibility. But I'll speak to him as soon as possible. Ideally, sometime tomorrow, we'll charge Ensign Wells with two counts of attempted murder."

Since her hell on earth was a step closer to over, Harper should have been relieved. Instead, she felt a keening loss. Of what? A man who had tried to murder her?

Still reeling from Hennessey's bombshell, a belated realization hit her. "Updating them on what, exactly, detective?"

"Surveillance reports. A couple more things, Miss Inez then I'll leave you until our conference call in the morning.

One more thing could collapse her. "Sure."

"Do you recognize the name Earl Maddox?"

The innocuous question made her uneasy, and she gripped the arm of the sofa. "No, not at all. Who is he?"

"An ex-con. Not important by itself, but according to your financials, he's contracted to perform a renovation on your Florida property."

At her side, Landon scribbled notes on the hotel stationary, writing down the name.

She had no clue what Ensign might have planned for her beach house. When his acting roles had withered away, she had asked him to manage her real estate investments to help him feel useful. According to her accountant, he had done very well.

"Renovation of what?" she asked.

"I'd hoped you could tell me. We'll check him out."

The beginnings of a migraine built pressure inside her head, and Harper closed her eyes. "Our beach house does need a serious update. But I'm sorry, Ensign hadn't mentioned a project."

"It appears he had legal authorization to pay contractors?"

"Yes." Harper stifled a groan. "He had a limited power of attorney—now revoked."

She had no idea why she'd referred to the Pensacola cottage as jointly owned. Habit, she supposed. With the exception of the condo and Ensign's McLaren, all of her property was in her name. In bitter irony, he'd likely use her gifts of love—half the condo and the car—to fund his legal defense team.

"Okay, I'll know more after we question Maddox."

The detective *might* find a renovation project in Florida. Harper had heard enough. "Thank you. I'll be in touch after I view the video."

"One more thing, please, Miss Inez."

Almost afraid to respond, Harper rubbed her temple. "Yes?"

"We …" Hennessey hesitated, signaling bad news. "We haven't been able to locate Mr. Wells since last evening."

There it was. The real reason security had swarmed the barn. Harper's blood ran cold. "I guess that explains tomorrow's meeting. Thanks."

"Yes. We'll talk more—"

She thumbed the call to a close and dropped her head back against the couch. Landon squeezed her hand and then sat quietly with saint-like patience, simply offering his presence.

Giving him a sad smile, she appreciated the moment to accept the awful truths of her life. "You were right. The video, Ensign's vanishing act, and the show of force at the barn—it all makes sense, now."

"Are you okay?"

"Yes—no." She didn't know what she was. A morbid laugh

bubbled up, and she met Landon's gaze. "I keep asking myself why he'd do it. How could he *hate* me that much? But I know."

Landon jutted his chin at her helmet, and an angry frown stamped his features. "There's no justification for what he did."

With his hand warm in hers, his fierce support kept any self-conscious feelings away.

"True enough. But Ensign and I had been in trouble for a while." She sighed. "My career soared and his stalled. He was jealous—of everything—other men, my success."

Landon grimaced. "Murder's a huge leap from jealousy."

"Yes it is. He must've spiraled even more than I could've imagined." She rubbed her eyes. The migraine was coming. "I tried to build him up. Nothing I did helped. Back in January, when I got a movie deal, I hid it from him—and he found out before I'd figured out how to tell him."

"And he didn't take it well."

She snorted. "That would be a big, fat no." Harper wished she could go back in time. If only she'd had the courage to leave Ensign that very day. Instead, she'd doubled down. "Then I got the brilliant idea to buy life insurance, hoping that if I showed my commitment, it would give him confidence in us. He was angry—insulted that I believed he needed me to take care of him."

"His motive wasn't about the money?" Landon asked, obviously still confused.

"Not in a way a sane person can understand. Or he'd have done the deed *after* the wedding." She covered her face with her hands. Maybe if she couldn't see, the world would go away—a luxury she could ill afford. Making a fist, she dug her fingernails into her palm. "Denial time is over. He's feeling the heat. Apparently, being married to me sounds better than life in prison."

Landon shook his head, and his lips parted. "He's a fool—"

Not up to condolences, she raised a halting hand. "Did you know that in New York, a wife cannot testify against her husband, unless he *allows* it?"

CHAPTER ELEVEN

*S*till on the sofa next to Luciana, Landon saw up close and personal how money couldn't make a person happy. Like anyone else, the rich and famous could be the most miserable people on earth. However, for them, loving someone carried risks most folks couldn't imagine.

A few tears had smudged the make up under her dark eyes. Suspecting she hadn't fully let go of her ex, he'd self-ishly wanted her singled up. Now, watching it unfold was killing him. At least she understood the motive behind Ensign's marriage proposal, and Landon's heart ached for her. "Luciana, I'm sorry."

He wrapped an arm around her, and she laid her head on his shoulder, not moving for several minutes. An occasional sniffle broke the silence. "Will you stay?"

Uncertain what she'd meant by *stay*, Landon shifted uneasily. He curled a finger under her chin. "I'm a friend, and I'll be here for you. You *will* get through this." He smiled. "I've seen your bull-headed streak. No one attacks a hill with more grit."

She smiled, and her eyes sparkled for the first time since they'd left the barn. "I was only showing off for you."

The invitation in her gaze threatened his gentleman's commitment, and he longed to close the distance with a kiss. But not now—not this way. Despite the small flair of bravado, she was emotionally brittle, and only a straight-up asshole would make a move in her weakest moment. Landon wouldn't settle for anything less than a whole and willing Luciana in his arms.

In a small concession to the lustful devil inside, he touched her fingers to his lips. "I know what we need. Red or white?"

"Red. How did you know I'm a wine girl?"

Landon rose and strode to the wet bar. "I'd like to say intuition, but I read it somewhere."

He opened the small fridge and pulled the solitary pinot noir split from the door shelf. A small bottle of *Molten Gold* sat between a Jameson and a Peat. Curious, he grabbed the local craft label and then plucked a goblet and a rocks glass from a shelf. The heavy glassware clinked together with the musical tone of leaded crystal. No plastic cups at the Lodge.

While he poured, she twisted around, resting an elbow on the back of the sofa. "Just how big of a fan *are* you, Mr. Macek?"

He laughed. "Put it this way. If I had a locker, Harper Inez wearing that little red string bikini would be taped up inside."

In mock astonishment, her eyes danced over a pouty open mouth. "Nooo!"

With a teasing grin, he handed her the glass of red wine and rejoined her on the couch. "But now that I know you, I think I'd rather have a picture of Luciana with marshmallow smeared on her nose as my phone's background." Amusement left him, and he put affection in his gaze. "You don't belong in anyone's locker."

Every generation had their Marylyn Monroe—the femme fatale that fired the male imagination. Luciana was as close to iconic as she could get without hitting the big screen. Landon wondered if he was man enough to have his woman be every other guy's fantasy. He swirled the ice in his glass, watching the amber liquid.

She rested a hand on his arm. "Modeling is a brutal business. My pin-up days may be over." She shrugged. "Honestly, I won't miss it."

Shocked, Landon couldn't imagine that she'd give up all the glitz and big paydays. "For real?"

"Fashion was never my life's ambition."

"That's unusual." According to her chat with Chelse, Juanita had been the aspiring model, but he didn't want to announce he'd been eaves dropping. "I thought all teen girls wanted to model."

"Not me, that is until Joni tossed out some big numbers." Luciana's smile didn't light her eyes. "After Papá returned to Argentina, things were tough. The money he sent wasn't enough to keep us afloat, but we got lucky. My first big job paid off our house the day before foreclosure."

Landon wanted to ask why papa had left his wife with two girls, but it happened all the time. Little more than a kid herself, she'd become the main breadwinner. All he'd done for his folks was to help Dad replace the deck. "I'd read you hit the big time in high school. But I didn't know that you'd supported your family."

"It's not public knowledge." She shrugged. "Don't get me wrong, I wouldn't change a thing. An incredible opportunity fell in my lap—but it wasn't my plan A."

"What *did* you want to do when you were a kid?" he asked, genuinely curious.

She snorted. "I never had time to figure that out, so I'm starting over." With a wistful gaze, she tapped a finger on her lips. "I've got this miraculous second chance at life—it's like a do-over. What I *choose* to do needs to *matter*."

Landon's heart filled to bursting for the generous woman in front of him. She'd taken the worst punishment that life could dish out, and instead of crumpling, she wanted to give back. He took her hand. "I'll bet on you."

She beamed. "Thank you. That means a lot."

Hennessey's call had squashed their enthusiasm for going out in public, and they'd discovered that the Gold Room delivered to the high-dollar suites. He couldn't help but be relieved that he could return the suit and slacks he'd grabbed at The Gift Shop.

One day, he'd take her on a real date—in the near future. After dinner, he'd go back to his room at Stick Pony. Hopefully, Fletcher had located someone to bring his truck to the Lodge, or Landon could catch a lift.

Sitting at a small table near the balcony windows, Landon cut a corner of an oozing, medium-rare filet and offered the forkful to Luciana. "This is the best steak I've ever had. You've got to try it."

She closed her lush lips around the tines and chewed with her eyes closed. "It's absolutely divine."

They casually traded bites back and forth, sampling Chef Wilson's best. Rabbit food didn't generally appeal to Landon, but he had to admit that a praline chicken salad could grow on him.

With his plate empty, and hers still holding neat half portions, Luciana set her leftovers to the side. She took a sip of her wine and grew serious. "I can't put it off any longer. I've got to download that video."

Watching someone try to kill her might damage Landon for life. Simply imagining her with a gunshot wound to her head put a ball of dread in his gut. "Do you want some privacy?"

She turned pleading eyes on him. "Stay? Hold my hand?"

If she had the guts, he could do no less. "If that's what you want."

"It's what I need."

He tossed back the rest of his drink and rose to get refills, reaching for her glass. "We might need more liquid courage."

When he joined her at the sofa, a blue arrow inside a circle shone large on the television. He'd figured they'd hover over her phone to watch it, but she'd cast the video to the big screen. Somehow, movie-sized attempted murder seemed more ominous. A healthy swallow of Molten Gold hit bottom hard—not helpful.

He sat closer to her this time and held her hand as he'd promised. With a glance at him, she took a deep breath. "Okay, this is it."

She tapped her phone, and the screen came to life. A man sat in a chair on the far side of a hospital bed, spearing his fingers through his short blond hair. Landon recognized Ensign Wells from the tabloids. Next to him, a square piece of equipment with a digital panel on top was visible near the head of the bed.

The nurse had focused the camera on the machine, and the bottom of the frame captured a patient's face and part of her shaved scalp. Plastic accordion hoses ran from a tube in her mouth to the ventilator. With taped eyes and bruised, puffy cheeks, the defenseless patient in the bed bore little resemblance to Luciana.

The man who'd brutalized her life sat right next to her in her most vulnerable state. Hot coals of impotent rage smoldered in Landon's chest. There was no way to protect her from the past or the horror of this video. His clenched jaw ached and reminded him of his purpose—to be supportive.

The video paused, and he shifted in his seat, trying to regain his composure.

"Sorry, I should've warned you." She squeezed his hand. "I looked pretty rough for a while."

Her banged-up, unrecognizable appearance had disturbed him, so he didn't comment. But he needed to get through this—for her. "To keep my sanity, I might pretend that's someone else up there."

"I wish I could do the same."

On screen, Ensign craned his neck, his gaze searching beyond the camera. Putting his hand through his hair again, he rose and turned to face the machine, blocking their view. Beeps sounded in time with his arm movements. Combined with the RN's testimony, any juror would believe he pressed buttons to change the ventilator settings.

Luciana gasped, and the picture cut to white. She sprang to her feet and, with an angry shriek, hurled her wine glass into the monitor. Shattering crystal and a low-pitched report shot through the room. Rage contorted the beautiful features mirrored in the cracked screen.

"You bastard," she screamed.

Already sickened watching her near murder, every muscle in Landon's body tensed with her pain. Then her devastated gaze met his in the reflection, and she teetered near collapse. Jumping up, he caught her and folded her into his arms. A single sob shook her frame and ripped into his heart.

He'd never felt so helpless. "I got you. Shhh now. I got you."

A sledgehammer fist pounded on the double doors to the suite. "Miss Rodriguez, I'm coming in."

Before the hallway sentry finished his bellowed warning, the mahogany panel thudded hard against the backstop, and a gorilla of a man in a snug gold polo burst into the living area.

Still cradling Luciana, Landon glared a warning at the beefy security guard and then stared at his nametag for a beat. "Gavin, she's upset and needs some privacy. Lock the door on your way out. Please."

"I'm sorry, sir. I can't do that." Gavin didn't move, appearing more battle ready than apologetic. "Miss Rodriguez needs to tell me that she's okay."

When Luciana offered no more than sniffles, he took a step closer, scrutinizing Landon as though certain he'd found the *bastard* responsible for her tears.

When his gaze landed on her, his features softened. "Miss Rodriguez, please look at me."

Kindness had replaced his authoritarian tone, and he scanned her head to toe, clearly assessing her well-being. The security guard was only doing his job, but his blatant suspicion made Landon want to put a fist through his face.

Wrestling his temper under control, he stroked her back. "Luciana, please tell Gavin you're okay. It'd be a damn shame if I've got to throw him out. He's a big 'un, and I might get an ass-whoopin'."

She half-sobbed and half-chuckled into his chest before raising a teary gaze to their intruder. "I *am* fine. But it was a really bad movie."

Landon snorted a laugh.

She'd recovered and didn't miss a beat with the guard. "Could you please ask maintenance to replace the television?"

Gavin tracked her gesture to the huge flat screen with spider-web cracks, and his eyes widened. "Um—sure thing." After a brief appraisal of the glass shards and red splatter on the rug, he raised a neutral expression. "They can be up in about fifteen minutes—housekeeping, too."

He'd said the last with only the slightest lift of his brows. Security at a place like this probably saw it all.

"The morning is fine. Please ask them to charge it to my room," Luciana said.

"Yes ma'am. I'll let them know." The bodyguard pulled the door shut behind him.

Neither of them spoke for several seconds, and then she dropped her forehead onto Landon's shoulder as though someone flipped a switch. "In my entire life, I've never thrown anything in anger."

"You did fine." He jutted his chin at the shattered screen. "Only a smidge off center—you'll hit the bullseye next time."

Slapping his chest, a shaky giggle bubbled up through her tears. "How can you make me laugh—now?"

Impressed by how well she'd rebounded from her meltdown, he smiled. "Sometimes a little humor makes hard things easier."

She glared at the big screen. "I might actually hate him and that's not who I want to be."

"I'd be worried if you didn't rage at him some." Despising Ensign right along with her, Landon cupped her cheek. "It's okay. Go ahead and hate on him for a while. He's earned it."

"I think I will. Thank you." She gave a tremulous smile and then wiped her nose with the back of her hand. With an arm around her shoulders, Landon ushered her to the sofa, grabbing the box of tissues along the way. She blew her nose, and dabbed gingerly under her eyes the way women did when trying to salvage their makeup.

They reclaimed their seats, and she snuggled into him. He held her in the quiet for several minutes, and her breathing slowed before she tucked her feet up under her.

The stress had tanked her reserves. Landon scooted over to give her more room and then reached up to douse the lamp.

❦

The next morning, Harper used *The Scandal* to collect the shattered wine glass. Dropping the crystal shards and the tabloid into the wet bar's wastebasket, she enjoyed a small cathartic moment. Ensign and the gossip rags could go straight to hell.

Breakfast fare lined the eating bar, and small bottles of vinegar and hydrogen peroxide sat next to a fruit plate. Room service hadn't flinched at the odd side order. She snatched a corner of honeydew melon and popped it in her mouth before she got to work. It only took a minute to mix up a bowl of Mamá's tried and true peroxide spot remover. Grabbing a washcloth, she hoped the red stains hadn't permanently set.

If she hadn't dropped into a dead sleep in Landon's arms last night, she'd have taken care of this mess right away. No creepy-eye nightmares either—nothing but blissful slumber. She couldn't remember the last time she'd slept a full six hours.

He lay stretched out on his stomach with his face mashed into a throw pillow, and his boots had landed on the floor at the end of the sofa. His long frame filled every inch of the couch, leaving her curious how they'd both fit on it for most of the night. He'd wake up soon, so she slipped her helmet back on. After sleeping in it for several hours, her scalp had needed a break from the pressure.

On her hands and knees, comfortable in her yoga pants and tank top, she worked quietly on the rug below the television. Despite her efforts at silence, it wasn't long before Landon took a big breath and rolled to his side. Hoping she hadn't woken him, she met his sleepy gaze over the coffee table. "Good morning, sunshine."

Looking around, he appeared disoriented before grinning. "Good morning to you, too. I hope I didn't snore."

"No snoring, but your phone's blowing up. I turned the ringer off so you could sleep."

"Thanks." He propped up on an elbow and peered down at her. "You know, fancy places like this do have housekeeping."

She gave a half-smile. "True enough, but I have a secret recipe that works like a charm." After pouring another dose of Mamá's concoction on a stubborn spot, she shrugged. "Plus, it's my penance."

Landon frowned. "No guilt. After watching that horror show, you earned a free minute of crazy."

"Thanks." His accepting take on her outburst eased her worst fears. "Sometimes I worry that the bullet changed me into someone else—suspicious and resentful."

He shook his head. "You're not even close. Give yourself some time."

Maybe he had truly forgiven her freaky paranoia over the tabloids, and she returned a grateful smile. "You're kinda good for me, Mr. Macek."

Showing a hint of his dimples with a curve of his lips, his warm gaze brightened. His phone vibrated again next to his head, and he checked it.

"Oh, crap." With a quick motion, he sat up and tugged on his boots. "Man, eight-fifteen. I gotta get to the barn. The stock'll be kicking the walls down for breakfast."

Disappointed he was racing off, Harper tried to keep her tone light. "Thanks for staying last night."

Pausing with all kinds of caring in his gaze, he rose and approached her, offering a hand to pull her up from her knees. He tugged her to stand in front of him body-to-body close. "My pleasure, Luciana."

With his nearness, her insides came to life, and warmth

curled low in her belly. She splayed her hands on his chest. "Speaking of breakfast, help yourself to as much as you can hold."

The double entendre was less subtle than she'd intended, and heat flashed in his gaze. He moved a hand to the small of her back, inviting her to close the gap between them. Despite the luscious temptation, something held her in place, though she couldn't say what.

He touched his forehead to hers. "I think I might do that."

What in the world was she doing? Only the night before, she'd wallowed in sorrow over a love betrayed. Stepping from his arms, she gestured to the quiche sampler and fruit tray on the bar. "Help yourself. Want coffee? They stock to-go cups in the cupboard."

The separation fizzled the electricity between them, and he bowed his head as though collecting himself. He recovered with a nod. "Sure. Thanks."

Sweet Landon rolled with the inexplicable change, and Harper struggled with her own reactions. She had a hard time meeting his gaze. "I'm sorry. Maybe I'm emotionally crippled, too."

Tugging her to face him, he held her by the shoulders. "Listen to me—you're *not* crippled. But after what you've gone through—*are* going through—who wouldn't be a little fragile?" He cupped her cheek, and she almost believed that he saw into her damaged soul. "I'm not gonna lie, Luciana. I care for you. And I want you—bad. But only when you're one hundred percent certain you want me back."

After years of fending off sexual advances with big strings attached, Landon's simple expectation that she be true to herself was a marvel. This man wanted honesty, and he deserved it.

"That's sweet…thank you." Harper's throat tightened.

"Since we're in confession mode, I'm attracted to you, too. You're kind and seem sort of wise now and then."

He snorted. "That's me. The sage old cowboy."

With a smile teasing her mouth, she bit her lower lip. "A little hot, too."

"Only a little?" Full-on dimples appeared in his cheeks before the yummy hollows melted to a mock frown. "Looks like I'm gonna have to bring my A-game."

They laughed, and she savored the simple joy of being happy. Every time they were together, moments like this increased Landon's appeal. However, she didn't dare trust herself with his heart.

In her brittle rebound state, with nagging body image issues, maybe she only needed any man to find her desirable. If that was the case, why hadn't his confession cooled her off? Instead, she wanted to ask him to find someone else to feed the horses and stay.

In a sad concession, she decided to keep the light banter going. "A-game? I can't wait to see it."

Harper pulled a white plate from the cupboard, and Landon half sat on a barstool, leaving one boot planted on the floor. "Yep. I've got my work cut out for me." He kept his gaze locked to hers. "I'd better fuel up."

He picked up a miniature ham and broccoli quiche with his fingers and devoured it. She poured black coffee. "Cream or sugar?"

"Cream, please." He spoke with his mouth still partially full.

After stirring in vanilla creamer, she placed a lid on the paper cup. Too soon, he'd plucked his hat from the closet, and they stood at the suite's threshold.

"No therapy today?" he asked.

Harper got the impression that he prolonged their good-byes, and she didn't rush, either. "Not at Stick Pony. After the security meeting, I've got an appointment for regular physical therapy with Chad."

The elevator dinged down the hallway, and its doors slid open. An imposing, grim-faced man emerged, clearly on a mission, and at sight of them, he increased his pace. A familiar gold logo on his jacket announced his official Lodge status.

With neatly trimmed white hair and matching beard, he had too much muscle to need shoulder pads in his navy suit coat. The silver fox joined them, looking vaguely familiar.

He turned intelligent brown eyes on Harper. "Miss Rodriguez, I'm Deke Ward, the head of Lodge security. We met your first day here."

Shaking his hand, she recalled Ryder introducing him before a review of security protocol. "Oh yes, I remember."

"Macek." Deke's tone was matter-of-fact, if not pleasant.

"Ward," Landon responded. Apparently, they'd met.

"Glad you're up, Miss Rodriquez," Deke said. "Can I come in?"

"Sure." Stomach sinking, she stepped back, gesturing for him to enter. "If this is about the television—"

CHAPTER TWELVE

eke's gaze shifted briefly to the shattered screen without a flicker of concern. "No ma'am—not the TV."

His lack of interest in the television set off Harper's radar. His visit must be about Ensign. Landon followed the security chief into the suite, and she gave him a grateful smile. *Stay*, she mouthed for his eyes only.

"What's up, Ward?" he asked.

Deke studied Harper for an instant and then settled his attention on Landon. "It's probably best you join us, Macek."

"I plan on it." Landon reached for his phone. "Give me a minute to round up someone to feed the Stick Pony stock."

He had gone from supportive to protective, and as much as Harper wanted to view herself as independent, a weight eased from her shoulders.

Almost at the same time, Deke pulled out his cell and typed a text. "Ryder can find someone to feed his horses."

Since he hadn't bothered to wait for a response, he must've sent a command rather than a request. The tension was palpable, and Harper fidgeted with the hem of her top. Trying for a semblance of control, she slipped into hostess mode. "Coffee?"

The security chief shook his head and gestured to the couch. "Maybe we should sit down."

His no-nonsense manner heightened Harper's dread, and as she took her seat on the sofa, she reached for Landon. Deke claimed the adjacent armchair, and his gaze dropped to their joined hands. As head of security, someone had certainly told him that she and Landon had spent time together, but finding him leaving her suite in the early morning sent a new message.

After settling an intense gaze on Landon, Deke shuttered his expression to all business. There was tension between the two men. Maybe he had come to bust Landon for spending time with a customer. Harper parted her lips to blast him, but Landon gave a shake of his head.

He stared at Deke with a stony regard. "It looks like you're making assumptions." A hint of warning laced his tone. "Don't make more out of me being here this morning than it is."

"Fair enough," Deke replied, not appearing the least intimidated. "But we've got more important things to discuss."

In her experience, most men couldn't wait to tell the world that they had it going on with a model. Instead, Landon tried to protect her reputation. He wasn't like any man she'd ever met.

"I'm sure we do." Certain Deke planned a later reprisal; Harper bristled and decided to pull her seldom-used celebrity card. "But to be clear, Landon's a good friend. And if anyone were to interfere with our friendship, I'd be *very* disappointed."

"Understood. Again, to other matters..." Tiny creases

bracketed his eyes, and his expression held unmistakable sympathy. "Hennessey called about an hour ago with some tough news."

Harper stiffened in her seat, grateful Landon hadn't left any earlier. If the video wasn't admissible …

"According to his people, late last night, Ensign Wells returned to his apartment," Deke told them. "At around five-thirty a.m. New York time, the surveillance team heard a gunshot and went in to investigate."

A million horrid possibilities flew through her mind, and she held her breath.

"I'm sorry to inform you Miss Inez, but it appears that Wells took his own life," he finished.

Harper covered a gasp with her fingers and then wrested her hand back to her lap. Profound relief washed through her, and an instant later, her selfish response produced a rush of shame. She struggled to find her voice. "I-I don't know what to say."

Landon squeezed her hand, and as though he'd read her heart, his gaze mirrored her inner pain. "You don't have to say anything at all." Putting a protective arm around her, he tucked her against him. "Deke, how does this change things for Luciana?"

In her numb state, Harper didn't have the energy to think past the next minute. She was grateful he'd asked the question.

"Hennessey's investigation is ongoing, so he's not ready to pull her security. He'll keep us informed." Deke pursed his lips, obviously holding something back.

"What else?" Luciana asked him.

"The weapon found at the scene was a *Glock 19*," he replied.

Even though Glock handguns showed up in the movies

all the time, the term was too familiar, and Harper's mouth fell open in shock.

He gave a slow nod. "Yes, the same model used in your assault. However, it's a common firearm."

In poetic justice, Ensign had used the same weapon on both of them. She bowed her head but couldn't find a prayer to offer up for him. What did that make her? "Oh God."

Landon squeezed her hand in quiet support.

"Hennessey's running ballistics to match it to the round already in evidence," Deke added. The bullet they had removed from her brain.

"I understand," she replied. If Ensign had killed himself, maybe he'd felt some remorse. Harper wasn't sure why that mattered to her. "Was there anything else? Like a note?"

Deke shook his head. "Not at the scene. Maybe they'll find more when they search his computer."

In reflex, Harper checked her phone for any overlooked emails or texts from Ensign. Nothing — only, the bogus marriage proposal he'd sent to save his own skin. In the end, not even an apology.

Was she supposed to grieve for him? She didn't know. However, with his death, maybe she could move on with her life. "Is the meeting still on?"

"No." The security chief took a deep breath as though relieved his task was over. "The red alert is cancelled, but the detective wants us to maintain our present security level until he gets the final lab report."

"I see." She took a shaky breath. "Deke, thank you for notifying me in person."

After a few pleasantries, she and Landon showed him out. She pushed the door closed and the quiet snick echoed in the silence. Harper dropped back against the mahogany panel, emotionally spent, and uncharted feelings tightened her throat—maybe this was what people called *closure*.

"I don't know what's wrong with me," she said.

Landon shook his head. "There's nothing *wrong* with you. You feel what you need to feel."

He enfolded her into his arms, and she rested her head on his shoulder. She'd never needed a hug so badly in her life. "I don't mourn him. Not in a way that makes sense. For the last six months, I never truly believed that he'd tried to kill me." She sighed. "The video solved that mystery. Now this? What a devastating waste—for him, me, and his poor family. His parents do *not* deserve this."

Landon rubbed slow circles into her back, and she took in his scent. No artificial cologne—simply warm, all-natural male. For a moment, she imagined an ordinary life with a regular guy who truly cared for her. The kind of love that happened for other people—a small house with a yard, a dog, and a couple babies with runny noses wearing diapers. Some even had horses in the back yard. She'd seen it.

"I need a day of normal. Plain old boring without drama." She spoke into his shirt, reluctant to leave the security of his embrace.

"Hmm—boring." Landon smiled, keeping his hands on her waist. "Let's see, we could go for a ride. Nothing too crazy, but there's a pretty creek near Stick Pony. We could even pack a humdrum lunch—I make a mean PB&J."

She pulled back and grinned. "Actually, that would be spectacular."

His eyes danced. "Let me guess, you haven't had peanut butter in…"

She laughed. "It *is* a guilty pleasure—on celery."

"I'll see if the store has any rabbit food." Showing his dimples, Landon pulled out his phone. "And I'll need a way to keep you informed of our upcoming tedious activities."

After they traded contacts, her first thought was to schedule security for any horseback ride outside of her hippotherapy appointments. But Ensign was gone, and she didn't need any ballistics report to know the truth. She was done with denial. More importantly, it was past time to move on. "I've been hostage for months. Let's fill up the calendar."

Landon grinned. "That's my girl."

She didn't want him to leave. However, with her head in chaos over Ensign's death, she didn't dare ask Landon to stay. She pressed her lips to his cheek and lingered, savoring the sensation of his masculine stubble against her skin. "Thank you—for everything."

Landon waved at Gavin's replacement on his way out, fighting an urge to touch the warm spot on his face. After the elevator doors closed, he gave in and grazed fingers down his cheek. The chaste kiss had held an unspoken promise, and despite the rash of grave events, he dared to hope for more. But he needed to hold his horses.

She'd endured weeks of therapy trying to recover—the video and now Ensign's suicide. It was important for them both that she took the lead in any intimacy. People didn't turn love on and off like a light switch, no matter the sins committed.

Landon planned to sidestep that emotional quicksand. However, being patient while she worked through her feelings might drive him nuts. The elevator dinged as though supporting his decision. He stepped into the lobby and strode to the valet desk.

Fletch had come through, and the attendant called for Landon's vehicle. Outside, Landon passed a young valet wearing a blue polo a five and climbed into his truck for the ride back to Stick Pony.

To make good use of the drive, he called his partner Burl Fitzgibbons to check on the home place. "Hey Fitch, how's it going?"

"Fair enough. The square bales came in." Fitchy's voice came from the Ram's speakers. "We partnered up with Jones on some temp labor. Unloaded the hay at our place in the morning and did his after lunch."

"Good thinking."

"I finished off the sixty days on Bowman's colt. He seems happy enough with him. That cleared our waitlist, so we've got our first empty stall."

Winning go-rounds had kept their barn full of roping prospects this year. Now, with Landon losing ground in the tie-down standings, it appeared horse-owners already shopped for training elsewhere. Fitchy always put in extra labor while Landon was on the road. Landon needed to pull his weight for their training business to make it over the hump.

He hit his turn signal at the Stick Pony sign. "Look, I contracted to tune up a few head out here, so I'll meet my part of the expenses—the same sixty percent as if I were rodeoing. Email me the balance sheet."

"I figured you were good for it." Fitchy chuckled. "But I sure did wonder where you'd get it. By the way, do you know when Rocket can travel?"

Landon hesitated. Most of the time, he hadn't been interested in leaving Colorado, so he hadn't bothered to ask. "This Doc Spencer's brought him along real nice, but he needs a few more weeks." He'd made that up, but somehow, saying *I met a girl* didn't seem like a good idea, either. "I'll try to nail down a timeframe."

They signed off, and Landon parked behind the main office building at the staff quarters entry. Not bad for free lodging. He shared the common areas with Tad and Callie, and with only the three of them onsite, each had a bedroom and a private bath.

He slid his passkey through the scanner, and his phone pinged with a text.

Luciana: For your locker.

Unable to wait until he got inside, he tapped the attachment. The delectable image of Luciana smiling from ear to ear with a dab of melted marshmallow on her nose filled his screen. With a couple taps, he saved his phone's new background, and his heart swelled up in his chest. He walked on air all the way down the hall and paused before entering their small kitchen, unable to resist another look at the picture.

Tad closed the fridge with a can of soda in one hand. "Mornin'. Aren't you all too happy." A crooked grin lifted one corner of his mouth. "We got overnight security guards. Protective custody at the *Lodge* go okay?"

Even the knowing jibe didn't dampen Landon's spirits. He pocketed his phone and smothered a lingering smile. "It was a long night."

"Right." The kid smirked and headed for the TV room where Callie sat on the sofa.

She waved with a big grin. "Hi, there. How's Luciana?"

"She's good, considering," Landon replied. "Thanks for checking on us last night."

The last time they'd seen him, he'd climbed into the back of an SUV with Luciana. Standing there in yesterday's clothes, he didn't bother telling a *nothing-happened* story. The ribbing was inevitable. Hopefully, they took their non-disclosure contracts seriously.

Still in the kitchen, he pulled out his phone—again. The racy supermodel Harper Inez was no more than a two-dimensional facsimile of the woman wearing creamy marshmallow. Luciana was kind and vulnerable, and at the same time, the most courageous woman he'd ever met.

Even if Bingham reconsidered his offer to lease Opie, Landon wasn't sure he'd leave Spencer. Not now. He had an important, boring date to plan. He searched the cupboard. Peanut butter and strawberry jam—check. He'd grab a fresh loaf of bread and some celery at the store in town. Horses… he needed two, and his was lame. "Callie?"

CHAPTER THIRTEEN

The next afternoon, Landon loosened Pongo's cinch outside the tack room, pleased Luciana had lingered after her first pleasure ride. She released the strap of her blue riding helmet and then spoiled the horse, as usual, giving him another handful of carrot sticks.

"Did you have a good time?" he asked.

"Yes, but Callie kept us on the wheelchair accessible paths around the cabin sites. Now I'm way pumped for our trail ride into the mountains." She gave him a pretty smile, and the appy nuzzled her pocket, searching for more carrots. "Thanks for the lift up the hill, Pongo."

Landon cringed.

When he'd asked to borrow Pongo and Dixie, Callie had sputtered before she could speak. "*Any* rider—even you—can fall off of *any* horse. Including Pongo," she'd said, telling him what he already knew. "You are aware that Luciana's missing a section of skull—with only scalp covering her brain? That's why she's wearing the orthotic helmet. Sorry, dude. Riding mountain trails will have to wait."

He should have guessed as much, but Luciana hadn't

offered that detail, and he hadn't asked. Working inside an arena with a sidewalker and horse handler, they'd minimized her risk for therapy, but not eliminated it. Landon should have known better.

Eager to share his love of horses with her, he'd wanted to show her the beauty of the Rockies from horseback. However, Callie was right. Nothing was worth even a small chance of Luciana reinjuring her brain. Now he'd have to disappoint her.

Tad led Dixie in through the main entry, saving Landon for the moment. He slid the Aussie saddle from the appy's back.

Tad stopped cold, letting out a bark of laughter. "Oh, that's rich, Luciana. Let *him* unsaddle your horse."

Biting her lower lip, Luciana trapped a wayward grin with her teeth, and a hint of rose darkened her cheeks. "Busted." She tilted her head at Landon's Stetson. "What can I say? It's the hat."

Her chuckle broke free, and Tad plucked his baseball cap off, studying it. "What? You don't like the Dodgers?"

Landon adjusted his hat, still curious about their banter, especially since it appeared they discussed him. "One of you gonna explain that?"

"Not me," Tad replied.

With a good-natured smile, the kid tethered Dixie to a post and stowed Callie's gear in the tack room before he led the mare toward the back of the barn.

Landon strode into the tack room and returned Pongo's saddle to its rack. The horse hadn't broken a sweat in the comfortable afternoon, so he grabbed a currycomb on his way out. He arched an expectant brow at Luciana. "You're not off the hook."

She bit her lip again, shaking her head. "You don't need to know *everything*, Mr. Macek."

Now Landon really wanted the story—maybe Tad would spill his guts later. Fletcher walked past the entry and gave a casual wave, making a round of the small barn. Beyond him, Tad strolled toward the office building.

Reasonably assured of privacy, Landon took a fortifying breath. "Hey, about our ride … maybe we should find another way to see the mountains."

Frowning, she knitted her brows. "What do you mean?"

"I got to thinking, out in the woods there's more to spook a horse. Even one as solid as Pongo. If you *did* take a fall …" He gestured to her helmet, fearing that he might hurt her feelings. "Well, I'd never forgive myself for letting it happen."

Luciana pressed her lips together. "I see."

"Not saying we can't go. But maybe ride up in the Gator, and then when a spot catches our eye, we can take a short hike to look around."

Her eyes lit up. "Oh, you don't want to cancel?"

"What?" Surprised, he smiled, relieved that she didn't seem disappointed. "Never. I promised days of boredom, and I plan to deliver."

She gave an easy laugh and then stepped in close enough that he caught a hint of spicy vanilla. Thoughts of tasting the smooth bronze skin in the hollow of her jaw consumed him.

"I'll hold you to that, sir." Closing the distance between them, she placed an open hand on his chest. "Hours of monotony, doing the same ho-hum things over and over."

The woman's eyes smoldered, and male awareness blazed through him. With fingers lightly stroking his cheek, she tilted her head and pressed lush full lips to his. To hell with Fletcher—Landon returned the kiss, savoring the softness of her mouth with unhurried indulgence. The intimacy of kissing a woman almost his height was a welcome surprise. He nuzzled her cheek, fearing he might drown in her provocative, spiced-vanilla scent.

The brim of his Stetson tapped her helmet, and she giggled against his lips. Not hampered by the amusing interruption, he tossed his beloved hat Frisbee-style to the bench and then gently pulled her in close to his body. Her slender frame made her seem delicate.

When she wrapped her welcoming arms around his neck, he teased her lips apart with his tongue. Wanting this moment to last forever, he took his time exploring, nibbling and nipping, indulging in her heady fragrance.

Her warm breath puffed against his ear. "I think I like your style, cowboy."

He cupped her face and gazed into her fathomless obsidian eyes. "I've wanted to kiss you since the first day we met."

Biting her plump lower lip, she could have looked shy, except that his mind had wandered into sultry territory.

"I wanted you to."

With a chuckle, he nipped at her finger pad. "I was just a straight-up coward."

She giggled. "Afraid of the big bad model? I'm not buying it. You seem a lot tougher than that."

In truth, with his growing attachment to Luciana, he feared that in her emotional confusion, she'd love him and then leave him shredded. "You're pretty famous." Cocking his head, he kept his tone light. "Currying horses with me this week. Come Monday, Austin B. Dunaway might give you a call..."

She snorted. "If you'd ever met the creep, you would *not* say that."

In an unexpected break into acting, Landon had doubled for the self-absorbed leading man because the idiot couldn't manage to swing a rope. He laughed. "Truth—I have met him, but I bet he actually remembers your name."

Her eyes danced over a mock frown. "Likely. Only because I wasn't very nice to him. But I'll be nice to you."

Grinning, Landon rubbed his nose to hers. "That's good news, because I've decided to risk my fragile heart."

❧

After a few days anticipating their outing, Harper soaked in the crisp mountain air while she and Landon hiked to a scenic spot recommended by Fletcher. The bodyguard's team had scouted the area and deemed it safe before signing off and making themselves scarce. The near pristine wilderness almost made her forget the security detail's presence.

Pine and hints of loamy earth filled her senses, and a Blue Jay cawed a warning from the safety of an aspen. Tree roots broke the path's surface every few yards, and she trod with care. Her left leg may never be one hundred percent.

Clear blue skies peeked through the canopy of leaves above, promising warmer temps in the afternoon. Since she'd opted for jeans rather than shorts, she hoped it didn't get too warm. She pulled off her windbreaker and tied it around her waist. "Three months ago, I didn't think I'd ever hike again. But here we are, and it's gorgeous."

Landon reached for her hand and squeezed. His smile hinted that he understood the importance of the moment. "You've got this." They paced in silence for a few yards, and he shifted a backpack from one shoulder to the other. "Fletcher seemed more relaxed, today. Did the ballistics come back?"

"Not yet, but Hennessey's still checking out the contractor. So far, other than the upfront money for a kitchen remodel, they haven't found any connection to Ensign. The guy complained he'd bought materials and demanded another payment before he'd start the work." She wished she'd paid more attention to her investments. "I suppose I need to call him and find out more about the plan before I pay for it."

Landon chuckled. "That's a good start. How much longer on the ballistics?"

"Hennessey said any time." She plucked an aspen leaf and twirled it from green to silver, noting hints of autumn gold outlining the veins. "I'm anxious for the final word. Fletch is nice and all, but I'm tired of no privacy. Like now. He's probably watching from somewhere, and it's creepy."

Leafy branches reached over them from either side of the narrow dirt path, creating an arched walkway. Tree roots broke the surface of the trail along with an occasional exposed stone section. The uneven ground didn't intimidate her as it once would have, and she navigated the terrain with only a few wobbles.

They reached a trickle of water no more than two feet wide, and Landon stepped across before turning back to help her. Instead of offering a hand, he simply lifted her over as though she weighed nothing.

She giggled. "I could've managed."

"But would that have been as much fun?"

Enjoying the firm warmth of his shoulders under her touch, she allowed her hands to linger. "Maybe not."

They resumed their hike at a leisurely pace. He wore his hat and jeans, as always, and he had traded his regular cowboy boots for a pair that looked like a dog had chewed on them. The day before their outing, she'd scored new hiking boots in an unpretentious Lodge boutique named The Gift Shop. If they explored the mountains again, maybe she'd scope out a pair for Landon.

Aspens and maples lined the trail. "Is it my imagination, or are the trees ready to turn?"

"Some are getting a little color. Temps dipped into the

mid-thirties last night. Hard to believe next weekend is
Labor Day already."

"Yes it is," she said, her voice subdued by a tightness in her
chest. She took a cleansing breath. "This will be my last week
of therapy—the intensive stuff, anyway."

Time in Colorado had flown by. Early that morning, an
email reminder for her flight home had shaken her. After
their first, real kiss in the barn, Harper wanted to give this
thing—this chemistry— with Landon a chance to flourish.
They had the start of something, or the thought of leaving
him wouldn't make her this miserable.

The grade steepened, but she held her own without
sucking air. It helped that Landon subtly eased their pace.
His jawline hardened, and she wondered if he shared her
dread of separation. She snugged her fingers tighter
with his.

Holding back a branch for her to pass, he gave a tense
smile. "I suspected you might be nearly finished at Stick
Pony. I mean look at you." His features relaxed, and he waved
at the forest around them. "You've come a long ways from
barely making the hill to the barn. Now, you're hiking in the
woods."

His praise made her smile. "After I left the hospital, I
transferred to acute rehab—inpatient therapy for people
with banged-up noggins. I was terrified." She always avoided
thinking about those awful weeks, however she preferred the
tender subject to talk of the calendar. Recalling those initial
days made her shudder. "Compared to some patients at the
center, I was in great shape. I was wobbly, but I could walk. I
was extremely lucky."

"Based on what I've seen of your recovery, it's hard to call
you lucky. I'm real grateful things weren't much, much
worse," Landon told her as he pointed out a tree root.

People often said, *it can't get any worse*. There were all

kinds of worse. She stepped over the woody speed bump. "Yeah, me too."

During her rehab, she'd had a pathological need to concentrate on the future— because the past and present had sucked. As a result, her long-term progress had seldom crossed her mind. Today, the difficult memories were a gift, bringing her accomplishment into focus. Filled with pride, she hiked a mountain trail without a cane.

"It's hard to admit this to you, but when Rocket got hurt, I'd believed I'd gotten a tough break." His solemn gaze intensified. "But watching you bring it every day put things in perspective, right quick."

When men interacted with Harper, most saw only what the camera lens showed them. Unlike others, Landon seemed to read her character and respected her. His open approval overwhelmed her, making her glow inside. "That's—thank you."

A bird warbled above as they approached an abrupt incline. The dirt path gave way to limestone, and he took her hand. She held on tight for safety.

For an elite athlete, losing a world championship had to be devastating. She recalled his shattered expression after he'd failed to lease that roping horse. "Dreams give us purpose, make us who we are. Don't belittle yours. What happened to Rocket and your dream *was* a tough break."

"I suppose so." He shrugged. "Still, you never know what window will open up. As it happened, I met you. Now that's what I call *lucky*."

Flushing warm under his adoring gaze, her stomach did a little flip. "You're a charmer, Mr. Macek."

He gave a low chuckle. "Only because you make it so easy."

Again, he'd made her feel special and all warm inside. She

returned a smile. Getting on a plane for New York without him would be torture.

The forest path ended, opening to a small grassy clearing set high up on the side of the mountain. Landon held her hand long after she didn't need his support, leading her to what appeared to be a seldom-used campsite.

Far below their vantage point, a few mares with foals enjoyed a meadow cradled within the massive Rockies. A dun-colored baby suckled his mother, getting lunch, and a pair of rambunctious colts played bump and run in a tight circle around the small herd. The delightful sight made her smile.

"Do they always play like that?" she asked, truly curious.

"When they're not hungry. But like any kids, play is how they learn the world. The babies figure out real quick who's the boss." He pointed at the running colts. "See how the little chestnut doesn't pull ahead of the sorrel?"

"A horseman's perspective." She smiled. "All I see is adorable cuteness."

He curled a finger under her chin. "Oh, I see adorable, all right."

His dimples melted her, and warmth flushed her cheeks before he leaned in and touched a feathery kiss to her lips. Her heart soared, breaking in the same instant. Now that she seemed able to move forward with her life and wanted more time with him, she was supposed to go back to New York. He'd return to California. Then what?

Trying to ignore her glum thoughts, she threaded her fingers with his.

The Rockies made the New York skyline look insignificant and cold. Sun and shadow imbued the peaks and crags with a warm, living quality, as though the land here had a pulse of its own. The mountains called to her, as did the man at her side.

"The mountains do have magic, just like you said."

"They are beautiful. Remind me to thank Fletch. This spot is great. Want to eat here?"

She quickly agreed.

Landon shrugged off his backpack and unzipped it, extracting a blanket that looked suspiciously like a bedspread. They selected a level spot and laid it out over the tall grass.

When she lowered to take a seat on the coverlet, a spasm in her lower leg dropped her awkwardly to the ground. Like lightning, Landon placed a steadying hand on her upper arm, keeping her upright.

Instead of being embarrassed, she chuckled and rubbed her taut calf. "I'd better ask Chad for some ideas on how to sit at ground level."

Giving her a half-smile, Landon dug in his backpack. "That's in the master class." Seeming to forget her near tumble, he set out paper plates along with several sandwiches. "If I recall, I promised a gourmet lunch. Well, a boring gourmet lunch to be exact."

Harper sniffed the air and her stomach rumbled. "Do I smell *peanut butter*?"

"You do. And do I hear approval?" With a big grin aimed at her noisy midriff, he handed her a plastic knife. "I know how you like variety. We can cut them into fourths—"

Holding her stomach as though she could silence her insides, she laughed. "You remembered."

"Of course, I did. Now, we've got all the classics. Peanut butter and strawberry or grape jam—or bananas." He raised a sandwich between them. "And for the adventurous—we have pickles."

Her jaw dropped. "How did you know? I love peanut butter and pickles."

With dimples punctuating his smile, he handed her a

plated sandwich. "I knew you had a wild streak hidden somewhere. One PB&P for the free spirit." He raised an index finger before reaching into the backpack, and with a flourish, he presented a bottle of red wine. "Did you know that five-star chefs recommend a ruby port to accompany peanut butter?"

Balancing her plate on her crossed legs, Harper laughed, enjoying the ease of being with him. "Sounds yummy."

His casual acceptance was his magic. From the very first therapy session, facing the challenges of her new life, his quiet approval had helped her to accept herself—a true gift.

A dragonfly hummed past them to light on a seed-head perch and above, a wheedling birdsong drifted on the cooling breeze. Simple pleasures she used to take for granted.

After opening the bottle, he filled a cup for her and then one for himself. He raised his glass. "To you, Luciana."

Relationships had taken on new importance, too. Putting affection into her gaze, she touched the plastic rim of her cup to his. "And to you, Landon. You make my days brighter."

With the briefest flare in his eyes, he seemed caught off guard, and a belated smile hinted at a chink in his confidence. Like her, maybe he sensed time closing in on special moments that would never happen. Could they reset the clock?

Jutting his chin at her sandwich, his dimples appeared, and the whisper of insecurity vanished. "My secret's out— knock 'em dead with peanut butter."

"Here I thought it was the port." Chuckling, she tore off a corner of her sandwich, ensuring a choice pickle made the cut, and popped it in her mouth. Savoring the tangy-sweet richness, she chewed slowly before chasing the tidbit down with a sip of wine. "This tastes like heaven."

He wore his Stetson with the rugged Rockies behind him, and Harper couldn't imagine Landon in New York

City. Not for any real length of time, anyway. With an appearance in October and reconstructive surgery scheduled in November, she wondered how long she could linger in Colorado.

"You're thinking pretty hard," he said.

Suspecting her glum reverie showed on her face, she promptly added a smile. "I know this is only our second *real* date, but I feel like I know you much better than that."

"Same here." He rested his elbows on his knees, leaning in. "You had a rough stretch of road, and hard times show how people are made, real fast." He gave a slight shake of his head. "You've got an inner grit that shames most of us—impressed the hell out of me."

At the time, she'd felt more damaged than impressive. "Thanks for the props—and your support. When I was the most lost, you were so kind. I don't think I could've gotten through it without you."

Ever since she'd received the video of Ensign, Landon had stayed at her side, never asking anything of her. Phone calls to Juanita had helped, too. However, he'd had her back during the bleakest moments.

His lips curved in that small way that she'd grown to love, and Harper realized why his half-smile had captured her attention from the very first. He'd always shown her the real Landon—no ingratiating public persona, only him.

"That's what friends do." He studied the distant mountains a moment and turned to her. "Luciana, you sound like you're trying to tell me goodbye. Am I wrong?"

She parted her lips to tell him how much she dreaded their farewells, and hesitating, she feigned interest in the meadow below, unable to share her heart. After only a single date, she didn't have the right to ask him to disrupt his life.

Playing in the grassy waves, a foal wandered too far from his mother and trumpeted a distraught whinny. The mare's responding nicker held an unmistakable fear of loss, resonating with the ache in Harper's heart.

Her feelings had grown to more than a simple attraction. Landon had a quiet, magnetic quality—a combination of confidence and kindness. She found the whole package irresistible.

"Not goodbye." She offered a sad smile. "The three-thousand miles between New York and California is bugging me. Plus, my agent's been working on some things…" Hoping she didn't presume too much about his feelings for her, she mustered her courage. "I suspect that you and I might want more than video calls between spotty weekends."

"I told you how I feel—and that hasn't changed." He rubbed the back of his neck, and lines bracketed his frown. "Yeah, I'd want more."

He was so honest, and he cared for her. Holding in an immature squeal of happiness, she tried to ignore the elated butterflies doing somersaults in her stomach.

"This one thing in October is important to me—and I still can't believe Joni pulled it off. But I'm not close to camera ready." She groaned. "I'll have to pay my personal trainer a bonus to make me presentable."

Landon's half-smile re-appeared, and his hooded gaze held equal parts affection and heat. "You look finer than you ever have."

Enjoying his brazen come-on, her smile made her cheeks hurt. "The camera is not nearly as forgiving as you are, Mr. Macek."

"This *thing* you have cooking—is there any way you can manage it from Spencer?" He cocked his head, and all kinds of subtext layered his question. He was no player. Like her, he probably wanted to see where their budding romance could go.

"My fitness trainer's in New York." Colorado could work

for nearly everything, except that some changes required more courage. Harper plucked a tall stem of grass with a seed head and twirled it between her fingers. "It's scary to think of working with someone new."

"I see." As though she'd shot him down, defeat showed in his brief frown. "What are your plans?"

Along with the loss of the flirty banter, his disappointment tempered her excitement. The rapid-fire negotiations had wrapped up the night before, and she hadn't even told her family about her big break. She hoped Landon would understand the personal significance of this engagement. "Joni landed me a spot on *Adele*."

His eyes widened and then he whistled. "That's impressive."

She surveyed the snowcapped mountains crossing the horizon, knowing the next chapter in her life would *matter*. "Yeah, it's a huge deal, especially for someone in the modeling industry. But I don't want to waste the opportunity on a career that I don't *need* anymore."

Landon came to attention at her side. "You've given this some thought. Vogue and, hell I don't know who all, it's a lot to put in the rearview mirror. Are you looking harder at acting?"

"My long-term plans are still vague. Acting? Maybe." She shrugged. "These last months have been really hard. Some days, the black tunnel stretched forever, and I didn't want to get out of bed."

Landon took her hand and squeezed.

Encouraged by his quiet support, she forged ahead, her excitement racing ahead of her doubts. "There are a lot of people with brain injuries. Like me. On *Adele*, I can show others that there *is* light at the end of that tunnel."

With open admiration in his gaze, Landon's smile widened. "You'll be an inspiration—you inspire me."

"Thanks." Embarrassed by his praise, she took a sip of wine to gather herself. "If I can help even a few people get up in the morning and focus on getting better …"

"Using your celebrity in such a classy way…that's right nice."

"Many do, and I've done charity gigs in the past. This is different." She supposed a brush with death reorganized a person's priorities. Patting her chest, her own passion surprised her. "It's from in here. I simply want to make a difference for someone."

"You do. Every day," he said.

Something in his hazel eyes let her believe she made a difference to *him*, and her own future consumed her thoughts. "Do you know when you're going back to California?"

His grin had a sheepish quality to it. "Rocket's been able to travel for a while. I've hung around…" He pulled her into his arms, and for the first time, a hint of vulnerability shone in his gaze. "Should I pack up my horse and leave, Luciana?"

Heart pounding, she wasn't sure her voice would work. "Stay … please." Whispering against his lips, she almost added *forever*. She closed her entreaty with a light kiss. "If you're here, I'll find a way to work from Spencer."

His brilliant smile showed full-on dimples. "The little town of Spencer is growing on me by the minute."

He slanted his mouth over hers in an unhurried taking, teasing and nipping, and the earth moved sideways under her feet. The promise in his passionate kiss flushed her girl parts with heat, and she nipped at his ear. "I think I want to go back to my suite—*now*, please."

Landon pulled back with a lined brow and studied her. "What?"

She bit her lower lip and widened her eyes.

With dawning awareness, his smile spread. "Now's good."

.   .   .

The Gator could not move fast enough to suit Harper, and during the trip down the mountain, she kept Landon's focus with a teasing hand on his thigh. He hit the gas, and the breeze nearly stole his hat. The Stetson rested on her lap until they arrived at the Lodge.

Finally back in her suite's kitchenette, she made a pretense of offering him a whiskey, pouring his favored Molten Gold into a shot glass. Fiery green glinted in his gaze as he took a polite sip. He set the shot glass down with an audible crack—before pulling her in for a devouring kiss. At some point, he fumbled his hat onto the counter.

With her arms draped around his neck, she pressed her body into his, savoring the whiskey's sweet, nutty taste on his silky tongue. The crisp mountain air clinging to him combined with his clean male scent intoxicated her—she didn't need any wine. They held each other while they explored, tasted, and nibbled.

He lowered his forehead to hers, and their breath mingled. "I want you—I have ever since that day you asked me to call you *Luciana*."

With his words feathering against her lips, she smiled. "And I love the way you say it. I want you, too."

He scooped her legs from under her, and cradling her in his arms, he strode to the bedroom. Halting at the bed, he held her to him and kissed her again before laying her on top of the comforter. With a leisurely perusal down her body and back again, his lips slowly parted.

"Perfect," he whispered on a sigh and then smiled.

The affirmation sent a wave of relief through her. Nude photo shoots hadn't stressed her as much as her angst over this man's opinion of her body. The *deficits* and *defects* had stolen her self-confidence. Or maybe Landon's approval meant more than anyone else's ever had.

Sinking onto the mattress next to her hips, he leaned in, caging her with a hand on either side. The need carved into his expression sent a warm shudder through her insides. He framed her face with his hands, gently placing tender kisses on her cheeks before taking her mouth with his.

The rough contrast of his calloused fingers to his soft lips curled warm desire in her most private places. Every touch made her yearn for more of him. He traced the helmet's strap with a fingertip and released the clasp.

Anxiety shot through her, and she tensed under his touch.

He pressed his palms to the sides of her helmet. "I want you naked."

With a panicked gasp, she grabbed his hands, preventing any movement. Her hair had grown, but her misshapen head might make him turn on his heel and walk out. "Uh…"

A gentle smile put crinkles at the corners of his eyes, and he rubbed his nose to hers. "Baby, I used to think Harper Inez was the most beautiful woman in the world—"

Not feeling at all like that fictitious, confident woman, she grappled for a dose of courage and failed, miserably. Her pulse thundered in her ears. "I'm not ready …"

He put a finger to her lips. "But then I met a gutsy knockout named Luciana. Don't hide yourself from me, not now. *Trust* me."

Any hint of disappointment in his features might melt her into a puddle. She had never felt so vulnerable. Praying he was the man she believed him to be, Harper tucked her chin, giving consent.

Slowly, he pushed the helmet off her head and set it to the side. His expression didn't change, and she trembled while he ran a hand over her pixie haircut, pausing briefly at the missing section of skull. His gaze hardened for a brief instant, so fleeting, that she thought she had imagined it.

Afternoon sunlight streamed into the room, and she regretted their timing. Evening mood lighting would have been more flattering. Anxiety darkened the edges of her vision.

His barely there smile gave her the acceptance that she desperately craved, and he brushed a kiss to her forehead. Cupping her face with both hands, he pressed his lips tenderly to hers. "Short is a good look for you. But anything would work with those midnight eyes."

Recovering her wits, she nuzzled his cheek. "I thought—I thought you might leave."

His intense gaze fixed on hers. "Never."

Threading his fingers into her short hair, he slid a hand behind her head and took charge of their kiss. The firm touches roaming her scalp sent warm tingles skittering to her shoulders and surprisingly beaded her nipples. He'd been right to ask her to lose the helmet.

After being so frightened of his reaction to her bare head, she melted into him with new confidence, running her hands over the supple planes of his chest. His lips parted, and his breath hitched. Emboldened by the need carved into his expression, she pulled him down into her arms.

With each caress and murmured endearment, her heart soared higher—on the wings of hope.

His tongue teased her lips apart and she opened for him, *trusting* him.

CHAPTER FOURTEEN

*A*fter three weeks of dating Luciana, Landon was still tempted to pinch himself. During the days, she'd prepared for her *Adele* appearance and worked with her new personal trainer in Spencer while he'd schooled the fresh Stick Pony stock to carry patients. He lived for the evenings when they had hit local attractions, and later, when they had cuddled, making love long into the night.

When the rodeo came to town with the county fair, he'd used his connections to score premium front-row seats for a double date with Ryder and his wife Vianna. Attending a rodeo was bittersweet, but he wouldn't have it any other way. He wanted to share his love of the sport with Luciana, hoping she would develop a passion for it, too.

The four of them arrived well before the Saturday afternoon performance and watched the go-round runs that didn't fit into the rodeo's two-hour schedule. The slack, a little-known part of the sport, was generally not open to the public. During the break before the main performance, the girls had gone off shopping for souvenirs.

Ryder propped his foot up on the cement ledge in front of

him. "Nice perk, you getting us in early. I'm surprised that some of the top names ride in the slack."

"Yeah, they keep it fair. A lottery decides who rides for the public." Landon waved at another familiar face in the thin crowd. "Most of the competitors like it better than the rodeo. The rodeo audience is fun, but without all the theatrics, it's pure, straight-up competition."

Ryder leaned in over one of the empty seats between them. "Deke said ballistics confirmed Ensign was the shooter?"

He kept his voice low, and Landon appreciated his discretion. "Yep, we're both relieved. It's helped Luciana move on," Landon replied. "I think it gave her some closure— the New York detective has all but closed the case."

"That's great news." Ryder cocked his head toward Fletcher's empty station near the exit. He and a new guy escorted the shopping women. "What's with the bodyguard detail then?"

"I guess she always has security at public events with a crowd. I sure wish she didn't need them, but at least she's got a little more privacy. Deke pulled the security from outside her suite."

"That's too bad. Sorry man. But I suppose it's better than before."

Recalling how Gavin crashed in the door, Landon had to agree. "Yeah it is."

"I've heard she's getting out some. People have seen you two around—a lot." He arched a brow. "Spencer's still a small town."

Gossip likely followed Luciana no matter what. Landon would have to get used to it or find a new girl. Not happening. He shrugged. "Colorado's working out pretty good, so far."

Shifting in his seat, Ryder smirked. "Well, if you're going to date a celeb, Spencer's the place to do it."

The reality that Landon was dating *Harper Inez* hit home—again. Luciana's unpretentious nature made it easy to forget who she was to the world. Recalling her willowy curves and the cradle of her hips, he wondered if he would wake up the next morning and find out he'd been dreaming all along.

"We've gone out some. Finally made it to the Wild Card—played darts, danced," Landon said, keeping his tone casual. Though anytime he thought about how he felt when he was with her, barn swallows swooped around in his stomach.

Ryder chuckled. "Yeah, I heard."

Being a gossip topic gave Landon an uneasy feeling, but he supposed it was inevitable. "By the way, I'll be in L.A. a few days next week. Tad agreed to do chores for me."

"Thanks for arranging coverage," Ryder said, and a slow grin split his face. "Let me guess, you and Luciana are getting away?"

Thinking about the trip with Luciana almost made Landon giddy. He reined in his besotted teenager reaction. "It's her first public appearance since the shooting. I'm trying to be supportive."

"Yeah? What's she doing? If it's not private, I mean."

"The preliminary ads will start in a few days," Landon told him, unable keep the pride from his voice. "She's got a spot on the *Adele* show."

Ryder's lips parted. "Wow, that's some gig."

"Yeah, it kinda blew me away, too." Landon shook his head. "She's doing great."

"You're going with her." Ryder snorted. "I'd say that sounds serious."

Landon smothered a grin. "I'm not complaining."

The ladies returned with bags in tow. Luciana descended

the aisle stairs with a careful, steady gait, keeping a hand on the rail. Tight jeans hugged those long legs and disappeared into high-fashioned, saggy cowboy boots. Their brass zippers and loose buckled straps didn't appear to have a true function. She'd called them *slouchy*.

Later, he would unzip those fancy boots and peel the stretchy denim off, one leg at a time. Later.

With Vianna close behind her, Luciana sidled in front of Ryder, and Landon rose to take her packages. He stowed them under their seats, and she settled next to him. She handed him a rodeo program. "Look what I found."

Amused at her enthusiasm, he chuckled. "Thanks. I've seen a few."

"But this one has your name in it." She bumped her shoulder to his. "I thought it was cool."

At sight of his wife, Ryder's face lit up, and he took her shopping haul, fussing over her. "You need to get off your feet."

Giggling, Vianna shook her head of dark curls and screwed up her face in an adorable frown. "See, Luciana, I told you, he's been unbearable."

"I say, enjoy it," Luciana replied with a smile.

As Ryder re-claimed his seat, he extracted a big-eyed plush kitty out of a shopping tote. The fluffy-orange fur ball purred with the slightest movement.

He dropped the baby toy back into the bag. "Landon, I bet there're over twenty stuffed animals in here." He widened his eyes at his wife. "Do they have anything left to sell?"

"Of course they do. But don't worry, I have another shot on our way out," Vianna quipped, rubbing her tummy. "Our baby's going to have everything I never did."

Landon had wondered if the two women would find anything to talk about, slow to realize the magnetic power of a pregnancy. Sitting between him and Ryder, they huddled over a phone viewing designer nursery photographs.

Catching his friend's eye, he grinned. "You saw what they did in only ten minutes. You're going to be so damned broke after these two get done tomorrow."

With a good-natured smile, Ryder retook his seat. "I've given up—"

Spirited band music blasted from the PA system, cutting him off, and the announcer's voice-over introduced the grand entry parade. Pretty girls wearing matching sparkling white western outfits galloped their palomino mounts in pairs down the center of the arena, splitting apart at the far end to circle back.

When competing in a rodeo, the high-energy parade usually signaled the beginnings of Landon's final prep for his ride. Today, sitting in the stands instead of checking his gear, the lively beat gave him the sense of a false start. He shook off the odd feeling and flipped open the program to the national standings.

Jenkins had the top spot, but he only led the number two and three cowboys by eight-thousand dollars. Since Landon's departure, they had split the wins between them. He skimmed down the list of familiar names, and halted his finger at the fourteenth spot. *Landon Macek.*

If no one knocked him down to sixteenth place in the next four days, he would still qualify for the finals. Stifling a groan over the irony, he shoved the program into a sack under his seat and returned his attention to the arena.

After the presentation of the colors, the announcer added a plug for the Audrey Knox concert planned later that evening. While the parade horses made their exit, the chute helpers set up the bareback bronc riding—an event not included in the slack. With pit-crew speed, they loaded stock into the chutes and launched the bucking horses, keeping the cowboys safe.

Luciana and Vianna seemed to take in everything and asked good questions, too.

"We might have two new rodeo fans," Ryder said.

Landon laughed. "I think so."

"I'm a fan, all right," Luciana replied, and she leaned over and gave him a peck on the cheek. "Of one cowboy in particular."

The woman melted his insides, and a broad smile cramped up his jowls. It was time to admit it— he was hooked. With their homes on opposite coasts, they needed to bring their lives together. Uncertain that she wanted the same, he tried not to think too far into the future, but usually failed, because every time he looked at her, his heart swelled up.

After the broncs, the crew set up for steer wrestling, allowing only a minute or two between events. Without a favorite, Landon cheered for riders by name, glad Jenkins had bypassed Spencer.

The lost championship aside, Landon was living the dream, spending the whole day at the rodeo, and tonight, country music with Luciana. He squeezed her thigh. "Okay, this next event is the one where the header ropes the horns and the heeler snags the two hind legs."

She gave him an amused smile. "I remember."

"I guess I said that already." A smidge embarrassed, he grinned and tried to rein in his eagerness for her to enjoy the rodeo. "We're rootin' for this cowboy getting set in the box. That's my buddy Colt. He's got a good year goin'. He and his teammate might even make it to Vegas."

"What's in Vegas?" Luciana asked.

He swallowed, regretting he'd mentioned it. "The

National Finals Rodeo, the NFR. We *all* want to be in Vegas in December."

Colt and his partner handily caught their steer, and Landon's rail-side cheering section drew his friend's attention. As Colt rode by with a big grin, he doffed his hat at their group, and they waved back with whoops and hollers.

"Isn't he the one who hooked you up on the Opie deal?" Ryder asked.

"Yep." Keeping his reply short, Landon wasn't interested in re-living his failed Hail Mary, especially while he watched a rodeo from the stands.

Luciana squeezed his hand.

So much for his nonchalant front—she'd detected his gloomy cringe. He lifted her fingers to his lips in a sort-of thank you. "You can't come to the rodeo without having a chili dog. And don't say you can't eat one. A hot—"

"I know, I know." She laughed. "A hotdog a decade won't ruin me."

The pair rose to seek out a concession stand, and Landon settled his hat back on his head, allowing Luciana to step past him. When they reached the aisle, he did the possessive male thing, placing his hand in the small of her back, and though she seldom lost her balance anymore, if needed, he could steady her.

A few in the audience recognized her and smiled. She would always draw attention. A fifty-something, heavyset man even gave Landon a thumbs up. With open envy on his face, all the big guy saw was the supermodel, Harper Inez, the woman in *Sports Illustrated*—not Luciana. A few months ago, Landon had been no different.

Now, with the warmth of her body against his hand, the NFR didn't seem like such a great loss.

En route to the arena entrance, hand in hand with Landon, Harper felt lighter of spirit than she had in years as they strolled the corridor of concession stands and souvenir booths. Ryder and Vianna kept pace beside them, pointing out local artisans along the way. The whole town had turned out for the Audrey Knox evening concert, and the fair's outdoor venue thrummed with energy.

A few strides ahead, Fletcher led the way, and Sage, a big guy with long dark hair, trailed behind. Harper didn't know the other two men walking on either side, they'd only come to provide coverage for the concert. Between the four body-guards, they kept the thick crowd at a safe distance.

A booth displaying baby outfits and a hodgepodge of other unique wares caught her eye. "Oh wow. Gotta stop. Give me a minute, guys."

As she detoured, chuckles sounded behind her. Fletch had likely spotted the shopping magnet first thing, and he shifted smoothly to pace at her side. He was learning her habits.

After a quick perusal, she snagged T-shirts featuring Audrey at a mic and a mega pack of digital album codes to share with the group. In a brilliant stroke of luck, she spotted a yellow Audrey onesie and a pair of coordinating ombré cowboy boots handmade with lambskin for delicate newborn feet.

She returned to the group and passed out the impromptu mementos.

Vianna fingered the two-tone ochre leather. "This is lovely. You-you didn't need to do this."

Her friend's near speechless surprise and heartfelt reac-tion sent warmth through Harper. "You're very welcome. Besides, who can resist shopping for a baby?"

It had been ages since she'd had a girlfriend who didn't want to talk about the latest designer. The petite woman was endearing, and nothing delighted Harper more than giving a gift to people she cared for.

Vianna held the baby outfit up for Ryder. "Do you know Audrey? Can we get her to sign it?"

Ryder chuckled. "Yeah, I know her." He nodded at Harper. "Thanks, I hope the little darling wears them for longer than a week."

Wistful, Harper wondered what it would feel like to shop for her own babies one day. "They'll make a good hand-me-down."

Carefully folding the onesie and returning the boots to their miniature boot box, Vianna shook her head. "The whole outfit will be a keepsake."

Resuming their way to the entrance, the foursome ambled leisurely, allowing the crowd to pass by on either side. In tacit agreement, they'd slowed their pace so that Vianna didn't become too fatigued.

A cluster of teen girls wearing matching pink cowboy boots line danced their way toward the main entry, singing an a cappella rendition of Knox's big hit, *Maybe I'm The One*. The girls had talent. Scattered applause erupted among bystanders, and Harper cheered them on. The last several months of hiding had made her claustrophobic, and she reveled in the crowd's energy.

Fresh popcorn aroma and hints of fried pastry tantalized her senses, and Landon gestured to a funnel cake booth. "I forgot. We need a stack of those, too."

She groaned. "You're going to kill me off. Do they have a juice stand anywhere?"

He knitted his brows. "What's that?"

Fighting an eye roll, she sighed. "You're hopeless."

Vianna leaned in near Harper's ear. "Thanks for the limo drop-off. I'd never ridden in one before. It's kind of nice having the big guys part the crowd, too. Do you always have a security detail?"

Harper laughed. At least someone liked the bodyguards. When Landon had spotted Fletch's team, he had frowned, making it clear he wished them gone. A niggle of worry ate at her. Her security needs had returned to baseline, so hopefully, he could adjust.

She smiled wide, making a mental note to call Vianna in the morning to confirm their afternoon shopping date. "Only for big venues like a concert. We won't need anyone tomorrow in Spencer—but we'll keep the limo."

Vianna raised a hand for a high-five. "That's what I'm talking about."

Billboard-sized photos at the entry touted the hometown girl who had made it big. Harper pointed at one. "Spencer sure loves their Audrey."

"You bet we do." Ryder laughed. "Her family owns the ranch across the road from Stick Pony. You probably get a bunch of attention back home, too. Where're you from?"

"Redding, California. No parades, yet," she said with a smile. "I did do an appearance at Kemp Auto's grand opening, though. A friend of Mamá's. She was so proud, I thought she'd burst. The whole County Memorial housekeeping department showed up *en masse*."

Landon's kind gaze belied his intuitive nature, giving the impression he had read between the lines. "Moms are good for that."

There were no landowners in Harper's background. Compared to other California communities, Redding wasn't a particularly wealthy town, either. In truth, Mamá had never even met Mr. Kemp, but she had cleaned his house for a few years. Knowing Harper was coming home for a visit, his wife had recommended her as an added draw for the event.

A slender man in his mid-thirties approached with an impressive full-sized camera hanging from his neck and extended a business card to Luciana. "Excuse me, Miss Inez. My name is Linc Simmons. I wondered if—"

Before she could react, Landon stepped in front of her. In the same instant, Fletcher dropped back to intercept the photographer.

Unlike the scowling Landon, the bodyguard smiled, not appearing the least bit concerned. "Hi Linc. Covering the concert?"

Mr. Simmons glanced from one man to the other, clearly uncomfortable. "Yes. Miranda asked me to provide a little color for the Herald's fair insert." Peering between the two men, Simmons beamed at Luciana. "Earlier at the rodeo, I captured a lovely shot of you and your gentleman friend. I'd hoped you'd both give your consent for us to use it."

Being in public meant being in front of a camera—a fact of life for Harper. Now, Landon had to endure it, too. Worried over his reaction to his first paparazzi encounter, she threaded her fingers in his. Few people had the fortitude for the incessant public attention given to celebrities.

After a minute, his jaw relaxed, and he gave her hand a squeeze. She let out a held breath. Even though she was a little annoyed, at least Simmons wasn't from a despicable gossip rag. Not true paparazzi, really—he had asked permission.

She pursed her lips, and then tried for a polite tone. "I appreciate that but—"

"I understand." Obviously anticipating her refusal, Mr. Simmons nodded with kind eyes and tilted his camera towards her and Landon. "Just take a look. You might like it."

Simmons had caught her kissing Landon's cheek right after she had declared herself as his number-one fangirl. His animated smile in full-dimple mode filled the small hi-def screen, broadcasting his besotted reaction.

Struck by the charming candor, Harper covered her lips before an *aww* could escape. If she'd had any doubt about his feelings for her, the tiny photo said it all.

Landon laughed, and a little color tinged his cheeks. "Oh boy, you busted me good."

People on their way to the concert slowed as they passed by, eyeing Harper and her friends before moving on with smiles.

Ryder shook his head, chuckling. "Man, you look like—"

Placing a hand on his forearm, Vianna halted his taunt. "He's absolutely smitten. It's the sweetest thing I've ever seen."

Grateful for her sensitivity, Harper didn't want Landon to feel embarrassed. But she agreed—he did look *smitten*. The love on his face made her insides flutter and no matter what she had to do to get it—she would own that photo.

Simmons seemed to understand the personal nature of the delightfully candid shot. Too many didn't. More important to her, he'd been totally prepared to give up publishing the image. She motioned for Fletcher to join her off to the side. "Fletch, how well do you know Mr. Simmons?"

"He's a decent sort. Owns Old Time Photos in Olde Town. In fact, he shot my sister's wedding last spring," he replied.

"Thanks." She returned to the group and reached for the photographer's card. "Mr. Simmons, when do you go to print?"

Instantly alert, Simmons squared his shoulders. "My deadline is tomorrow at one. The issue releases Tuesday."

"Give me a minute, will you?" she asked.

The photographer beamed. "Take your time."

Harper pulled Landon a few feet away, leaving the group

to entertain Mr. Simmons as they could. From their affable conversation, it was clear they all knew each other.

Landon rubbed the back of his neck. "Are you really thinking of letting them use that?"

"Your image belongs to you, not me. So it's your decision. But hear me out." She put affection in her gaze. "It's only a matter of time before a tabloid catches a picture of us, and some gossip rag tells our story how *they* want to tell it."

"You think a small-town paper in Spencer is likely to be respectful."

His near frown hinted at skepticism, and she wanted to reassure him. "When dealing with the media, controlling the narrative is key. Plus, if Simmons got a picture, at least ten cell phones caught us, too."

The corners of Landon's mouth tightened. "I hadn't figured on that, at all."

"Social media posts are usually no big deal." Harper shrugged, not caring who saw her kiss Landon. "But the *Spencer Herald* won't speculate about Ensign's motives, or if I'll ever work again, or the other garbage the tabloids spew. A local paper will showcase their rodeo and the Audrey Knox concert."

"You're not worried about sending the wrong message? Like we're a …?"

Realization dawned that Landon did not know how important he was in her life. She tilted her head and bit her lip. "A couple?"

"Yeah," he said on a sigh and then smiled. "Like a couple."

She pressed a kiss to his lips. "If you're ready, I want to tell the world about us, and this might be a really good way to do it."

Landon grinned with full dimples and returned her kiss. "Is this how a celebrity asks someone to go steady?"

"With all the time we've spent together, I sort-of assumed

we were exclusive. We'd better straighten this out right now."
She giggled, stroking a finger along his lower lip. "Will you
be my guy?"

Dimples appeared, and jade flecks brightened his hazel
gaze. "Exclusive—damn straight, we are," he murmured at
her ear. He pulled back and scanned the area, seeming to
realize they had a furtive audience. "I suppose this means
that we need to figure out the East Coast-West Coast thing."

Taking the next step and thinking about a possible future
with this kind and gentle man almost made her explode with
happiness. "Yes, I think it does."

Keeping his cheek next to hers, he spoke quietly. "I'll leave
it up to you if we let Simmons use that photo."

"He did catch your personality—everyone will know right
away what I see in you."

"Nah, they'll know I'm stuck on you."

Over Landon's shoulder, a college-aged guy pocketed his
phone and moved on. Her relationship with Landon would
be public within the hour, so the *Herald's* article would only
confirm social media accounts. She trailed a finger pad along
his jawline. "And tomorrow, I'm going to have a new wall-
paper for *my* phone."

Landon snorted. "I guess I owe you one."

CHAPTER FIFTEEN

*B*y the following Tuesday after the fair, most of Spencer's residents had seen Landon's lovesick mug either in the *Herald* or on any one of a groundswell of social media postings. He took some expected ribbing at the Wild Card from Ryder and Fletch. However, strangers regularly identifying him on sight unnerved him.

Every now and then, a casual rodeo fan said hello and asked about his horse or for roping advice. The Harper Inez following seemed bolder, or maybe the sheer volume of attention overwhelmed him. Possibly, because he wasn't an actual celebrity, some of the locals had assumed he was fair game. A shameless few greeted him with a version of, "Hey, aren't you that guy with Harper Inez?" Others gave him knowing smiles.

After a few days of that nonsense, he welcomed the anonymity outside of Spencer. No one at the airports recognized him, nor did the flight attendant in first class.

He was a nobody in L.A., too, and he was fine with that. He and Luciana followed an escort through the television studio's back hallway, and two admin types converged on her from either side. Landon dropped back to follow in their wake.

Defying convention, *Adele* was broadcast live and her fans ate up the authenticity of the candid interactions. A mid-twenties man with bright red hair offered Luciana last minute updates regarding her interview, and then with a big grin, he asked her to sign a photo.

She turned those dark eyes on him and the poor kid's whole face flushed red, matching his hair. Luciana beamed at him, appearing to fight a chuckle. "What's your name, sweetie?"

He handed her an eight-by-ten copy of the epic red bikini shot. "Dexter."

Landon's favorite. He clenched his jaw. If he wanted a long-term relationship with Luciana, he would have to adjust to sharing her public persona with her fans.

At her other side, a mid-twenties woman with over-sized glasses provided a rundown of an abbreviated fashion show to follow the interview. "Miss T said Claude and two dressers—I think she meant attendants— will be in the dressing room. The commercial break runs three minutes-fifty seconds."

Luciana laughed. "I can change three times in three minutes. That will be plenty of time."

She was in her element, and Landon couldn't be prouder.

The corridor was a gallery of sorts. Images of the famous African American talk show host posing with too many celebrities to count adorned the walls. Maybe she would add one of Luciana to the collection.

The entourage ahead of him turned left and caught Landon lingering among the displays. He hustled to catch up. As he neared the wide entry to what appeared to be a receiving lounge, a uniformed man pulled the double doors shut and took a wide stance in front of them. "I'm sorry sir, staff only past this point."

With heat flushing his face, Landon searched the corridor for someone to vouch for him, surprised to be excluded. Suspecting the guard had made an error, he didn't want to draw any negative attention. "If I'm not allowed in, is there a place I can wait?"

"There's the main reception area you walked through at the front entrance." With a lanyard identifying him as J. Smith, the twenty-something security guard appeared genuinely sympathetic. "Truthfully, sir, I'm not sure how you got this far."

Becoming more frustrated than embarrassed, Landon repositioned his hat. He had no idea where the limo had deposited them, and he hadn't seen any damned waiting room. "I don't think I came in that way."

Smith's brows wedged together, showing the first hint of suspicion. "You didn't get a visitor tag?"

"I'm with Harper Inez, if that helps."

The guard's mouth tightened short of a smirk, his doubt clear, and then he reached for a radio at his hip.

One of the doors opened behind him, and Luciana poked her head out. "Landon, there you are. I wondered what happened to you." She fixed the startled security with her dark gaze and frowned. "This is Mr. Macek. He's with me."

"Yes, ma'am— Miss Inez. Apologies, sir," Smith stammered as Landon, feeling like an afterthought, stepped into the forbidden territory.

Out of his element, he couldn't help being touchy. But Smith had only protected Luciana. Along with everyone else in the United States, he had to know that only a few months ago, someone had tried to kill her. Hell, that's how they got here in the first place. How had Landon forgotten?

Instead of irritated, he should be grateful. He turned back

to the threshold and extended a hand. "We're good, Smith. Any creep could claim he's with her. You're doing the job she needs you to do."

Tension visibly drained from the guard's taut frame, and belatedly, Landon considered the possible consequences to him. Pissing off a big-name guest or their friends might not go well, especially with a jerk celeb like Austin B. Dunaway. Landon vowed to be more tolerant.

The young guy's palm was damp. "I'll know you next time, sir."

Feeling a little guilty, Landon left Smith to resume his post and turned to join Luciana.

"What was that about?" she asked.

"Nothing." He gave her a half-smile. "Glad you came back for me."

Inside, square upholstered chairs formed bigger squares around low tables. He supposed some decorator intended the seating arrangements to be *cozy*, but all the sharp angles reminded him of holding pens. On the far wall, a hospitality spread of fresh fruit and calorie-free beverages invited guests to help themselves. Landon didn't feel welcomed, either.

Like the furniture, the people had a sleek appearance, as though body fat was a sin. No matter their age, everyone in the room was unusually attractive and slender. Probably none had eaten a roasted marshmallow since childhood, if at all.

Luciana flagged down a tall, middle-aged brunette who scribbled furiously on a clipboard. "Tabitha, this is my friend Landon. Can you make sure that he's taken care of?"

Tabitha smiled, and her frenetic demeanor morphed to calm congenial. "Absolutely, Miss Inez." She waved at a petite, curvy woman leaning over a four-legged desk, studying an electronic tablet. "Anna? Join us please?"

As Anna approached, it became clear she wasn't petite at

all—more like five-seven-ish. Nor was she overweight. She only appeared short and plump in the room filled with tall and thin. Tabitha made introductions, and Anna pushed her oversized glasses up with an index finger.

She extended a hand with a pleasant smile. "Nice to meet you, Mr. Macek."

"Likewise. But Landon works fine."

With her nod, the blue frames promptly slid back down.

A tall, muscular man wearing a snug T-shirt and stretchy jeans emerged from a door near the buffet, commanding the room's attention. He wore his dark hair shaved at the sides with the top gelled into short spikes. A rooster's coxcomb came to mind.

The dandy's gaze zeroed in on them, or rather Luciana, and he strode toward her with an athletic swagger. A couple people in the room made eye contact with him as though they expected a greeting, but he ignored all until he reached her. He touched her elbow and led her off to the buffet table to chat.

With sharp attention, Tabitha tracked the popinjay's path. "Anna, please ensure that chilled Perrier and frosted animal crackers are backstage for Mr. Claude."

The muscled-up metrosexual had to be the designer Luciana had mentioned. Claude of Paris. The big cheese wanted animal crackers. Landon fought a smirk.

Claude huddled with her near the buffet, speaking in low tones, and Landon took an instant dislike to him. A guy who wore a shirt announcing every muscle group was overcompensating for something. Landon unclenched his jaw, admitting that he might even feel a smidge threatened. Time to man up.

Anna belatedly dragged her gaze from the designer. "Already done, Miss T. Adele wants your entire team well cared for—especially Mr. Claude. If you and yours need anything, please let me know."

After a brisk nod to Anna, Tabitha beamed full-wattage-fake geniality at Landon. "Mr. Macek, I'll leave you in Anna's capable hands."

The *Adele* interview was huge for Luciana, and Landon wanted to be supportive of her first public appearance since the shooting. He didn't belong here. Not one bit.

However, he would do it for her.

Adele herself entered from the rear door, wearing a classy burnt-orange tunic and dark slacks, with short jet hair sleek against her scalp and large hoop earrings. At sight of her, Anna snapped to subtle attention at his side.

With amiable greetings for the mix of guests and employees, Adele worked her way around the room, seeming to know everyone by name. "Tabitha, you've done a great job organizing everyone."

She even stopped to say hello to Landon before circling back to the buffet. "Harper darling, Claude, come with me."

The door closed behind the trio, and as though their exit triggered a silent fire alarm, the room emptied, leaving Landon and Anna alone. He accepted the glass of ice tea she offered.

Anna gestured to a couch positioned in front of a large screen on the wall and snatched a remote from the low coffee table. "Let's watch the interview, shall we?"

An energetic jazz soundtrack played over an intro clip of the Los Angeles skyline and mountainous background. Wanting the best view, Landon sat next to Anna on the sofa. On screen, the program cut to a studio set where the famous host occupied one of two armchairs angled together.

After a brief monologue, Adele clapped her hands together. "Today, Harper Inez joins us—the Argentine Empress of the modeling industry for nearly a decade." The studio crowd applauded while she nodded encouragement. "As many of you know, she's had a rough year after suffering a gunshot wound to the head. Only about five percent of victims survive this type of injury, yet she has prevailed. Now, she's ready to share her return to the runway with us."

Music played, and Adele rose to greet Luciana, who strode in from off stage. Her agent had lobbied against the long olive green jacket and slacks outfit, but Landon had voted for it.

With Vianna's help, she had added a coordinating helmet and a fancy walking stick to the ensemble. After a brief hug and smiles, the two women on screen took their seats. Luciana crossed one lithe leg over the other.

Next to him, Anna gasped. "She rocks that outfit. First thing tomorrow, women will be buying helmets and fashion canes."

Landon snorted at the idea of helmets as fashion. But Luciana's remastered orthotic and walking stick gave off a subdued Vegas showgirl vibe. She was stunning. The admin might be onto something.

On screen, Adele gestured to the elaborate cane. "Check you out, all accessorized. Is that a ruby-throated hummingbird?"

With an amiable smile, Luciana raised the fancy porcelain handle that she'd found at an antique store, and a detail inset appeared in the corner of the television. Landon focused on her. More than beautiful, she exuded confidence.

"I suppose when you have something with you all the time, like eyewear—or even a helmet—you want stylish options. But not everything fashionable comes from a high-dollar boutique." Leaning in, she looked straight at the camera, indicating her peach and olive-green print helmet.

"Wrapping paper," she mouthed.

Quiet laughter came from the crowd.

"For fun extras, I highly recommend Aunt Cora's Attic in Spencer, Colorado. They have a wide selection of period cane handles and other vintage accessories."

"I'll be sure to stop in during my next visit." Adele leaned over the arm of her chair. "Now, between us girls...did I see you have a new love interest?"

Landon ran a hand down his face, stifling a groan. Anna chuckled beside him.

Biting her lower lip with dancing eyes, Luciana gave a cute little nod. "Landon Macek's a special guy. We met in Spencer while our careers were on hiatus."

Adele returned her smile and then engaged the audience. "Is she glowing or what?" After the applause died down, she returned her attention to Luciana. "I'm very happy for you, Harper. No one deserves a special guy more than you."

On the sofa next to him, Anna raised her glass in salute. "Go Landon."

Landon's gut clenched. Luciana had notified the entire nation that they were dating—or more likely the entire English-speaking world. The tasteful article in the *Spencer Herald* hadn't seemed like an invasion of his privacy, but the *Adele* show had millions of viewers.

After exploring Luciana's California childhood, Adele segued to her Argentine roots. "I love coming to America stories. Tell us yours."

Forgetting the dating reveal, Landon planted his elbows on his knees, eager to learn this part of her history and embarrassed over his ignorance. He'd never asked about her life before America.

"Being an interracial couple in Argentina, life was difficult for my parents. They immigrated to the U.S., hoping for tolerance. However, after a few years, my father worried that he'd deserted his family—and his people. My mother believed Juanita and I would have more opportunity here. In the end, they separated." She hesitated, appearing to compose herself. "I'm very proud of both of them."

"I should say so." Adele paused, giving Luciana a moment. "Your parents sound like remarkable people.

Recovered, Luciana gave a slight smile. "Yes, they are."

After a teaser about the shooting, followed by a commercial break, the talk show host dove in. "Harper, this spring, you suffered a grievous assault…"

Landon held his breath, fearing how the recall would affect Luciana. However, Adele deftly avoided direct references to the actual shooting, and he let out a relieved gust of air.

Luciana gave poised and thoughtful responses to the very personal questions. "Applying mascara is still a challenge, and I take medicine every day to prevent muscle spasms. It works most of the time." She chuckled, briefly engaging the camera. "Hopefully, I won't fall down on live TV."

Adding subtle plugs for Stick Pony, she even narrated videos marking her progress, not shying away from how the brain injury had affected her gait. Landon could not have been prouder of his classy lady.

At the close of the therapy clip, Adele took a deep breath. "What an *incredible* story." She waited for the applause to die off and then addressed Luciana with a slight tilt of her head. "Harper, through all of your challenges, what is the most valuable thing you've learned?"

Luciana tapped her lips with an index finger. "Wow, that's a long list." The studio was dead silent awaiting her reply. "My biggest lesson was…that for every person who would profit from your pain, there are hundreds more who will help you. And a stellar few will risk everything to protect a stranger."

Without a doubt, she spoke of the unsung hero Angela whose interventions would forever remain hidden. How

Luciana could lose so much at the hands of others and still have such a grateful heart confounded Landon. He didn't know when it had happened, but he had fallen in love with her.

"A stellar few?" Adele raised her brows. "You tease us with a titillating secret. Care to share?"

Luciana shook her head. "That story isn't mine to tell. But I do have a message for the audience."

Adele gestured toward the viewers. "By all means."

The camera closed in on Luciana and her fathomless dark eyes. "Today's interview isn't really about *my* comeback. If you've suffered brain trauma, know that *you* can rejoin the world. Things are not the same. But you can have a full life and have fun doing it."

With the genuine caring that had made her a household name, Adele squeezed Luciana's hand, clearly fighting emotion. "Thank you for being with us and sharing your story."

Luciana held their connection. "Absolutely my pleasure. Thank you for having me."

Adele gave the camera audience her full attention. "People, right after this message from our sponsors, Harper will share her incredible progress. Get ready to feast your eyes on the latest fashions by the brilliant, up and coming sensation, Claude of Paris."

Anna pointed the remote at the television and the screen went dark. She leapt to her feet. "That's our cue. Come on. Let's go backstage where the action is."

Startled by this new development, Landon numbly followed the admin to a small sitting room with a portable clothes rack jammed against a sofa. In front of the hanging garments, attendants fussed around Luciana while she stood mannequin-still in a shimmering taupe dress. The silky number stopped at her upper thigh, and its plunging neck-line dove to her waist.

He muffled a lusty groan.

She smiled at him, but Claude emerged from behind the clothes rack, breaking their connection. He wore a suit — sort of. An embroidered peach jacket with a stand-up collar hung open over a fishnet shirt, exposing his pumped-up torso. Landon struggled to keep the shock from his expression.

Standing at his side, a distracted Anna hugged her electronic tablet to her chest and kept her gaze riveted on the fashion peacock, clearly engrossed in the show.

"Mr. Claude himself came for this event. He's simply divine," she said on a sigh. Landon doubted she spoke to him.

The designer had made a distinct impression, but *divine* hadn't crossed Landon's mind.

❦

Very aware of Landon's presence, Harper remained stock still while Claude tapped his fingertips to his chin, scruti-nizing her breasts. "No-no. Zees will not do. Paulette, bigger tape."

The dresser in charge of tape jumped like a scared rabbit and produced two rolls for his highness. Claude repositioned the fabric over Harper's breasts and tsked. "Ze bias is cut wrong."

The pretentious accent made her want to laugh. According to the biz grapevine, he had actually grown up in Jersey. However, she maintained her impassive expression. Profes-sionalism demanded that she act the part of a mannequin and allow the designer to display his creation to best advantage.

Claude slid his fingers under the fabric covering her

breast and grazed his knuckle over her bare nipple, adding a little extra motion. Shocked, she broke with protocol and sent him a warning glare.

His return gaze held the subtlest of heat, confirming his lewd intent. "Unlike zee other statuesque beauties, you have zee natural bounty, *mademoiselle*." Giving Landon a dismissive shrug, he lifted her *bounty*, using his thumb to secure more tape. "We must take care, no?"

Models had whispered about the designer's proclivities long before he became *Claude of Paris*, but this was a new twist. The freak liked an audience.

Impotent fury rushed heat to her cheeks, and it took every bit of her self-control to hold her tongue. A stolen feel, nor her injured pride, would derail her purpose. Claude be damned. Her trip down the runway had to happen for the people who struggled with a walker.

Over Claude's shoulder, deep lines of rage carved Landon's features, and sure knowledge flashed in his hazel eyes. The designer had blocked his view, so her expression must have given away the letch caress. A touch of nausea swirled in her stomach.

Landon made a noise close to a growl and took a big step toward Claude in the tight quarters. Frantic to keep the show on track, Harper gave a curt shake of her head. Landon halted, his taut frame fairly vibrating with fury. Though grateful for his desire to protect her, she hoped he kept his fragile control.

Every model had grope stories like this one. She had lost count of her own. However, with her success, few acted with Claude's brazen sense of impunity. Not so, for the other models who dreamed of making it big in a cutthroat industry. Young girls like Chelse.

The more she thought about it, anger pooled in her stomach. She should let Landon beat the snot out of the pompous jerk. A luxury she couldn't afford—the ensuing scandal would overshadow her message of hope. She had to defuse the situation.

Claude snorted. "Your *le petit ami* seems upset."

"He's a *good* man." She glared at him. "So a guy fondling his girlfriend doesn't set so well."

The designer sneered. "You insult me, *mademoiselle*. Had I *fondled* you, make no mistake." He leaned in, pressing his lips to her ear. "You would have enjoyed it."

No one reacted to Claude's whispered comment. However, a dresser hoping to keep her job with a top designer might ignore his lewd activities. Maybe Harper should change her message— give the letch pigs what they deserve.

She hauled back and slapped him, and a glaring red hand-print blossomed on his cheek.

The dresser in charge of tape gasped. "Miss Inez!"

Harper was so done with this crap. "Make yourself useful, Paulette. Mr. Claude needs makeup."

Determined to convey her hopeful message, she shoved past everyone in a blaze of fury, uttering an angry noise as she rushed through the doorway. She stopped short, narrowly avoiding a collision with Dexter waiting in the hallway.

Wearing headphones, the assistant producer looked up from an electronic tablet with a huge smile that promptly evaporated. "Are you able to go on?"

Knowing she probably looked like a crazed banshee, she took a deep breath and tried for composure, relaxing her features. "Of course. It's just business as usual in the fashion industry."

Clearly, Dexter had overcome his early fascination with her, and with his raised brows, he didn't appear the least convinced she was sane.

She'd forgotten her coordinating walking stick. "Oh crap. Wait."

Not only had she left her cane behind, she had forgotten Landon. She pushed the door open. Inside, a purple-faced Claude hugged his stomach, appearing dangerously close to losing his lunch. A step away, Landon shook out his hand with a grimace.

Harper gasped, and without any concern for the letch designer, she scanned the room. No one brandished a cell phone. With some luck, the tabloids wouldn't get wind of this fiasco. Correction, a lot of luck. She grabbed her cane and handed Landon his hat.

They turned toward the door, and a tension-breaking chuckle bubbled up in her throat. "I can't believe you punched him. Thank heavens you didn't give him a black eye."

"Baby, that felt *really* good." Landon took her arm in his and added a rakish grin. "How was it for you?"

"You. Are. Awful." She laughed, and they strode toward the open door arm in arm. "But yeah, it was super-good for me, too."

Dexter stood in the threshold with his mouth hanging open. Snapping to life, his gaze darted from Landon to Harper. "We're good—?" He snorted a laugh. "I mean okay?"

Failing to stifle a snicker, Harper nodded, and the producer led them at a brisk pace to the backstage ramp access. Holding Landon's arm out of affection rather than a need for support reminded her of how far she'd come.

Heavy footfalls pounded in the hall behind them. "Someone's late for his entry." Chuckling, Dexter lifted his tablet up, showing the tail end of a household-cleaner commercial. "We're in good shape, though."

A minute later, Adele's voice carried backstage along with Claude's fabricated personal history. The designer would try to make trouble, but Harper's modeling career was safe. He couldn't change history.

Standing at the base of the ramp on the *Adele* show, a profound sense of accomplishment filled her. Modeling in a premier venue most could only dream about, she wore a top designer's dress—even if he was a pig.

Her mojo was back.

Landon seemed to sense her triumphant moment, and hugged her. His hazel eyes sparkled. "That dress is smokin', you know that, right? You'll knock 'em dead."

High on success and still riding the adrenalin rush from the dressing-room drama, she threw her arms around Landon's neck. The last couple months had been the happiest she could ever remember—because of him.

The world slowed, and she lost herself in his hazel gaze. "I think I might be in love with you, Mr. Macek."

His eyes lit up an instant before his smile widened with dimples, and he lowered his lips to hers. "I love you—"

Mid-sentence, Paulette arrived in a tizzy, having sprinted to catch up. With a half-smile, Landon dropped his arms and stepped back, and Harper cursed the dresser's timing.

The dresser grimaced at Harper's neckline, and then raised a tentative gaze. "May I?"

Her simple question was foreign in the fashion industry, and consenting to be touched was a novel experience for Harper. She found it empowering.

While the dresser fussed with the folds at her deep neckline, Dexter monitored Claude's interview on his tablet. Harper tugged at her golden helmet to show more of her eyes and looped the strap of the designer cane around her wrist. The faceted Lucite knob flashed in the backstage light.

"Miss Inez, in three," Dexter declared barely above a whisper. "…two…one."

An effervescent instrumental track filled the space and

black curtains parted to a sea of smoke. With head high, Harper followed red tape on the floor into the glaring stage lights, strutting down the ramp built out into the studio seating.

The sassy beat vibrated the wood under her spike heels, and the studio audience roared, drowning out Claude's fashion commentary. Row after row rose to their feet.

Having never experienced such a connection to the crowd, she discarded her pouty runway façade and smiled from ear to ear at the shadowy figures. They cheered for *her*, not the dress. Every few strides down the catwalk, she tapped her golden walking stick on the ramp more for show than need.

"Way to go, Harper!" a male voice shouted from the audience.

She patted her chest before blowing a kiss at her unseen supporter. With the strap around her wrist, she twirled the cane at her side and then planted its rubber tip on the floor for her well-practiced turn.

❧

Luciana only needed her cane for the pivot part of her routine, and she nailed it. Landon released a held breath.

Serenaded by wild cheers, she made her return trip down the catwalk, glowing with happiness. This was her moment, her world, and she'd brought the whole damn house down. Immeasurable pride made Landon's insides feel weightless.

As she cleared the curtain, he spread his arms, waiting to congratulate her with a hug, but Paulette and another woman rushed her. Feeling awkward, he dropped his hands to his sides. He rubbed the back of his neck in a self-conscious habit.

With a tiny grimace, Luciana mouthed, *"I'm sorry."*

The two attendants stripped her down to tape before she stepped into another Claude creation, and the lack of modesty struck Landon anew. With a brief smile for him, she strutted up the ramp again. He was so proud of her.

He loved an amazing, successful woman, and incredibly, she loved him back.

CHAPTER SIXTEEN

In the week since her Adele appearance, Luciana and Landon had returned to Spencer but without a moment's peace. Her phone chimed nonstop. Worse, the calls came in at all hours from time zones worldwide.

Her agent Joni worked relentlessly to capitalize on the zealous response.

The constant interruptions grated on Landon's nerves. But he supposed that if he had millions of dollars in deals pending, he'd answer the phone every twenty minutes, too. If she started flying the globe for photo shoots, the East Coast-West Coast problem might be the least of their challenges.

With the snow-covered roads, they should've left early. Instead, he'd waited in her suite while she'd exchanged yet another text with an *associate*, and now they were late for Ryder's pre-open house walkthrough.

Irritated over their delay, he depressed the pedal of his Ram 3500 gas-hog. "Is there some reason you couldn't have handled your business on the way?"

An annoying smile tugged at her lips. She probably

thought he was being petty. "I suppose, but I know the Lodge's network is secure. Plus I wanted some privacy."

Like the cab of his truck was crowded. Or, maybe she hid something from him. A return to New York—without him? Madness lay with that line of thinking, and Landon tossed it aside. "Could you text Ryder our ETA?" he asked. "Please?"

Her eyes danced at a joke that he didn't get, and she pulled out her phone. "I'll tell him not to start without you."

He needed to chill, but he also wanted Luciana to take his obligations seriously, even if he didn't have an interview with Adele. "Stick Pony's open house is a big deal to Ryder, and I promised him I'd look things over." This was more than a routine social visit to Landon. He valued good friends. "When Rocket got hurt, and I couldn't get my horse home, he took care of us. I want to do the same, you know?"

Luciana tucked her phone in her purse and then reached for his hand. "You have. Callie loves the horses you've trained for the camp. She said that the gray mare you just sent to her might end up being as good as Pongo."

At the Stick Pony sign, he flipped on his turn signal, slowing early in case he found a slick spot in the road. "Pearl's a level-headed girl."

"Admit it. You like working with the therapy horses."

He shrugged. "Yeah, in a different way. When I'm schooling the Stick Pony stock, I always see a *patient* aboard. Somehow, it seems more important than teaching them to chase calves."

Luciana turned in her seat to face him. "You know, Callie wants you to give up rodeo and become a horse-handler."

Recalling her near tumble and the first touch of her skin, Landon gave her a teasing grin. "I prefer the side-walker job. That way I can catch the pretty ladies when they fall."

"Oh, really?" She pursed her lips in mock reprimand. "I

think you should walk behind the horse and drive, unless I'm in the saddle."

Her sparkling eyes belied her pouty frown, and Landon laughed as he navigated the truck onto the camp property. Down at the end of the main drive, the new state-of-the-art hippotherapy facility rose up, dwarfing the surrounding outbuildings.

"I joked about the horse-handler thing. But maybe after Rocket and I retire …"

Settling back against her seat, she puffed air through pursed lips. "I know what you mean. I need a retirement job, too."

Landon snorted. "Listen to us. Neither of us has even hit thirty, and we're talking about retirement."

"Pro athletes are kind of stuck. Experience gives you an edge over the younger competitors—for a while. The more successful models are staying in the business longer, but I'm ready for something new."

An ATV approached the main drive, coming from the direction of the cabins under construction. Landon waved at the driver. "The way your phone's been going off, I think the fashionistas want you to stick around."

"Ah, thanks. I'm not quite ready to say no to a big job. Modeling's lucrative, and fun, too. But I want to do something meaningful." She paused, tapping her phone to her chin. "I'll consider acting again. I'd like to do a movie that inspires people—a film that *matters*."

She'd explained why she had endured Claude's assault— to prevent scandal from burying her message. His driven lady wanted to give hope to others with brain injuries. Landon didn't doubt she would land the right movie deal, either.

With a half-smile, he shifted his gaze from the road. "I'll bet on you."

Glowing under his regard, a sweet dusty rose flared in her cheeks. "Thanks."

"Before I met you, I'd rooted for you to make a movie. Others probably did, too. Maybe a film about overcoming adversity?" he asked.

"Exactly." Her eyes sparkled with enthusiasm—a charisma the camera lens never captured. "Okay, I have a plan. And you? How long will you rodeo?"

It was a good question. He had never had a reason to do anything else. "Oh, I don't know. We'll see. But I'd like at least one world championship." He laughed. "Okay, maybe two or three."

With an odd smile, Luciana tapped on her phone, sending yet another text. Whatever she was working on must be big. A tandem horse trailer hitched to a familiar red Ford F350 blocked a good portion of the front row parking. Colt would be in Texas this weekend, so the rig couldn't be his.

Landon found a spot on the far side of the lot. He jutted his chin at the trailer. "Looks like Ryder found another horse."

She lowered her cell and grinned. "Mm-hmm. Looks like."

Landon got out and handed her down from the tall vehicle. He needed some running boards. As they strolled to the main visitor entrance, she kept her hand in the crook of his arm. He cherished these private moments with her, and the way her simple touch warmed him inside.

A construction worker with graying brown hair and wearing coveralls inspected a downspout at the far corner of the barn. The brand-spanking new building needed repair already? The man slanted his eyes in their direction—or rather at Luciana.

Most of the contractor's hired help stayed in their designated areas, but every male on the planet wanted a gander at Harper Inez. The few who strayed all wore the same stupid, gawky expressions—not this guy's steely-eyed bearing. Landon fixed him in his sights.

The workman snapped his attention to his tool belt and patted the loops, apparently missing a needed implement. Abandoning his project, he strode toward the same ATV that had come from the cabin construction site. Creeps like him had made Landon warm to the bodyguards. He tracked the ATV's departure.

Luciana tugged at his arm. "Doesn't the place look great?"

Fall crews had finished the landscaping, and evergreen shrubs and river rock peeked through a blanket of snow along the front of the building. They followed the neatly shoveled walk to welcoming bales of straw and pumpkins on either side of the open double doors. A scarecrow on the right gestured them into the building with posed flourish.

Inside the wide entryway, a burnt-wood relief of a simple stick horse and rider hung on the wall above a bench. Ryder emerged from an adjoining office wearing a dark blue baseball cap embroidered with the same childlike drawing in silver—the Stick Pony logo.

He wore a huge smile and appeared more excited than stressed. "Hey man, glad you could make it."

Landon took in the scent of new wood and sweet alfalfa, offering a fist bump. "After watching this shed go up all summer, I'm ready to see the finished product."

"Shed? Watch yourself, friend," Ryder replied, adding a mock glare.

"Had to slip a burr under your saddle at least once." Landon laughed. "I snuck in here early on, right after the rafters went up."

After some small talk, Ryder gave them a quick tour of

the office and handicapped-accessible locker rooms near the front of the building. While they lingered in the main corridor, his enthusiasm for his project infected Landon.

"I'm real happy with the arena," Ryder said. "Oh, Landon, if you've got a few extra minutes, I want your opinion on a new arrival."

"I saw the trailer and wondered." Landon had been eager to see the medical facilities, but he supposed it was natural Ryder wanted a horseman's opinion on the equine aspects of the operation. "Lead on."

He exchanged grins with Luciana, and her eyes held an impish gleam. Before Landon could react, his friend turned on his heel and led them across the main passageway to the indoor arena, and he dismissed the odd exchange.

At the far end of the high-ceiling enclosure, a two-story wall of windows framed the snowcapped Rockies, and daylight filled the large space. Stick Pony's unique design would allow patients to enjoy the splendor of the mountains year-round while riding in a safe and comfortable environment.

Landon tipped his hat back in amazement. "Damn Ryder. This set up is really something."

"It's gorgeous," Luciana added.

"Thanks. Glad you approve," Ryder replied, appearing pleased with their stunned reactions.

A horse nickered in a tone too high to be relaxed. Tethered to a post and all saddled up, a sorrel quarter horse tossed his nose up and down at them. The fidgety gelding appeared on edge, not surprising after a trailer ride. Landon normally gave a new arrival a day to acclimate to its surroundings before saddling up.

"That your new one?" he asked, eyeing the well-balanced animal—and the tack. "Is that *my* gear?"

Luciana giggled behind him, and Ryder wore an odd grin. "Yeah, he got in this morning. Thought you'd prefer your own saddle."

Forgetting the gear, Landon sensed he was the butt of a joke. Too bad, he didn't get it. However, the more he studied the gelding, the less he worried about the joke. This wasn't their usual donated pleasure horse needing a retirement home. The beast was athletic as hell.

"Don't be shy. Mount up and tell me what you think." Ryder waved, urging him on, but Landon was already moving.

Keeping his hands at his sides, he approached the well-muscled sorrel slow and easy until he was close enough for the gelding to sniff him. After the horse lost interest in snuffling his shirt, Landon gently lifted its upper lip. The angle of the horse's teeth put him at over ten, at least.

"That's a good fella, Red," Landon murmured.

He unclipped the halter and led the animal away from the wall. Roping reins. Ryder had grabbed *all* of his gear.

Landon planted a foot in the stirrup, and swung into the saddle. Even being a little skittish, Red didn't move. In fact, having a rider aboard actually seemed to settle him down. Landon took the gelding through a warm up jog and lope routine. Pushing a little harder, they loped a figure eight, performing a flying lead change without a hitch.

"All right, you've got some moves. What else you got?" Landon asked, forgetting his audience. The horse was extremely well broke, and he wanted to see what else the critter could do.

He leaned forward, and Red blasted the length of the arena, reversing directions in a perfect rollback over his haunches and then sprinted toward Ryder. On cue, the gelding slid to a well-coordinated stop near him and

Luciana. For one last test, Landon asked the horse to sit and do a couple spins. With a release of leg pressure, Red stopped on a dime.

Ryder stared at the gelding with lips parted, clearly impressed. Odd, that the horse's abilities surprised him. Maybe he hadn't bothered to ride a donated horse. Even more strange—who donated such a well-trained animal?

Next to him, Luciana beamed up at Landon. "Do you like him?"

No one simply let this horse go. If Red here was even half the athlete that Landon suspected, the gelding might make a decent roping horse. He had already learned the hard way a guy needed a respectable back-up mount.

"I think I do," he told her. He spoke plainly to his friend. "Ryder, how much do you want for him?"

"Oh, the horse isn't mine to sell." Giving Luciana a crooked smile, Ryder left him hanging. "I think he really likes him."

She clapped her hands like a schoolgirl. "I think so, too."

Colt stepped into the arena from the adjoining stable wearing blue jeans, a plaid flannel shirt, and his favored brown leather hat. The red F350 with the two-horse trailer in the lot had been his, after all. He had hauled this horse to Spencer.

The *confidential* texts, Luciana's sly smiles— she had pulled a fast one. Landon sat aboard *Opie*, and he'd never seen it coming.

If the plain-Jane sorrel had had any white on him, Landon would've recognized the horse right off. However, aside from his athletic confirmation, the gelding looked like thousands of other ginger-colored Quarter Horses. The implications of Opie's surprise arrival ricocheted in his mind.

Colt had worked a lease after all, and Luciana had been in

on it. He'd used her celebrity status to make the deal, and Landon didn't like it one bit. If Bingham had behaved like most men, he fell all over himself talking with *Harper Inez*. Now, he had a story to tell the boys hanging around the cattle chutes.

Landon had an earful ready for Colt at the first opportunity. He dismounted, eyeing his friend. "Hi, there. I thought that truck seemed familiar. Shouldn't you be in Texas?"

With a shit-eating grin, Colt hooked his thumbs in his jeans pockets. "I had a little business nearby. Thought I'd stop in and see the new place."

Landon snorted. "Yeah, right."

Luciana rushed him and wrapped her arms around his neck. "You do like the horse, don't you?"

At the moment, he liked the horse a whole lot more than Colt, and he nodded. "His name's *Opie*?"

"The one and only." Her eyes sparkled like a little kid who couldn't wait for someone to unwrap their present. She was absolutely thrilled with herself. "Your friends helped me."

In the face of her enthusiasm, Landon couldn't help but smile, warming to the idea of getting back on the circuit. He doubted Ryder had done much more than let the horse on his place. Maybe he would forgive Colt, after all. "I bet you didn't need any help to charm Davey Bingham."

"This is not my first rodeo, cowboy." She planted a hand on her hip. "Mr. Bingham didn't even know my name until he got his copy of the signed contract. Every time I buy something in person, the price goes up."

A sick feeling hit Landon's gut. She had *purchased* Opie? He could cover a lease, but his bank balance hadn't changed. He didn't have the cash to buy the horse outright. Colt knew that, too. Landon hoped like hell that his friend hadn't preyed on Luciana's lack of horse knowledge.

Adding up Opie's price and the cost to haul him to Spencer, his heart sank. With dread cinching his chest, he cupped her cheek. "Baby, please tell me that you did not *buy* this horse."

With a dazzling smile, she kissed the palm of his hand. "Colt told me that you hung on and qualified for Vegas. Why didn't you say something?"

Not wanting to think about his lost opportunity, he hadn't said a word to anyone. Landon shook his head. "Because it didn't matter."

"Dreams always matter." Her gaze searched him. "Colt says with Opie, you have a real shot at the championship. I want that for you—so bad."

Stepping back, Landon rubbed his jaw, trying to find the words to explain why he could not accept such an expensive gift. In truth, he didn't understand it himself.

He glared at his soon-to-be ex-friend. "You got her a good price?"

Colt slapped his hat against his thigh with a scowl, clearly offended. "Bingham had another buyer."

Meaning that she had paid ninety-five thousand—or possibly more. Landon's innards twisted up.

Gaze darting from one man to the other, a tiny V formed between Luciana's brows. "Landon, is something wrong?"

Vexed over what she'd paid for the horse, and stunned that she'd bought him in the first place, Landon struggled for words. "Look, Opie's incredible. I'm overwhelmed, really. But it's way too much money. I can't ever get you something like this."

The joy drained from her expression. "I'd never expect you to. I love you, and I want you to go after your dream." She placed a hand on his arm. "Gifts aren't about money. If you could, you'd do the same for me, wouldn't you?"

Instead of soothing him, her mollifying comment poked

at a deeper, invisible wound—he *could not* do the same for her. "Of course, but that's not the point. I can't accept a gift like this. It would be…"

The small wedge in her forehead deepened. "What exactly is your *point*?"

Moving at a good clip, Ryder and Colt stole from the arena. No doubt, they both thought Landon was an ungrateful jerk. He sure felt like one.

Relieved to have the privacy, he met her turbulent gaze. "I'm not a jetsetter like you. People in my world do *not* spend tens of thousands on presents for anyone." From the lift of her chin, his feelings of inadequacy made no sense to her. He had to make her understand. "It makes me feel—I don't know —like I'm being *kept* or something."

Her black eyes flashed, and she fisted her hands at her hips. "You think I need to *pay* a guy to be with me?"

He had stepped in it big time with no way to recover. But everything in him rebelled against accepting such a high-dollar gift. "Baby, that's not what I meant at all."

"No, it's how you *feel*. You said that, Mr. Macek," she hissed. In her fury, the snide formal address lost all of its flirty charm.

That she would spend ninety-five thousand dollars on a gift for him had never entered his mind. Worse, being propped up on a world-champion horse grated on a nerve he hadn't known existed. He couldn't explain why, or how exactly, but having Opie handed to him cheapened the win.

She glared at him expectantly, but he could see the hurt in her eyes.

They would never be on equal ground. He had believed he could deal with their lopsided incomes. Her celebrity status hadn't intimidated him, or so he'd thought. The extravagant gift put everything in a new perspective. If they stayed together, she would always pay his share. Everyone would know it, too.

Still, money alone shouldn't come between them. The media, the public appearances like the *Adele* show, where he would always be the odd man out—stopped at the door like an unwelcome gatecrasher.

She had told him she loved him, and he'd convinced himself they could make it. The part of him that wanted *forever* with Luciana railed against his cowardice—man up, problem solved. However, the daunting prospect of attending a lifetime of Harper Inez celebrity events won out.

Meeting her dejected gaze put an ache in his chest. "Maybe we should take some time apart—I need to get my head on straight. Our worlds…"

Her eyes widened over parted lips. "You want to break up? Why?"

A split had never crossed his mind. At least he hadn't thought so. Nor could he explain what he didn't understand himself. "I think I need some space." He placed a hand on Opie's neck. "And I can't take this kind of help."

She swiped a tear from her cheek. "I bought the horse because I *love* you. Nothing more."

Even if he swallowed his pride and took Opie on the circuit, the next tabloid headline could read *Harper Inez Puts Macek on the Leaderboard*. He rubbed the back of his neck. Without making sense of his own reactions, he had no hope to explain himself.

Landon studied the arena floor, conflicted and hurting. Finally, he met Luciana's eyes, putting all the feelings that didn't have words into his gaze. "Baby, I love you, too, always."

The defeat in her dark pools crushed him. "Isn't love enough?"

Maybe it wasn't. Landon parted his lips and couldn't form words.

Having read his answer in his expression, she gave him her back and trudged toward the exit. After a few yards, she squared her shoulders and lengthened her stride, disappearing into the stable. Opie's soughing breaths echoed in the empty arena.

CHAPTER SEVENTEEN

*H*arper found the ladies' room near the barn's entry and dried her eyes with a paper towel. When she got to her suite, she would allow herself a good, sobbing cry. As an afterthought, she stuffed a paper towel in her pocket.

She sought out Ryder in his office, and found him in quiet conversation with Colt. No doubt, they discussed her Opie gift fail. Not wanting to hear a word, she halted at the threshold. Both men fell silent. Likely, Colt wanted to know if the sale was still on. Tough luck for him. She didn't have the energy to talk business.

"Ryder, can you give me a lift to the Lodge, please?" she asked.

"Sure thing." Ryder stood, grabbing his keys from the desk and then plucked his Stick Pony cap from a hook near the door.

Harper strode toward the exit, but Ryder took his time. Impatient, she hovered near the bench in the entry.

"Colt, I'll be back in thirty. Pick any open stall for Opie.

We'll get you a bed somewhere." Ryder's quiet voice carried into the hall.

"Thanks, but don't bunk me too close to Macek. I think he wants to give me a whoopin'," Colt replied.

"Yeah, and me right along with you," Ryder mumbled before he emerged from the office.

At sight of her, his gaze flared, likely worried that she'd overheard them. Her own heart hurt too much to worry about any rift between the men. She exited to the lot and strode to Ryder's Blazer.

During their trip back to the Lodge, Ryder had not said a word, and Harper was grateful. Getting shot down with an audience had stung enough, and a follow up discussion would have made it worse. Now she needed to get through the rest of the day.

It wasn't as if she had never been dumped before. However, there had been clues that Ensign had lost interest. Landon's *need for space* had floored her, and she had missed any hints that he had been unhappy. Nor had she felt *a need for space*. The dumpee was always the last to get it. At least this time, she hadn't taken a bullet to the head.

Landon *had* said he loved her. Taking a break may have meant only that.

She replayed the Opie disaster over and over, trying to figure out what she'd done wrong. Nothing. Except buy a gift for someone she loved. Now, what to do with the darned horse. Maybe she could return him.

After moping around the rest of the morning, it took all the fortitude she could muster to attend her afternoon physical therapy session. The hour with Chad had kept her mind occupied until she returned to her overly quiet suite.

She closed the mahogany door behind her and set the alarm. Landon usually arrived about this time, right before dinner, and they would have cocktails. The silence was killing her. She flipped on the big screen for background noise.

Boy-trouble required sisterly support. After gathering her composure and pouring a hefty glass of wine, she called Juanita. Harper made a pretense of a few minutes of small talk and then spilled out her woes.

Juanita's sigh filled the room from her cell phone speaker. "How much did you pay for the damn horse, anyway?"

Bristling, Harper glared at the phone. "The price *isn't* important."

"Right *there*. That's why he broke things off. The cost of the gift *is* significant to *him*."

Where was the sisterly commiseration? She crossed her arms, indignant. "It shouldn't be. When you love someone, money doesn't matter."

"True—in theory. But despite our equal rights, male pride is a real thing. You should be glad he has some. The fact that he wouldn't accept your exorbitant gift means that he loves *you*, not your money."

Juanita had blasted her for giving Ensign the McLaren. In the end, her intuition had been more accurate than Harper wanted to admit. Truth and love went hand in hand, and sisterly advice did not necessarily come in pretty packaging.

Her irritation lost some steam. "You're always so suspicious. Landon's not about money. At least I didn't think so until he wouldn't take Opie."

"Sis, I love you, and I'm there for you, even when I *should* say no. That's what *I* do when I love someone." Juanita's gentle tone stole the last of her annoyance.

Staying with Harper through months of rehab, she had nearly lost her job. Harper had needed her so badly that she couldn't even feel guilty over it. "I know, and I love you right back."

"Aww…" Juanita's tone had a smile in it. "But my point is

this— even back when we had nothing, your love language was always gift-giving. So when you give me some over-the-top present for no reason, I get that it's just you telling me that you love me."

No one understood Harper like her sister did, and she wished she could hug her. "Does that mean you're keeping the Porsche?"

"Damn straight it does." Juanita laughed. "But the rest of the world doesn't know what to do with that, and lavish gifts make them uncomfortable."

She paused, and Harper didn't respond, giving her insights some thought. Juanita had raised her gifting habit before, but Harper hadn't paid much attention—until now.

Her friends in New York and Ensign had always enjoyed receiving presents. Of course, those relationships all ended so well, speaking volumes for her love language.

"By the way, your cowboy's sounding better to me than he ever did. Just sayin'," Juanita added.

"Yeah, me too."

However, Landon needed time apart. The Rockies filling the suite's panoramic view had lost their magic, and Harper's fragile mood collapsed into a sulk.

"You need a weekend away, I can tell," said Juanita.

After conferencing in Mamá for a family chat, the three women planned a Chicago get-together in mid-November before signing off. From the Windy City, Harper would fly to New York for her fixer-upper surgery.

Anticipation of a family weekend and losing her helmet for good should have lifted her spirits. She took another sip of wine, wishing that Landon sat next to her. Calling him was out of the question. He needed *space* and she would give it to him. Exhausted by the day, she turned in early.

That night, Harper slept fitfully, enduring another terrifying dream of menacing eyes. Bolting upright in bed and panting in fear, she was grateful for the morning light seeping around the blackout curtains. The nightmare was Landon's fault. When he had spooned his body with hers while they slept, the dead eyes had stayed in the ether. If he had been where he belonged…

Like it was *his* job to keep the nightmares away. She slowed her breathing. Their separation had warped her thinking. Her shrink in New York would have a field day with this scenario. Reluctant to continue analyzing her crap relationship with Ensign, she hadn't resumed counseling in Colorado. It was time for her to take charge of her life.

As much as she dreaded sharing her mistakes with someone new, she considered scheduling an appointment with that Dr. Rasmussen Callie had mentioned.

On the other side of the bed—Landon's side—the cover lay undisturbed. Her big, quiet cowboy was worth a few counseling sessions.

Her phone pinged, and hope that the text was from him surged her heart into a gallop. She snatched the cell from the nightstand.

Colt: When you get a minute, call me. Thanks.

Heaving a disappointed sigh, she chastised herself for being so weak and flopped back onto the mattress to tap in her reply.

Harper: Will do. Is an hour okay?

Colt: Sure thing. Ryder put me up at Stick Pony. Having coffee, no rush.

After a quick shower and making her own coffee, she settled onto a stool at the counter. Harper rifled through Opie's purchase paperwork that she'd left stacked on the island. A stapled section titled Purchase Agreement looked like a good place to start. She took a fortifying sip of caramel roast before scanning the text.

The contract addressed the horse's registration information, price, terms, and finally a disclosure of Opie's health history. No section on a return policy. However, a "vet check" clause stated that if a veterinarian found a significant health problem within two weeks, the buyer could nullify the sale.

Since Opie looked *as healthy as a horse*, as the saying went, a surprise ailment appeared unlikely. However, a veterinary examination made sense, so she added a call to Ryder's cousin Jackson to her to-do list. She flipped to a back page that she had believed was blank and discovered a short addendum at the top.

> *Said quarter horse Opie is purchased as a gift, and the recipient of said gift, Landon Macek, will maintain final approval of this purchase. Should the recipient decline the gift, this purchase agreement is null and void. The undersigned buyer will return said horse Opie to the seller at her own expense.*

The added clause, drafted in a different font, read as though written by a layman pretending to be a lawyer. Further, though her signature hovered above the *buyer line*, Harper did not recall signing it. In her excitement to get the horse to Colorado in time for the next rodeo, she had simply signed by the Xs.

Colt must have added this paragraph, and she owed him a ninety-five-thousand-dollar thank you.

Something about the addendum nagged at her, and she read it again. The team roper dreamed of a rodeo championship, too, and yet, he'd thought to include this clause. Even Landon's good friend had known he might decline the horse. With a groan, she dropped her head into her hands.

She pulled out her phone.

Harper: I want to talk to Landon again. Can you give me a few hours?

Colt: Sure. But he's bull-headed about some weird stuff. Good luck.

When Landon had told her about the NFR in Vegas, he had gone all melancholy. He wanted a world championship, and he wanted Opie. Harper needed a more creative way to support his dream. She could fix this.

❧

The mid-morning sun had done little to warm the day, and Harper left Fletcher with the limo in the Stick Pony stable's parking lot. Her breath made puffy clouds in the cold air. Surprised to see Landon working a horse outside with the indoor arena only yards away, she stuffed her pride in her back pocket and used her cane to trudge up the low grade.

The whine of a power saw coming from inside the big barn at her back answered her question. The noise would have spooked the saddled palomino he drove with longlines. As she neared, doubts plagued her.

He had always seemed so confident and driven by the joy of achieving his goals rather than money. She couldn't be wrong about who Landon was, and she believed he loved her.

Despite his comment about "being kept", a man with his strong character would not allow an extravagant gift to bruise his ego. Another issue had to be at play here, and the unknown threat frightened her.

As Harper approached, he lifted his chin in greeting. That was something. She tugged her hood up over her helmet and then crossed her arms on the top rail of the arena fence, waiting for his full attention.

He tied the horse to a post and then joined her, tipping his hat with a gloved hand. "Morning."

Trying to read him, she couldn't tell if he was pleased to see her or not. The half-smile was missing.

"Good morning," she replied.

He rested an elbow on the fence. "I still can't accept the horse."

If he wanted to dive right in, so could she. "I know. I wanted to apologize. It hadn't crossed my mind it might make you feel like a creepy boy toy."

He snorted. "I'm sorry, too. I didn't handle things well, at all."

The admission soothed her a little. "For a lot of years now, I've had more money than time. Sending a gift was all I could do to show people that I cared about them. Some habits die hard." With her admission, she smiled, hoping he would understand. "In the future, I'll try not to smother you with presents."

"For the record, Opie was a great gift—a thoughtful gift, a loving gift. Really, I didn't mean to hurt your feelings by declining."

They had both apologized, but he had not said anything to make her believe *the break* was off. The hidden threat loomed large and tied her stomach in knots.

"It took a while, and some tough-sister love, but I get why you said no." Truth was crucial, no matter how painful. Harper sought courage from the indomitable mountain range in the distance. "But there's more to this than a price limit on gifts, isn't there?"

He clenched his jaw, his thoughts seeming to steal his attention. "Yeah, but it's my problem, not yours. You're great."

"But not so great that you can tell me what's wrong?"

Hesitating, his hazel gaze brimmed with sadness. "You deserve honesty." He gave her cheek a tentative touch. "Baby, you can't change that you're a celebrity any more than I can change that I love you."

The paparazzi and bodyguards. Her notoriety had been a plus for Ensign and her New York posse. When the cameras had trailed them, they had all hoped for a little press. But not Landon. He had never sought any publicity.

His only national exposure had been the flattering SI article—until she came along. Thinking back, ever since they'd returned from taping the *Adele* interview, he had avoided going out, preferring private walks or calling for room service. She should have seen this coming.

Instead, Harper had envisioned them together, raising little boys in cowboy hats and chaps riding their ponies. Her imagined future filled with love grew hazy, and a band circling her chest squeezed the air from her lungs.

"We could keep to ourselves." Swallowing, she tried to subdue the anxiety in her voice. "I don't want to model anymore, and I don't need a movie deal."

Tiny lines bracketed his eyes, and he shook his head.

With his strong confidence, she'd believed he was the one great guy in the world who could deal with the spotlight that stalked her—but she had been wrong. Maybe she expected too much of him.

Desperation clawed at her throat. "The public will forget about me in a matter of months."

Pain filled Landon's gaze, and he traced a leather-clad finger along her jaw. "Damn your generous spirit. You'd support my dreams and give up your own."

"You're more important to me than a movie deal."

As though his hand weighed too much, he dropped his arm to his side. "We both know it's more than a movie. My need for a normal life isn't more important than your message." His brows drew together. "Don't you see? If you give up who you are—your dreams—eventually, it'll ruin both of us."

They could have talked out a misunderstanding over Opie. But this? He might think he needed some space. However, if Harper didn't quit movies and modeling, the paparazzi would always follow her. Unless one of them made big changes, this break would turn into a long-term split.

Her throat tightened and she nodded, buying a moment while her heart broke. One day she would learn that love isn't enough.

However, today was not that day. She wanted to give people with brain injuries hope, but the man in front of her had put a more personal future in her head. Somehow, she could do both. Nor did she intend to play fair. She'd be damned if she let him walk away.

Wrestling her emotions under control, she pasted on a fake smile. "A break might do me some good, too."

The surprise in his gaze was perversely satisfying. Let him imagine what she would do with their time *apart*. And she'd only profess her love again when he was in her arms for good. Petty thoughts, but her breaking heart didn't care.

Landon straightened. "If it's okay, I'd like to stay in touch."

He wanted to be friends? Never happening. They needed to love each other more than rodeo championships and movie deals. She would not settle for less. However, long term anything required *some* contact.

"Sure. You have my number." Reconciliation plan A had failed. Time for plan B. "Before I go back to New York, I could use your help with a small problem."

The smile she loved returned. "What do you need?"

After misjudging him over Opie once, her doubts almost squashed acting ability. She tried for a teasing tone.

"Well, as it happens, I've got this super-great roping horse without a home."

His smile dropped away. "I'm really not—"

Discarding her attempt at banter, a shake of her head interrupted him. "I can return the horse, so it's your choice. But hear me out."

Landon's sigh came out in a cloud of steam. "Okay…"

His frown ate at her confidence, but she mustered her courage for their future and plowed ahead. "What about a partnership? I finance, you ride. We split the profits fifty-fifty. After Vegas, I'll give you a limited time to buy me out at cost—including my transportation expenses."

His brows shot up before he became serious. "Shipping costs, too?"

Seconds ticked off. "I'd like to say take your time, but Colt can't stay in town much longer."

"Fair enough. I'm good with buying the horse later, but I don't know about a fifty-fifty split," he told her, cocking his head. "Half seems slanted in your favor. I mean, I'll be doing all the work."

He had apparently warmed to her idea, but if she made it too easy on him that darned male pride could rear its ugly head. Readying to turn on her heel, she lifted her chin. "Okay. I'll tell Colt to take him back to South Dakota."

As she planted her cane for a step, Landon raised his hand. "Now, wait a minute." Making a show of rubbing his stubbled jaw, he focused on the muddy snow. He finally lifted a solemn gaze. "I can make that work. But we do paperwork and everything, understood?"

Landon would have Opie. They would still speak during their *break*. With less satisfaction than she had anticipated, Harper extended a hand. "Absolutely."

. . .

Later back in her suite, Harper sipped wine alone—again—besieged by second thoughts over their partnership. A second glass of red inspired a brutal bout of honesty. Landon needed a break, and instead of respecting his wishes, she spun a financial string to keep them connected—hardly the space Landon needed.

Another dismal thought came to her. Did she *truly* give gifts out of love, or did she use them to keep people close?

Undoing her mistakes was impossible, but she could minimize the damage. She grabbed her phone and tapped a text to Juanita.

Harper: Okay if I come early? Like tomorrow evening early?

CHAPTER EIGHTEEN

*T*he clock on Landon's dashboard said eight-forty. He depressed the gas pedal. Maybe he could catch a minute or two with Luciana in the parking lot before their nine a.m. appointment with the attorney.

Over the last four days of *taking a break*, he had missed her something fierce. Their intimate evenings had been the most treasured part of his day—of his life. He'd hoped they would be a part of his future, too. Now, other than a few practical texts about contract details, they'd had no contact. He'd known a separation would be tough. Living it was inconceivably worse.

He turned into the parking lot of an elegant home converted into a chic office building. No sign of the Lodge limo or Fletch, so he'd beat her here. Everything in this part of Spencer was high-end, and the law firm's digs met the local standards. Landon parked and entered through a set of wooden doors with brass knockers.

At check in, he declined the receptionist's offer of coffee or bottled water and then claimed a seat near the waiting room's stone fireplace. The upholstered wingback chair ensured a view of the front entrance. He didn't want to miss Luciana's arrival.

At first, the idea of a partnership had seemed complicated —a painful reminder of the disparity in their incomes. But after getting used to the idea, he looked forward to working with her. They would be a rodeo team—like some of the big-name cowboys with corporate sponsors. Best of all, he'd still have an excuse to talk to her on a regular basis.

He tried not to examine his need to see her too closely. Loving her was easy. Determining what their break would gain him wasn't so cut and dry. A breather from the media was important. But then what? He didn't know. At some point, he'd have to decide if he could live in her world. She was worth it. But was he man enough?

Flames danced over the fake logs, and Landon checked the time. Nine-fifteen. The delay could be anything, but she was seldom late. He opened the text screen.

The receptionist left her seat and approached with a gracious smile. "Sir, Mr. Beacham apologizes for the wait. He's available now. Would you come with me, please?"

Landon followed her down a wide hallway to Beacham's office. Inside, tall oak bookcases with beveled glass doors on each shelf lined one wall, and on the opposite side, sunlight from a picture window brightened the space. Though the furnishings appeared newer, the room still gave a sense of the 1800s.

A tall, suited man with salt and pepper hair rose from a leather chair and stepped around an imposing period desk. He extended a hand. "Mr. Macek, I'm Ed Beacham. Nice to meet you."

They exchanged a handshake, and Beacham retook his seat, gesturing at one of two office chairs in front of the desk. The leather seat creaked as Landon settled across from him. "Mr. Beacham, good to meet you, too."

"Call me Ed. Jakob Spencer says good things about you."

The comment grabbed Landon's interest. "Really? I haven't met the man."

"I'm not surprised." The attorney shrugged. "He keeps tabs on everyone related to the Lodge and then some. Miss Inez had asked him for a referral to set up your partnership, so he probably did a little digging."

A less than gentle reminder of why Landon needed some distance from Luciana's fame. Of course, he'd known that Deke Ward had done a background check, but now it appeared Jakob Spencer had shared their findings with a complete stranger.

The attorney handed Landon a stapled sheaf of legal-sized paper. "I'll walk you through this. Feel free to stop me anytime—"

"Shouldn't we wait for Miss Inez?" Stifling his irritation, Landon strained to hear footsteps in the hallway. "She should be right along."

"What?" Beacham cocked his head. "She told me she's in Chicago, but we can handle signatures with the mail."

Staring at the attorney, Landon realized his mouth hung open. "You know for a fact she's in Chicago?"

Embarrassed that he'd barked the question, he clasped his hands over his stomach, relaxing his posture. From the flicker of awareness in Beacham's expression, Landon's attempt at composure had failed.

Luciana left town without saying goodbye.

"I'm sorry." The other man studied him and shifted in his chair. "I was under the impression that you knew her pretty well."

Sympathy filled the attorney's gaze, and humiliation took Landon's voice. He cleared his throat. "We're good friends. I hadn't known she was leaving, is all. I'll give her a shout later."

He might have imagined the subtle flare in Beacham's gaze. No doubt, the attorney believed that Harper Inez had singled Landon up right in front of him. Hell, maybe she had. Or had she thought taking a break actually meant splitting up?

Regardless, telling Beacham that he and Luciana were *good friends* had nearly ripped his heart out. The rest of the meeting was a blur.

Beacham handed him the legal paperwork in a heavy folder stamped with the firm's logo and secured with a gold elastic band. "Read this over tonight and come in tomorrow to sign. It has to be notarized. My personal cell number is on the card inside if you have questions this evening."

The red-carpet treatment reminded Landon of the attorney fees. According to the contract, he owed half. "Thanks, Ed. I should be good."

A few hours later at his Stick Pony quarters, Landon stared at his phone's display, having backspaced over three texts to Luciana. They had all sounded like an indignant lover left behind. He finally grabbed one of the sofa's print pillows to use as a desk. They were on hiatus, and she didn't have any obligation to report off to him before leaving town.

He'd needed time apart, and he still did. Total strangers gabbed about his love life, in print no less, and dug into his business, all because he loved the wrong woman—or rather the right woman with a *household name*. If she'd been a millionaire guest, things might have been easier.

Later, after people became aware of their couple status, security guards would let him into hospitality suites. Plain and simple, he didn't want to share their lives with the media, and the constant public intrusions had worn him out. Being painfully honest, he hated that the whole world would watch him living on her dime. The admission made it easier to type.

Landon: I met with the attorney today. They'll send you the signed contract tomorrow.

Proud of his matter-of-fact tone, he grabbed a bottle of water from the fridge, grateful to have the place to himself. Callie and Tad must have gone into town. He watched a few minutes of the evening news, checking his phone more often than was healthy. When his cell vibrated, he snatched it from the sofa.

Luciana: Thanks for handling the paperwork. I wanted to make it, but it didn't work out.

Landon: How's Juanita?

He grabbed a beer this time—and waited. Clearly, she was busy and texting Landon was not a priority.

Luciana: Good. We're going shopping tomorrow.

The stilted exchange said it all. They were officially on break. Just like he'd wanted. His cell buzzed again.

Ryder: We're waiting on your ass. Get moving bro.

Unloading a semi-truck load of hay in sub-freezing temps sounded better than putting up an all's-normal front at a send-off party. But Ryder and Vianna had arranged this. Jackson and his wife would be there, too. And Landon had grown close to Callie and Tad. A few drinks at the Wild Card wouldn't kill him. At least no one would ask why Luciana hadn't joined him. They all knew.

Landon: On the way.

A couple days after the attorney finalized the Opie partnership, Landon took to the road. His first stop—Colt's home place in the Texas panhandle to offer an apology.

Striding from his barn wearing a jean jacket, Colt waved Landon over to park alongside the stable and then greeted him as he exited his truck.

"Hi, did you bring this lousy cold front from Colorado?" Colt asked.

"Not me. Seems pretty nice compared to the mountains." Landon chuckled. "Thanks for letting me stop in."

He slipped on a down vest before unloading Opie. Colt led them into the barn and then slid a stall door open. "Put the big guy in here."

He tossed a couple leafs of alfalfa into the corner hay feeder, not showing any hint he held a grudge. Landon had screwed up, and he needed to get things square with his friend right away.

After closing the stall door, he paused until he had Colt's attention. "Hey, I didn't want to apologize over the phone. Luciana told me about the gift clause. Good thinking. I should have had more faith in you, and I'm sorry. No excuses."

"No worries. I just figured you'd lost your damn mind." Colt snorted and took Landon's extended hand, pulling him into a backslapping shoulder hug. "Watchin' you say *no* to a woman the likes of Harper Inez? What sane man…?"

He hadn't known the half of it, and Landon wouldn't enlighten him. He clenched his jaw. "It's complicated," he bit out, unwilling to talk about his complex relationship with Luciana. "Thanks for helping her. Opie's a good horse."

"Finally he shows appreciation." Offering his classic shit-eating grin, Colt's rabid sense of humor appeared unde-terred. "That wasn't so hard, now, was it?"

More than ready to skip past his inept handling of Luciana's gift, Landon put a warning in his gaze.

"Oh, I see. We're still a little tender about the pretty lady." Colt laughed, poking the bear one more time. "I'll make you feel better—wanna see how Opie does with a calf?"

Now he had Landon's interest, and a smile tugged at his lips. No one with a roping setup lived near Spencer, so he itched to toss a loop from his new mount. "That'd be right nice. You keep a few calves?"

"Nah only steers on my place. But a friend down the road a piece just got in fifteen head—never seen a rope," Colt told him. "Indoor arena, too. He said to come on down around two this afternoon."

Fresh calves like the rodeo stock—a great test for Opie, and Landon could use some serious practice, too. His pulse sped up. Colt had really come through. Before Landon had even apologized, his friend had arranged a roping session. Humbled and truly grateful, tension seeped out of his shoulders. "Thanks, man."

"You're welcome," Colt said with a level gaze. Never serious for long, one corner of his mouth rose. "No such thing as a free calf, though. Don't be surprised if'n he asks you for some schooling—for him and his horse."

Hardly a big demand—ropers practicing together helped each other, anyway. "All good. I'll appreciate the use of his place."

Later that day, Landon and Opie neatly caught their first calf together—followed by a dozen more. The gelding showed his chops in the arena, boosting Landon's hopes for Vegas.

❦

A couple weeks after leaving Colt's place, Landon traveled down I35, and a royal-blue baseball cap on his truck's dash still made him smile. At the Wild Card, Ryder had handed him the Stick Pony hat, saying, "So you don't forget about us after you're a bigtime rodeo champ."

They hadn't forgotten him. Minutes after his first win at Fort Worth, Landon's phone had exploded with congratulatory texts. Apparently, they had monitored the tie-down scores on the net. A message from Juanita had surprised him

—she included the schedule for Luciana's reconstructive surgery.

Since then, time had flown by in a flurry of Texas rodeos, and her operation had come up fast. He needed to make arrangements. Yesterday, he had asked her to call him. As though he might have missed a ringtone in the last hour, he checked his phone again. Nothing.

A break hadn't meant he'd quit caring for her, and dammit, he was done pretending. Twenty-four hours was long enough to wait. He hit the phone's mic to dictate.

Landon: I want to be there for you Thursday.

The video of Ensign messing with her ventilator played over in his mind. Another brain surgery and stint in the ICU had to scare her. It terrified Landon. After forever, his phone buzzed.

Luciana: Thanks, but not a big deal. Juanita's flying in.

He had wanted time apart, or so he'd believed. Now with her pending surgery, he needed to hold her hand and tell her he would be waiting for her when she woke up. Nurse Angela would need a grenade to get him out of her room.

Deciding to fill up the top half of his tank, he pulled into a gas station and hooked up. He typed while the pump ran.

Landon: I'm worried. I need to be there.

Luciana: Don't stress. I'm good. Get us that championship.

Landon: There are rodeos out east, too. I'm coming.

Rodeos on the East Coast outnumbered unicorns by about seven or so. He'd leave his truck and horse at Colt's place and fly out of Amarillo. Minutes passed, and Opie stomped inside the trailer, rocking the rig. Landon returned the gas pump nozzle to its home and checked on his horse through the side door. "A few more miles, Opie. We'll bed down early tonight."

He missed Rocket and Buck. The little burro always ran

loose in the big trailer, and Landon hadn't realized how much he'd enjoyed the little donkey's nosey greetings.

After checking his phone, he strode into the station for a soda and a slice of pizza and then waited in line at the checkout, scanning the tabloids out of habit.

Luciana's dark eyes stared back at him from the rack, and unsurprised, he plucked this week's issue of *Do Tell* from the pile. He had resigned himself to finding her everywhere. This time, her famous jet locks curved over her shoulders, so they'd used a file photo from before the shooting. The caption read, *Has Harper's Cowboy Ridden Off Into the Sunset?* At least they hadn't used his picture.

He folded the paper and tucked it under his arm to pull out his phone. In contrast to the tabloid image, her fun-filled broad smile and sparkling midnight gaze glowed back at Landon from his phone. Still no response.

After checking out at the register, he returned to his truck and got back on the road. A few miles later, Harper's *It's Your Love* ringtone sounded, and his heart stopped. He turned off the heater and radio before opening the call. "Hello, Luciana."

"Hi."

In the last three weeks, he'd only spoken with her accountant. The sound of her voice, quiet, almost shy, made Landon want to pull her into his arms.

"Why…" He cleared gravel from his throat. "Why don't you want me in New York for your surgery?"

Her sigh filled the cab of his truck. "I lied. I *am* nervous."

Not daring to talk to her and drive, he pulled off onto the shoulder. Traffic whizzed past, and an eighteen-wheeler blew by, sending a shudder through his rig.

"Me, too. I want to be there for you. I need to be there," he said.

"That's sweet, but have you seen *Do Tell's* latest article?"

Despite her caution, he could hear the smile in her tone.

He dared to hope she'd needed to hear his voice, too. "Yeah, I haven't read it yet."

"It's crap, like all their stuff. But someone pings my publicist every day for updates on our relationship." Maybe she would give him an update on their relationship. "The *no comments* are wearing thin. If you're here, the gossip press *will* find you."

"I'm more worried about you than any damn stalker reporters." He scowled at the tabloid lying on the passenger seat and then flipped it over to hide the mocking headline. The relentless paparazzi would never leave her alone. "I do love you. That hasn't changed."

"I lo …" She sighed.

Waiting expectantly for her to finish, Landon's heart sank when she trailed off. She'd almost said *I love you*. This separation sucked for her, too. He had to see her. "I can make it there, easy."

"Honestly, this surgery's nothing like the last one. Les said he won't even go into the brain. The actual risk is low, so it's not worth creating more tabloid fodder."

"Les?"

"My brain surgeon."

Providing Luciana hadn't minimized the dangers of the procedure, the return to the ICU likely frightened her more than the surgery. Landon's protective instincts rose and hammered away at him. "Will you at least have Juanita call me? Keep me informed? I'm dying here."

She chuckled. "Yes."

They said their goodbyes, and Landon choked back another *I love you*. Technically, she had left him hanging, so he wouldn't push. However, her slip lightened his mood, energizing him.

After confirming Colt would take Opie for a few days, Landon opened a travel app and booked a Wednesday flight

out of Amarillo. He pulled back into traffic. One more win in
Lubbock and five days before he saw Luciana.

The morning of his flight to New York, Landon rested his
forearm on Colt's large living-room window, taking in the
soundless predawn twilight. Icy frost edged the glass,
framing a snow-globe wonderland, and outside, a rolling
blanket of white glittered under the barn's yellow yard light.
Lacking appreciation of the Christmas-card view, he raised a
steaming mug of coffee to his lips.

The wind had howled all night long, matching his mood
as a sadistic Mother Nature corralled him in Texas. The
morning stillness sat at odds with a pointless need to act
beating at him. His heavy sigh clouded the glass pane.

Footsteps descended the stairs behind him, and Colt's
blurry reflection appeared in the glass, his mouth a grim line.
For once, his sense of humor took a rest. "I'm sorry, man. We
never have snow like this."

The rain pattering his windshield the evening before
hadn't worried him, nor had the prediction of a light flurry.
Snow did not stick in Texas for any length of time—unless a
record six inches fell. Landon had woken to a flight-cancella-
tion text.

He turned from the window. "How long do you think
before the roads are clear?

Colt frowned. "The county has a few plows, but this far
out from the city, mostly they wait for the snow to melt."

Landon's heart sunk. With forecasted temperatures in the
twenties for the next two days, he could not ignore the grim
reality. Even if the airport opened up and offered a flight, he
couldn't get to Amarillo.

❧

Staring at dropped ceiling tiles overhead, Harper lay on a gurney in New York City General's pre-anesthesia unit with a dry mouth and the beginnings of a caffeine-withdrawal headache. With any luck, she would be out cold soon and miss it.

Juanita squeezed her hand and a V formed between her perfect eyebrows. "You're sure you want them to shave your whole head? There's still time to change your mind."

"No. Les said they'd have to clip the full right side, anyway." Losing hair did not come close to topping Harper's list of worries. "Either way, I'll have to wear a turban. I'm so over hair, maybe I'll go au natural, who knows."

Juanita nodded and pulled a chair to the side of the gurney. She settled and pulled out her cell, leaving Harper to mull over her recent pre-surgery discussion with Les.

He had reviewed possible complications—infection, seizures, blood clot on the brain—and no matter how many times she asked, he refused to guarantee no ventilator post op. A sense of foreboding tightened her throat, and she swallowed hard. Funny how fear brought a person's regrets into clear focus.

Had she really given Landon space? Or had her wounded pride made her resentful? At every turn, the tabloids taunted her with his rejection, and she had blamed him. When he had reached out, she had pushed him away. No wonder he'd so easily given up on coming to New York.

A raindrops ringtone interrupted her thought, and Juanita lifted her phone to her ear, smiling. "Hello...yep, she's right here."

Mamá had called earlier, and Harper's hopes soared that Landon waited on the line. Juanita's devilish smile all but confirmed it, and Harper resisted the urge to snatch the phone from her hand. She casually lifted the device to her ear. "Hello."

"Hi, baby. How're you doin'?" he murmured.

Concern filled his tone, and his baritone ran through her insides like thick warm honey. Wrapped in the comfort of his voice, she smiled ear to ear. "Okay. A little jittery, but not bad," she lied. "Where are you at?"

Knowing he was in Texas, she held her breath, anyway, hoping he would say he was in the hospital elevator. After taking an extra beat to respond, he sighed. "I'm supposed to be with you, holding your hand, but Mother Nature had other ideas. I'm snowed in north of Amarillo at Colt's place."

Hiding her disappointment from her sister, Harper turned to her side and tugged the sheet up over her shoulder. "You decided to come anyway?"

"I couldn't stay away. Almost made it, too."

"It snows in Texas?"

"Not often. I got lucky."

"I know I told you not to come, that this wasn't a big deal." She had so much to say to Landon. An apology hovered on her lips, but she needed to see him. "It means a lot to me that you tried."

His low chuckle filled the line. "I'm getting better at reading your bull-headed moments."

Two women in scrubs entered the room, and one with a floral bouffant hat and a clipboard approached the head of the gurney. "Are we ready to do this, Miss Inez?"

Cursing the interruption, Harper raised a finger, silently asking for a minute. "Landon, they're here for me."

"Okay, baby. You'll do great. As soon as you're awake enough to manage a phone, call me. I'll need to hear your voice."

CHAPTER NINETEEN

*L*andon jogged his horse up and down the back alley of the Thomas & Mack Center in Vegas, taking a few warm-up swings with his rope. He still didn't feel as one with Opie, not the way he had with Rocket. A horse and rider melded together over time, and there was no substitute for training your own mount.

However, he couldn't complain about their results. They had both done their part, slugging through a blur of rodeos and improving their times. He'd tuned Opie up for this rodeo, and his efforts on the road had paid off. He and Jenkins were tied up in the finals. Unbelievably, Landon had a shot at the title.

Still, the wins weren't as sweet as he'd remembered. Over the past several weeks, Landon had faked his way through a multitude of post-rodeo parties, checking his phone way too often for the infrequent, business-related texts from Luciana.

He'd had no idea what *a break* would be like, but he sure hadn't planned on the hollow feeling that invaded everything. After ten sleepless nights in a lonely Vegas hotel, he just wanted to go home—if only he could figure out where that was.

Reaching the pinnacle of his sport should have him pumped to the max. But ever since he'd missed the opportunity to see Luciana, backing into the box hadn't flooded his veins with adrenalin—and the wins were only a task completed. He lacked intensity. He had lost his focus.

Jenkins came around the bullpens aboard his black gelding and halted near the passageway into the arena. He coiled his rope and waved. "Hope you're bringin' your best tonight, Macek. Everything's on the line."

Landon jutted his chin in greeting, cueing his horse toward their competition. He parked the gelding head to tail alongside Jenkin's mount. "Opie's pulling his weight. I'll do the same."

He had a junk drawer full of trophy buckles back home, but he might actually wear a gold one stamped NFR. Especially if he sniped it from blow-hard Bart in the last go-round.

He gave a nod. "Good luck."

"Same to you." Jenkins shoved a thumb over his shoulder. "It's a full house out there."

Nearly twenty-thousand fans filled the Thomas & Mack coliseum from the rail-side seats up to the nosebleed sections. Clowns performed antics with a bull and a barrel between events, and beyond them, two women occupied seats at the arena rail—one wearing a glitzy gold turban. Though they were too far to make out their features for sure, Landon's heart soared. Luciana had come, he knew it, and she'd brought her sister.

The sneaky minx had texted him good luck but hadn't said a word about being in town. He smiled wide, even if he shouldn't be this excited over seeing a *business partner*.

Jenkins tracked Landon's line of sight. "What?"

Wanting to holler and wave like a little kid, Landon reined in his enthusiasm, hoping he appeared casual. "I see a couple friends out there, is all."

Jenkins scanned the sea of people, instantly honing in on Luciana. He must have spotted her earlier. "Oh, yeah. Your supermodel. Here, I reckoned you were a damn gelding—never messing with the fillies on the circuit." Finally pulling his gaze from her, he laughed. "You were only holding out for the good stuff."

Landon narrowed his eyes at his rodeo rival. "Careful, Jenkins."

"No offense, now. Imagine me, will ya? Feeling all sorry for you over losing Rocket with only three months left in the season." Jenkins gave a mock frown. "Next thing I know, I'm at the gas station grabbin' a burrito, and your face stares back at me from a magazine rack—with the hottest thing I've ever seen in a motorcycle helmet laying one on you."

Fuming inside, Landon tightened his fist around his rope. Having the whole world follow his love life rankled him, again. Worse, that included Bart Jenkins. Or maybe Landon was angry with himself for leaving her. And for what? Because she could buy a horse that he couldn't afford? A belt buckle? Even the gossip rags seemed a weak excuse.

"We're good friends—and she owns Opie," he added, realizing the most likely reason she had come to Vegas.

Luciana probably wanted to watch her investment pay off, not see the ex who needed privacy more than her loving. The couple of times she had called since her surgery, she'd seemed more herself, but she hadn't mentioned getting together—certainly not coming to Vegas.

"Friends? Dude. Your lie, tell it how you want. *Whipped* was written all over your face. At least you didn't leave empty-handed. Opie's a nice keepsake." Jenkins waggled his brows. "Since you're on the outs, you won't care if I try my luck, will you?"

Angry heat branded Landon's face, but Jenkins always tried to rattle the competition right before a ride. He'd struck a tender nerve this time, and Landon wanted to punch him. Recalling how easily Jenkins had gotten Dolly's phone number, Landon wrestled with his composure. "She's no buckle bunny like you're used to, but knock yourself out."

Jenkins ignored the jibe and laughed, apparently pleased he'd hit his target. "Relax, I'm only yanking your chain. I saw you're on deck first. Nice. I'll know right away how good I need to be."

Never happy to be in the leadoff spot, Landon growled. "My lucky day." Planting his hat on a little tighter, he wished he'd cut this short five minutes ago. The saddle broncs would move fast. "Speakin' of, I'd best get on over to the other side."

Jenkins built a loop with his rope and swung it once. "Oh, I'll be right behind you."

Ignoring Jenkins's subtle challenge, Landon's interest in their psychological warfare died out. What he really wanted to do was tie Opie to the nearest post and find a way into the stands.

The first bucking horse jumped out of the chute, which meant Landon was due in the box in about ten minutes. Cueing his mount to a jog, he circled around to the roping set up at the far end.

An alcove under the stadium opened to the arena, and he couldn't resist another glimpse of Luciana. Halting Opie, Landon stood up in his stirrups. Closer now, he could see her dark eyes and high cheekbones as she chatted with Juanita. If all went well, he'd tie his calf right in front of their seats. She could witness the return on her investment.

After the rodeo, he would find Luciana and put an end to this *break* tonight—if she still wanted him.

A man with mouse-brown hair descended the stairs and stopped to speak to her and Juanita. He seemed vaguely familiar, and Landon wondered where he might have seen him.

Luciana gave the guy a big smile, rising to join him, and then the pair climbed the stairs to the exit. After paying thousands for a premium box seat, she would miss his ride. Landon fought a stab of disappointment and nudged Opie to a brisk trot.

"Macek, you're up," a chute helper called out.

This was the ride of his career. Even in his funk, as he entered the box a surge of adrenalin hit, dimming the crowd noise and speeding up his heart. In a well-honed ritual, he gripped his piggin' string between his teeth and meticulously coiled his rope. He built a loop before backing Opie into the far corner of the starting box.

The gate clanged shut behind the calf, and the gateman waited for Landon's signal. He allowed his focus to slip long enough to check Luciana's section, hoping she'd returned.

Only about fifty feet away, Juanita's alarmed gaze collided with his, and her mouth dropped open. She leapt to her feet and bolted up a short flight of stairs two at a time.

Something was going down with Luciana. Every instinct Landon owned urged him to chase after Juanita. He even had the ludicrous fear that Ensign Wells had somehow defied death.

Before he could blink, Juanita raced back down the concrete aisle stairs, flagging an arm. "Landon!" Her terrified shriek echoed over the arena, and fans turned in their seats, tracking her path down to the rail. "He took her!"

Tossing his lariat aside, Landon spurred a startled Opie

through the string barrier and raced to the arena wall. He slid his mount to a stop, bringing him nearly face to face with Luciana's hysterical sister who gripped the railing.

The crowd murmured, and Landon ignored them. "Who?"

"I-I don't know. He said you wanted to talk to her. But then you—" Her words tumbled out on top of each other, and she waved an arm at the box. "She's *gone*. I called nine-one-one but..."

Landon reached up and gripped the top rail, pulling himself over, leaving Opie adrift in the arena. "Where's her bodyguard?"

He hit the cement aisle running, and with boots pounding the stairs, he raced up to the exit. Juanita followed on his heels.

"Ty couldn't come," she hollered at his back.

Fear quickened in his gut. He skidded to a stop in the main hall, frantically searching for any sign of Luciana.

Catching up and gasping for air, Juanita pointed down the corridor at a potted tree obscuring an emergency exit. "I didn't see that before."

As he jetted toward the door, panic threatened to close his throat. He hit the emergency bar at full speed, and a siren screamed. Outside, the parking lot's access lane was empty, and he feared a get-away vehicle had already whisked Luciana off. He slowed, searching the grounds.

Scuffling noises came from a section of tractor-trailer rigs. With new hope, he doubled his pace. The crisp outside wind took his hat, and footfalls too heavy to be Juanita's fell in behind him on the asphalt. Event security had joined the pursuit. Landon couldn't tell if the guards planned to help him or tackle him.

"Let me go!" Luciana's screams rang out over the quiet parking lot before something muffled her voice.

She was still here and alive. Relief washed through him.

The ruckus came from behind a parked big rig farther down the lane. Heart thudding in his chest, Landon raced towards it and rounded the tractor's front bumper.

An idling black minivan sat hidden on the other side of the eighteen-wheeler. The fit, middle-aged man from the stands held a rag over Luciana's face, fighting to push her through the van's open sliding door.

With only three car lengths left to reach her, she slumped limp in her attacker's arms. The kidnapper heaved her onto the floor of his vehicle with a thud. Horrified, Landon surged forward.

"Stop right there," he yelled, frantic to reach her.

"What did he do to her?" Juanita screamed behind Landon, running between the guards.

The goon leapt into the driver's seat, and Landon reached in to grab him. The bastard banged the door on Landon's arm and then again with more force. Pain shot up to his shoulder. The van jolted toward an empty expanse of parking lot, nearly shaking him loose. Desperate, he grappled for anything to hold, seizing the steering wheel.

The asphalt whizzed underneath him as he wedged a boot onto the floor's edge. Using sheer force of will, Landon hung on. One wrong move would send him under the wheels, and Luciana would be lost forever. He focused on the driver.

The careening van narrowly missed the two security guards who had cut across the lot, and one put a radio to his mouth. While the vehicle fishtailed, the sliding door rolled open and closed at Landon's back, and he feared Luciana would tumble out onto the road.

"You can't get away," he yelled, their noses a bare inch apart. "Give it up."

The thug released the steering wheel, and a gun material-ized in his hand. His breath came fast, smelling like garlic, and his glacial eyes held no emotion—insanity stared back at Landon.

"I think *you'll* give it up." The kidnapper's detached tone matched his cold gaze.

The fricking psycho would pull the trigger. Landon had to finish this, now.

He jerked the wheel, pulling the vehicle into a sharp inside turn. Centrifugal force sent the kidnapper falling sideways. The same gravitational pull catapulted Landon into the cab, and he landed between the driver and the steering wheel. A deafening report rang out, and searing heat burned his ribcage.

The van jumped a high curb, and the steering wheel crushed the wind from Landon's chest. Righting himself with Landon still wedged in front of him, the gunman hit the accelerator, and the engine roared. Earth thudded against the rear undercarriage.

With his gun hand sandwiched between Landon's ribs and his groin, the kidnapper wriggled his fingers. Avoiding the trigger or seeking it? No man fired a round that close to his male parts.

Landon had to risk it. If he didn't subdue the driver, he would never see Luciana again.

With the van rolling over bumpy ground, he dropped the full weight of his torso on the gun, and then jackhammered the goon with his elbow. He finally landed a lucky blow to the throat.

The man's steely eyes widened in eerie silence, and he clutched at his neck with both hands. Grotesquely mute, he worked his mouth, and ominous hiccup noises came from his throat. Terror filled his gaze, along with an unmistakable plea for help.

Mercy took time that Luciana didn't have.

After sideswiping a light pole, the van dropped and then rolled over a level surface. Landon lifted up and tossed the loose handgun to the floor before planting a boot on the kidnapper's hip. Giving a solid shove, he sent Luciana's attacker flailing out the swinging door.

Landon pulled himself upright behind the wheel, hitting the brakes, relieved to see open parking lot in front of him. Behind him, she jolted to her side and whimpered.

The sound of life was the most beautiful music he had ever heard. He rubbed a hand down his face, letting out a groan of relief.

Forgetting everything, he sidled between the seats back to the cargo area and dropped to his knees next to Luciana. Dim light from the parking lot illuminated her face, and the turban was gone. A freshly healed incision shaped like a horseshoe parted hair only a half-inch long on the side of her head.

Her lashes fanned her cheeks at half speed, and her eyes stared straight ahead. Recalling her tumble to the van floor sent terror to his heart. What if she had a concussion? Or even worse, had a bang to her head shoved that new plate into her brain?

"Look at me baby, please," he begged, heart pounding.

The door at his back rolled open, and Juanita's shadow fell across the floor.

"Is she alive?" she asked, her voice tremulous.

"Yes." Barely getting the word out, he hoped *alive* meant well.

Regret crashed through him, tightening his chest. He had thought his damned pride was so important. Money, body-guards, tabloid gossip—how could he have believed any of that mattered? His only reason for living lay on the floor in front of him. She blinked again.

Hope soared and a strangled noise came from his throat. He wanted to lift her and enfold her in his arms, but he didn't dare, fearing she'd taken a hit to the head. He leaned down and nuzzled her cheek. "Oh baby. We both have another chance at life. Let's do it together— Luciana, wake up for me, please."

Luciana groaned, and he cupped her face. "Open your eyes…." Adding a silent prayer, he cleared the gravel from his throat. "Can you hear me?"

Her starlit black gaze found him. "Yes. I heard you." A trembling smile shaped her lips. "Was I dreaming? Do you really want to try again?"

Ignoring the branding iron searing his ribcage, Landon buried his face in the hollow of her neck. "I love you," he murmured. "We'll do more than try. My word on it."

Luciana raised a hand to his face with tears glistening on her lashes. "I'll hold you to that, Mr. Macek."

Feeling whole again for the first time in weeks, he smiled and touched his forehead to hers. "I always keep my word, Miss Inez."

Quiet weeping behind him turned into hiccups of laughter from Juanita, who clutched the gold turban with both hands. "Way to go, cowboy. Way. To. Go."

Luciana slid her arms around his neck, and her parted lips invited his kiss. Uncaring of the audience, he took his time, savoring her taste. Pulling himself back took a considerable effort. "We need to get you someplace safe."

While he had ignored everything but Luciana, the lot had filled with cruisers, and strobed blue light pulsed over the entire area. Paramedics jogged toward them from an ambulance, and Landon waved them on. He and Juanita stepped out of the way. Barely. While they worked, she snapped out a report of Luciana's recent surgery, as if they might overlook the fresh incision on her head.

Near one of the cruisers, two guards held the cuffed kidnapper who was alive if not healthy. When he'd landed on the pavement and rolled to a stop like a ragdoll, Landon had thought he had killed him. He had a hard time caring one way or the other.

The ambulance crew placed Luciana on a heavy-duty gurney, and before they could raise the side rail, Landon leaned over her. She reached an arm around his waist and he leaned in for a brief kiss. Pulling from him, she raised a hand, squinting at her fingers in the poor light.

"What's…?" Blood coated her skin. "Landon, you're hurt!"

⚜

Harper couldn't let go of Landon's hand as he sat on the end of an emergency room gurney. A Doctor Tabbot cleaned the gunshot wound in his side and then showed Harper the bloody groove through Landon's muscle, explaining that the bullet hadn't entered the chest. Relief—or the sight of the ravaged red tissue— made her tighten her grip on the cart's side rail.

Tabbot applied a dressing and then smoothed the tape into place. "Mr. Macek, you were extremely lucky—a flesh wound. A couple inches to the inside, and that bullet might've ended you."

Landon grimaced. "Yeah, with this kind of luck, I'll steer clear of the craps tables."

They had been more than lucky. Unbelievably, she had dodged two assassination attempts—three counting the ventilator sabotage. This time, her brave cowboy had risked his life and allowed her to escape with only a couple bumps. Absently, Harper squeezed his hand.

Despite her earlier protests, Landon had stood there in his bloody shirt, refusing treatment until Dr. Tabbot examined her. After a cat scan and video consultation with a neurosurgeon, the ER doctor finally diagnosed Harper with a skinned elbow. She had drawn the line at staying overnight for observation.

"A Detective Sanchez is waiting with your sister." Dr. Tabbot removed his gloves and then washed his hands, speaking over his shoulder. "Are you ready to speak with him?"

Before she and Landon had gotten in the ambulance, the detective had taken Juanita to get her statement. Recalling the attack sent an unnatural chill through Harper. The gooseflesh traveling her arms was probably a natural reaction, though she wouldn't know. After the previous attempts on her life, she had been insensible for weeks and missed this part.

"Yes, we need to get this over with," she said.

Tabbot strode out of the exam room, and a minute later, Sanchez entered with Juanita at his side. The suited man with dark hair and a badge clipped to his belt stood a few inches shorter than Harper.

Juanita discreetly lifted her gold turban, and Harper shook her head. The disposable skullcap from the ER nurse hid her scalp stubble well enough. She had bigger priorities.

Sanchez carried a folder and flipped it open. "This won't take but a minute. Tomorrow, we'll do a formal line-up at the station."

He plucked a couple glossies from the file, and even though they were only photos, Harper's heart pounded in her chest. Landon slid off the exam table and curled an arm around her.

"It's hard, I know," Sanchez offered. "I promise that your assailant is locked up tight."

"I understand," she replied.

He held up two eight by ten photos. In the first image, officers on either side of the prisoner held him by the arms, and one gripped his jaw as if he had forced the man to face forward. Apparently, her attacker was camera shy. Sanchez slipped the other photo in front of her. The close up of the familiar dead eyes drained the blood from her head and her balance faltered.

Landon tightened his hold on her waist, exchanging a concerned look with Sanchez. "Baby, what is it?"

The detective studied her. "Miss Inez, do you know this man?"

Harper forced herself to stare at the suspect, and for a brief instant, a vision of the glass wall in her living room distracted her. Or rather, recall of the mirrored image on its shimmering surface. The stone-cold eyes in the reflection matched the ones in the photo. A shudder jolted through her. She refocused on the picture. "No. Yes. He tried to kidnap me."

"Miss Inez?" The detective's gaze bored into her, and then he cocked his head. "Have you seen him before?"

She pursed her lips, terrified by what her dreams meant. "Maybe."

"Okay, you seem uncertain. We'll come back to that." He inched in as though he feared missing a word. "Can you tell me what happened tonight?"

"Not all of it." Her shaky voice sounded childlike, and she leaned into Landon.

"Take your time. You're safe here," Sanchez said.

"At first, he was all friendly and nice. He didn't look like that." Speaking more to Landon, she pointed at the close-up, embarrassed by her poor judgment. "When he said that you'd asked to see me—I hoped that you—I was thrilled. I can't believe I was so naive."

Landon kissed her forehead. "When I saw you out there, I wanted to blast into the stands and hold you forever. But I had to get to the chutes."

Even though he recorded the interview, Sanchez listened with rapt attention, and when the personal moment passed, he nodded. "It's okay, Miss Inez. Anyone can be fooled by a con. Go on."

Bracing herself for the recall, she bit her lip. "When we got to the corridor, he said that Landon was outside, and my internal alarms went off—too late. I knew I was in deep trouble. I told him 'no' and tried to back away."

Events blurred together, and adrenalin pumped through her body. She hugged herself to hide her shaking hands.

"And?" Landon asked, low and gentle, giving her much-needed courage.

"He poked something into my side and said he'd shoot me. I didn't really see a gun. I almost didn't believe him. Maybe I should've screamed right away."

"You couldn't have known that. When you think a man has a gun, generally, you do what they say," Landon replied.

Relieved she had done something right; she took in a fortifying breath. "He walked me out an exit door, threatening to shoot me if I made noise. But when we got to the van, I *knew* it was a death sentence."

Juanita gasped, bringing a hand to her mouth. "*Never* go with your attacker."

"Exactly," Harper agreed. As teens, she and her sister had attended the same YWCA self-defense class. "Panic mode took over, and I kicked and screamed bloody murder."

Landon gave a hint of a smile. "I saw. You were magnificent."

His voice was rough, and she realized that he must have been terrified, too. "Since I'd gone quietly at first, I think I surprised him—or maybe he didn't *really* want to kill me—regardless, he didn't shoot me."

Sanchez jotted more notes on a pad. "You said you might've seen him before. Tell me about that."

She sought out Landon's gaze, he would understand. "Ensign had left for wine—*that* night. A while later I was standing at the window watching a young girl play with her dog at the park across the street.

"When the condo's elevator chimed, I thought it was Ensign with our wine. I didn't even turn around, but then—" A sob threatened and she covered her mouth, glancing at her kidnapper's photo. "That man was behind me. His reflection was in the window. Those dead eyes stared at me. He raised his arm and…"

Even as he held her tighter, graven lines carved Landon's face into a mask of rage. "You're sure?"

"One hundred percent." A new revelation crashed into her, and she gasped. "If he's the one who shot me, then how did Ensign get *his* gun?"

"I think I saw him at Ryder's walk-through." Landon glared at the criminal's image, honing in on his steely eyes. "Your kidnapper might actually be a hitman cleaning up loose ends. And if that's true, I doubt Ensign killed himself."

"Oh my god. He murdered him." The revelation took her breath, and she practically whispered. Landon's theory lined up with the facts, and it should have been obvious. "Of course."

The detective's brow furrowed. "Mr. Macek, you seem to know what all of this means."

"Yes sir. It means you need to contact Detective Roarke Hennessey at the NYPD. Tell him that you might have found his Florida ex-con. Name's Maddox?"

The detective's eyes widened. "Running a check now.

You're saying that this man was involved in Miss Inez's assault last spring?"

Landon glared at the photo. He'd never wanted to kill someone in his life—there was a first time for everything. "It's a pretty good bet."

Surprise lingered in the detective's expression. "Okay then. I'll get on the horn to Hennessey. We'll need a full statement first thing in the morning."

While her sister provided the detective with everyone's contact information, Harper dropped her head against Landon's shoulder. It was over. Again.

The detective offered an escort to her limo waiting in the parking lot. Three news vans parked on the perimeter, and one blocked the exit. An irritated hospital security guard directed the driver to move.

Glaring lights made it seem like daytime outside. The trio climbed into the back of the limo with Juanita taking the rear-facing seat. Landon closed the door, and Harper welcomed the quiet.

As their driver turned over the engine, Sanchez stepped away and spoke with an officer who handed him a large tote-style shopping bag and a very familiar cowboy hat. After a short exchange with the man, he raised a hand, signaling them to wait. Landon rolled down their window, and the noisy world intruded once more.

"Miss Inez, one more thing," Sanchez called.

When a detective said *one more thing*, something detonated. Harper stifled a groan. "Yes…"

With a couple quick strides, he closed the distance, and Landon opened the door.

"Thanks," he said as he accepted the hat and placed it on the seat next to him.

Sanchez handed the bag to Juanita. "A bystander retrieved

your purses. They're not evidence, so you're free to take them."

Nothing blew up. In a belated response, Harper offered a relieved smile. She hadn't given her belongings a thought. "Thank you, detective. We'll see you in the morning." She was seeing boogiemen everywhere. "Landon, let's get out of here. Please."

Landon closed the limo door. "Good idea."

CHAPTER TWENTY

*H*e pulled out his phone. "I gotta see what became of our prize roping horse. I sort of left him wandering in the arena."

Confused, she raised her brows. "What—"

Juanita straightened in her seat, pulling her attention from her phone. "You should've seen it, sis. He left his calf in the chute and jumped over the rail. The crowd's still wondering what possessed him."

Tension-breaking laughter filled the limo's interior. Even the driver joined in. Harper threaded her fingers with Landon's, incredulous over his sacrifice. "You left the rodeo to come after me?"

He tugged her closer and nuzzled her cheek. "I couldn't very well let some thug run off with my best girl, now could I?"

"But the world championship..." Harper could barely speak. "That's—I don't know what to say."

"There's always next year." His voice was hoarse. "Besides, sometimes dreams change."

"Well, we'll have to find another way for you to pay off

your debt." She leaned into his ear and whispered, "I can think of a few."

Desire flared in his gaze, and his dimples appeared. "I'd better get started right away. Don't want to ignore my obligations."

Harper rubbed noses with him—her cowboy with his rigid code and too much pride. This man would make the long haul, and she would do what she had to do to make it work.

Landon's phone chirped and he studied the incoming text before tapping in a reply. "Nice. Jenkins put Opie up after the go-round. But I still want to check on him."

"Poor Opie. I wish I had some carrots for him. We're only a few minutes away. We can swing by, easy," Harper said.

As the stretch navigated between the stables and livestock rigs, the few contestants on the grounds stopped and stared. Landon chuckled. "Not too many big limos find their way to the barns. Right here is fine."

The vehicle pulled up next to a side entrance on the long building, and he climbed out, waiving off the driver before he could leap out and open the door.

With their separation, inexplicable dread slammed into Harper. She couldn't tell if she feared more for herself or for Landon, but neither made sense. They had trapped the boogieman behind bars, and she should feel safe. Working through the logic didn't temper her irrational unease. It had to be adrenalin overload.

Seeming to sense her anxiety, Landon reached into the cabin for her hand. "Don't run off, now. If you're gone when I come back, my heart won't take it."

"I'll be here." She ignored his weak attempt at humor. Landon must be shaken up, too.

His smile dropped away. "Lock up. All I need to do is make sure he has feed and water."

After closing the limo door, he studied the area with a calculating intensity and then strode off at a crisp pace. The locks clicked of their own accord. Evidently, the driver agreed with him. Emotionally spent, Harper slumped back against the leather seat.

Juanita tracked Landon's path to the barn and then gave Harper a thumbs up. "He's a keeper, Luciana."

Resting her forearms on the window ledge, Harper gazed after him. "I think so."

Not only had he left his dream behind in the arena, he had risked his very life to save her. Had he been critically hurt or even killed… An involuntary shudder coursed through her body.

Juanita only used Harper's real name when she had the most important things to say. Mamá refused to use the name Harper even in public. Landon called her Luciana, and she loved when he said it.

The people who mattered used her given name, the name deemed too *ethnic* for the modeling agencies. Maybe she should, too.

After a few minutes, he returned to the car and climbed in next to her. "Jenkins left a note on Opie's stall door. He stowed my gear in his trailer, too. That guy's surprised me a few times."

Juanita snorted. "It's the least he could do after you handed him the championship."

Surprised that her sister had known anything about Landon's competition, Luciana arched a brow. "You followed things pretty close."

"*Me* following?" Her sister snorted. "It's all you've talked about for weeks."

With a smirk for Juanita, she refocused on Landon. "I'm so sorry you missed your go-round."

What could only be re-lived fear filled his gaze, and he

cleared his throat. "When I realized someone grabbed you, I found out real quick what mattered to me." Not breaking their connection, he lifted her fingers to his lips. "And her name's Luciana."

Recalling those horrifying seconds before she lost consciousness, she leaned in close to his ear. "When I fought him, I thought I'd never see you again—and I regretted all the time we've wasted apart. I'm sorry for pushing you away." Her voice cracked. "I felt rejected, and I think my pride got in the way of my heart."

Landon shifted to face her, his gaze full of concern. "Only because my bull-sized ego trampled you. When you gave me Opie, I panicked, all worried I couldn't measure up." He touched his forehead to hers. "I'm so sorry, baby. Forgive me?"

Throat tight and unable to speak, she nodded.

He tugged her in close and kissed the tender spot under her ear. "I gotta hold you until next year. That might not be long enough."

"All night." Finally, she held Landon in her arms. "I love you."

Absorbed in their reunion, Luciana had forgotten their lack of privacy. Juanita's faked indifference didn't fool her for a moment. Slumped over her phone on the opposite seat, she most assuredly strained to hear every word. Luciana caught her eye for an instant and imagined she saw approval there.

Her sister politely studied her cell, leaving Landon and Luciana to cuddle before they dropped her off at the Wyndham. As the women stood outside of the limo, Juanita gave Luciana a long hug. "I love you. Call me after you get to his hotel. Just cuz."

"I love you, too. For sure, I'll call. Just cuz." Luciana pulled back and gazed at her sister. "Starting this minute, I'm changing my life. Watch for a call from *Luciana*."

Juanita's eyes softened. "It's about damn time."

They hugged again before she strode through the hotel entry.

Luciana rejoined Landon in the limo and raised the privacy partition for the drive to the Do Stop Inn. The two minutes she had spent with her sister had been too long to be apart, and they snuggled together for the quiet ride.

❦

The next morning, lying in the motel's king-sized bed, Luciana rolled to the side and carefully draped an arm over Landon's hip, avoiding the tender wound over his ribs. She hadn't gone a minute during the night without touching him. Daylight creeped in across the blue carpet, and without really caring, she wondered what time it was.

He turned gingerly to face her and kissed her nose. "Good morning."

Tension in his jaw belied his discomfort, and she wished she could ease his pain. Light brought out the moss green in his eyes, and she caressed his face. "Good morning back at you. Would you like me to grab you a pain pill?"

He shook his head and then nuzzled her neck. "I don't want anything but you."

All during the night, they had made love tenderly and then snuggled, talking about their future, only to repeat. His face tensed with a grimace, though she suspected he tried to hide his discomfort. He was paying for their lovemaking.

"You're hurting. I can tell. We should have stuck to cuddling last night."

"Oh, hell no." Landon shook his head with a broad grin. "We *definitely* made the right call on that one."

With her guilt soothed, a giggle bubbled up. "If you say so."

The hotel phone rang a jarring note from the nightstand. Propping up on his elbow, Landon fumbled the receiver to his ear. "Hello." After a minute, he frowned. "Thanks for the heads up."

"Who was that?"

He dropped back onto the pillow and groaned. "The front desk. The clerk said a few journalists are camped in the lobby."

Luciana suspected the groan had nothing to do with his gunshot wound.

*L*andon's cell buzzed in his jeans pocket while he waited in the Martin's grocery checkout line.

Joni: Score another one! Stetson on board. Expect a delivery later this week.

Luciana's agent—and now Landon's— punctuated the text with a champagne bottle. After losing at the NFR, he would never have thought to hunt up representation, much less a publicist. However, the story behind his dramatic arena exit had captivated the public well beyond the rodeo world.

In a networking blitz, Joni had seized on the opportunity and provided Landon with a ready-made marketing team. Within days, she overnighted sponsorship contracts to sign. His new publicist had even given Opie and Rocket their own social media account.

Landon: All your hard work is paying off. Thank you and your team.

He grabbed the latest June issue of *The Scandal* from the impulse-buy rack and added it to his purchases. The Martin's clerk shook her head. "I always think it's weird when the person on the front page buys those."

"Me, too. Before I knew the people they wrote about, they were kind of fun. Now, they're part of the job."

As he exited the store, Jakob Spencer and his wife Willa strolled along the sidewalk. Both wore sweaters in the sunny but cool spring weather. Landon and Luciana had attended their small Super Bowl get together, and he had finally met Ryder's grandfather. The Spencer's business leader kept a tight rein on his corporation, but after getting to know him, the man had grown on Landon.

When the older couple saw him, they stopped to chat. He exchanged a handshake with Jakob, and Willa spread her arms for a hug.

"Hello, Landon." Holding him in place with a gentle hand on his arm, she cupped her mouth near his ear. "I'm dying to know if Nathaniel was able to help you with *you know what*."

The Spencer matriarch was an endearing sort, and Landon had fallen under her spell along with the rest of the town. "Like you promised, Mr. Reidel knows his stuff. In fact, I'm on my way to Denver right now.

With a young girl's enthusiasm for a secret, Willa crossed her heart. "Oh my, that's wonderful. I won't say a word."

Jakob beamed at his wife, and his affection shone in his eyes. "Nothing like a romance to get a woman all excited."

They said polite goodbyes, and after Landon got in his truck, he tracked their leisurely progress down the sidewalk. Holding hands, they didn't appear to have a destination, simply enjoying the sunshine.

The Spencers' obvious love for one another gave Landon a glimpse of a *'til death do us part* future. Years from now, Luciana's inner beauty would ensure he stayed every bit as hooked as Jakob. Landon couldn't help but wonder where their lives would lead, and his excitement over his trip to Denver grew.

A few hours later in an upscale Denver shopping district,

he put Fletcher's bodyguard instruction to good use, circling the block surrounding Reidel Creations. Landon scanned the area for anyone who appeared out of place before parking at the rear employee entrance as Mr. Reidel had advised.

Still not used to carrying a weapon, belated recall halted his exit from the vehicle. He grabbed a sports jacket he now kept in the cab and slipped it on, securing a single button to hide his holstered Smith & Wesson. A glimpse of the weapon might freak out the jeweler.

The more formal look with his jeans and hat had grown on Landon. The gun—not so much. Even a few months after his concealed carry course, he wasn't comfortable packing. But they had let their guard down once, and Luciana had nearly paid with her life. Never again.

He knocked on the service entrance, and an older bald man opened the metal door, greeting him with a smile. A white fringe of hair and matching mustache gave the jeweler an eccentric appearance, but his winning personality soon dispelled that first impression.

He waved Landon in with a flourish. "Come in, come in."

Landon followed him to a small showroom with enough space for a display case and a pair of upholstered chairs for clients. "It was right nice of you to make this visit so private."

Mr. Reidel gestured to a gray swivel chair. "It's nothing. Discretion's always important." While Landon took a seat, the older man unlocked an unseen compartment below the counter. He sat down and meticulously laid out a black velvet cloth before setting a deep red jewelry box on top of it. "Are you ready?"

Surprisingly nervous, Landon smiled and pulled his chair closer. "Yes sir."

The jeweler opened the box, and a radiant three-carat marquise diamond reflected shards of light. Smaller marquise stones, set at angles, flanked the center diamond on the platinum band and gave the piece an artistic quality Landon hadn't found anywhere else. The engagement ring was stunning, and his lips parted in awe.

Obviously amused by Landon's reaction, the quirky businessman's smile widened. "You made an excellent choice going with the flawless gem rather than a lesser quality five carat." Nathanial gestured to the ring. "Anything larger than this might overwhelm your lady's fine-boned hand."

Landon held the diamond ring next to his thicker finger and had to agree. "It's even prettier than your mock-up. Thank you."

He laid the ring on the velvet, trying to imagine Luciana's reaction.

Mr. Reidel reached below the counter and then placed a similarly sized loose diamond on the velvet next to the ring. "This is the clarity you'd have gotten with the larger stone." He rotated the gemstones under the fluorescents. "There is no substitute for a flawless diamond's fire."

The ring's reflected starlight made the loose stone appear yellow. "Wow. That is a difference."

The jeweler picked up the ring, holding it out between them. "Now, this is an original piece that any woman in Hollywood would be proud to wear. Over the years, Reidel jewelry *has* been worn on the red carpet."

Wondering when Joni might hear back on Luciana's debut big-screen project, Landon ran a fingertip over the facets. The story about a woman surviving the aftermath of Argentine slavery was made for her.

"Who knows? Maybe this one will, too," he replied.

The jeweler gave a wry smile. "Willa mentioned there was a possibility."

Landon gave a good-natured snort. "So *that's* how I got the friends and family discount."

A suppressed grin twitched a corner of Riedel's mustache, but he didn't comment.

After Landon viewed the flawless stone under a microscope, the jeweler took a documentation photograph. He rose from his rolling stool behind the counter. "I'll be back in a minute or two."

Luciana would wear this ring forever—that was Landon's plan.

Even with his endorsements, his portfolio would never be in her league. However, an engagement ring was special. He had paid off Opie with his winnings and his sponsorship income now sat in a tiny red velvet box. A ring she could wear with pride in her world had been imperative. He had no regrets.

A sliver of doubt intruded, churning his gut. He quelled the negative thoughts. Luciana would say yes. If she didn't, he would wait until she did.

A few minutes later, Mr. Reidel returned with an envelope of paperwork and a black gift bag stuffed with gold tissue and sparkles. "My best wishes to you both. If this is not absolutely perfect, you bring it right back."

While carrying the small bag back to his Ram, Landon surveyed the lot for anyone out of place. He half-regretted not asking one of the Lodge bodyguards to come with him. On the other hand, maybe he should have driven an armored truck. He climbed in and within minutes, he cruised the highway toward Spencer, hoping his new life with Luciana would begin this evening.

❦

Carrying a chilled bottle of champagne recommended by Chef Wilson, Landon mounted the wooden steps to Luciana's cozy Twin Owl Lake bungalow. The setting sun peeked through a stand of Aspens fronting the property, leaving the buff-colored cottage and covered front porch in shadow. Maybe later, they would snuggle under a blanket on the fan-backed porch swing.

The day after she had moved in, she'd snagged the hand-made piece in Old Towne and then searched the internet for hours to find the perfect coordinating pillows. Admitting that the porch swing with its buttoned cushions made a person want to sit a spell, he punched the security code into a keypad next to the cardinal-red entry door. The swing was a favorite cuddling spot—and might be a good place to pop the question.

A text buzzed at his hip.

Luciana: I'm in the hot tub. Come on in.

Erotic images scrolled through his head, dropping heat to his groin. Hooking the Reidel bag on a finger, he tucked the champagne into a football hold to type his response.

Landon: Please tell me you're naked.

Luciana: LOL sorry. Nope, not naked.

Damn. On the bright side, while she lounged in the hot tub, he could walk right in without hiding the gift bag.

Landon: In that case, I'll be a minute.

After he tapped the access code into the security panel, the lock released and he shouldered the door open. In the small foyer, he toed off his boots, pushing them to the corner of the parquet floor. He peered inside the gift bag for the tenth time. The ring sat in a deep red, flower-shaped bow, and he ran a finger over the stone. Simply touching the engagement ring sent his heart racing.

Trying to relax, he stowed his hat and holstered gun on the shelf inside the entry closet before padding to the bedroom. He set the bag down on the bed, gently laying the champagne next to it. Jostling a hundred-dollar bottle of bubbly was not a good idea.

He and Luciana didn't officially live together. However, Landon had claimed a small section of the walk-in closet as well as a couple drawers in a highboy chest. He changed into his swimsuit before heading to the kitchen where the sound of the whirring jets made him eager to join her.

Through the window above the sink, gas torches atop bamboo-like posts glowed around the patio. Barstools and a built-in counter edged the spa, and only a corner of the hot tub was visible, but he caught a glimpse of her arm stretched out on the edge.

After locating wineglasses, he struggled to tie the flower ribbon to a crystal stem. His trembling fingers simply refused to cooperate. Taking a cleansing breath, he tried for calm. She *would* say yes.

Finally, the ruby flower with a diamond center sat securely on the foot of the wine glass. Pleased with himself—and relieved—he popped the cork on the champagne.

The sun had dipped below the tree line, so if he carried the glasses carefully, he could likely get them to the hot tub without her seeing the ring. He braced himself for the sixty-degree evening chill and pushed open the back door. A tantalizing view halted him at the top of the stairs.

Raising a smoky gaze from her seat in the deep steaming water, Luciana's pouty lips formed a lusty bow. She rose from the pool, exposing her glistening upper body. Multiple strands of tiny light-colored pebbles draped from her neck, framing the smooth bronze of her cleavage before disappearing into the churning froth.

Landon had seen the twisted rope of necklaces before and his breath caught. "Lord have mercy."

Before he had finished the whispered prayer, she dropped below the water and then rose slowly with her short hair slicked back. Shimmering rivulets slid down her lithe body in the firelight. Landon wanted to follow the water's path with his tongue and taste each droplet one by one. She twirled a single strand of wet stones around a finger, and the sultry look in her black eyes nearly dropped him to his knees.

Thin red straps on her shoulders peeked through the beads, and matching strings rode high on her hips, criss-crossing up her slender waist to hold two small red triangles taut over her plump breasts. Underwater lighting gave him a glimpse of a third scrap of red at the apex of her thighs.

Practically shaking with desire, Landon dropped his arms slack at his sides and nearly lost his grip on the champagne. "Is *that* what I think it is?"

His voice tumbled with gravel, and the little minx had to know she owned him. Her eyes lit with an enticing call, and she bit her lower lip. "Do you like it?"

"*Oh, yeah.* But I swear, if you wear that in public, I might not recover."

She giggled. "I think the *public* has already seen it."

Landon's sexual fantasy had come to life right before his eyes—and like everything else about Luciana—she made the reality a thousand times better.

He could hardly croak out words. "*Oh, no they haven't.* Not like this."

❧

Thrilled with her successful seduction ploy, Luciana allowed herself a leisurely perusal of Landon, traveling from his eyes down his body and back. The patio torches cast shadows over the ridged muscle of his bare torso, and a puckered ridge of scar high on his right side gave a poignant reminder of his love. He had even turned himself into a bodyguard of sorts—for her. The hard-loving cowboy with his deep ethical code was a keeper.

Landon had given her real hope for a future. Their new home base in Spencer kept their private life mostly private, and with some creative adjustments, they had coordinated their careers. He and Rocket were back on the circuit, and Joni had landed her the perfect movie about a woman overcoming domestic hardships.

Luciana had a simple long-term plan. No matter where her callings led, the man in front of her would be first in her life.

Landon's close-cropped dark hair blending into his beard growth spoke to a hard-wired feminine part deep inside. When he reached for a towel, his thick biceps flexed, warming her in all the right places. He was straight-up hot.

She tracked the light dusting of hair down his torso until it disappeared into his swim trunks. The pattern emphasized the V-shape of his broad shoulders and narrow hips. Manscaped gym rats didn't have anything on a guy who wrestled calves for a living. His hazel gaze smoldered in the flickering firelight.

Wineglasses dangled upside down from Landon's loose fingers, and worry that he might let them crash onto the patio cooled Luciana's heated response. "Baby, are you going to drop those?"

He darted a glance at the stemware and smiled. "Oh, yeah. Thanks."

Descending the few steps, he held his arm stiff at his side as though hiding something. He set the glasses and a bottle of champagne on the teak bar and then quickly placed a towel beside them. The awkward movements made him look nervous.

Maybe resurrecting the SI bikini pin-up shot had been a bad idea. He had instantly recognized the wardrobe and liked it. She hadn't missed that. However, the reminder that she had posed close to naked may have pushed a button.

"Does the bikini bother you?" she asked, truly concerned.

Landon sat on the edge and slid into the bubbling water. As he neared her, heat filled his gaze. Gathering her in his arms, he kissed her long and slow. When their lips parted, only a hair's breadth separated them, and she savored a taste of sparkling fruity goodness. He had sampled the champagne.

"Oh, yeah. It bothers me." He traced a fingertip down a shoulder spaghetti strap. "I *love* the bikini."

She wrapped her arms around his neck and nipped at his fleshy lower lip, allowing their breath to mingle. "But don't wear it anywhere?"

Landon gripped her rump with both hands, pulling her into his body. "Not without duct tape holding it in place."

Her smile brushed his lips. "Duct tape. Check."

Pressing her against the smooth fiberglass wall, he lifted a strand of pebbles between them. "I'm going to peel this bikini off of you one string at a time."

Loving how he sparked her anticipation with a preview, she chuckled low in her throat. "Now let's not rush this. Do I see champagne?"

"Definitely not rushing." He kissed her again and reached over to fill the glasses with golden bubbly. Handing her one, he gave her a dimpled smile and raised his glass. "A toast, to the love of my life."

Glowing inside, she put all the love she could in her gaze and clinked the rim of her crystal to his. "I love you, too."

The bubbles tickled her nose, and she detected the familiar fruity note from their kiss before taking a small sample. "Very nice. We need to put this on our list."

In a clumsy grip more suited to a beer can, Landon held his wineglass by the stem's base, and his trembling pinky surprised her. Surely, the bikini hadn't rattled him that much.

As she thought to take another sip, he cleared his throat and traded glasses with her. Confused, she met his gaze and affection had replaced the heat.

Cupping her face, Landon's eyes welled with tenderness. "You've made me the luckiest man on earth."

"We've made each other lucky." Below her fingers, sparkles of light blossomed from the middle of a silk flower secured to the bottom of the glass. After a beat, she realized a *ring* was nestled in the bow— a marquise cut—her favorite. She cradled the goblet in front of her with unsteady hands. "Oh…oh."

As she tore her attention from the diamond, his loving gaze captured her. An uncertain curve of his lips belied his anxiety.

"Luciana, will you stay with me until the rodeos are over and all the movies are made?"

Unable to speak, tears welled in her eyes, and she nodded.

With the half-smile that she loved, he leaned in and kissed her gently on the cheek. He pressed his lips to her ear. "And years from now, after the fans have forgotten our names— and our children are grown—will you hold my hand for a walk in the park just to enjoy the sunshine?"

Imagining a future of loving this beautiful man filled Luciana with blissful expectation. *Joy.* "Yes. Yes. A thousand times, yes."

As though stunned by her response, Landon hesitated. Then a broad smile lit his eyes. "The luckiest man in the world—just got luckier."

He slanted his mouth over hers in a swoon-worthy kiss, and Luciana melted into his arms, boneless. Her best years lay ahead of her with Landon.

"Now, about those strings…" he murmured.

RODEO AND EQUINE TERMINOLOGY

For a comprehensive glossary of rodeo terms, check the Professional Rodeo Cowboy Association's rodeo terminology page at https://www.prorodeo.com/prorodeo/rodeo/rodeo-terminology

Appy: Slang term for an appaloosa horse. Appaloosas have a pattern of small spots, most often displayed on a section of white coat over their rump.

Barrier: A vertical plane at the front of the box marked by a string and flag. A contestant and his horse may not cross this plane until the steer or calf has the designated head start.

Box: Essentially, this is a horse and rider's starting block in timed events. A contestant backs his/her horse into a three-sided box for tie-down roping, steer wrestling, or team roping. The open side is the entry to the arena. Alternate: A spacious, square stall is known as a box stall.

Breaking the barrier: Refers to a penalty in the timed events. If a rider fails to give a calf or steer the allowable head start and leaves the box too soon (breaking the barrier), the contestant is assessed a 10-second penalty.

Bridle path: A clipped area of mane behind a horse's ears that allows the bridle to lay flush with the horse's head.

Bullfighter: Commonly called rodeo clowns due to their clown costumes, they are much more. After a bull rider dismounts, or the bull bucks him off, these athletes protect the cowboys. The bullfighters distract the dangerous bulls and encourage them towards the exit gate, often placing themselves between the bull and a vulnerable bull rider.

Calf roper: A tie-down roper.

Cantle: The raised, curved section at the rear of a saddle that helps hold the rider in place.

Chute: A pen that holds an animal safely in position

Flying lead change: When a loping or galloping horse changes his lead from one side to the other while in motion, this is known as a flying lead change or flying change of leads.

Gelding: A castrated male horse. Most male horses are castrated while young to make them safer to manage; both for their human handlers and other horses.

Go-round: Rodeos often have more than one round of competition. Each rotation through the competitors is called a go-round. All contestants participate in each go-round. Semi-finals and finals include only qualifying contestants.

Header/Heeler: The two partners in team roping. A header throws the first rope to catch a steer by the head or horns, and a heeler throws a second rope to catch the steer's hind legs. Securing only one leg results in a five-second penalty.

Hooey: The knot that a cowboy uses to finish tying any three of a calf's legs together in tie-down roping.

Lead: When a horse lopes, canters, or gallops, legs on one side of its body, or the other, strike the ground first and farther ahead of the other side. This is known as a left or right lead.

Nodding: A contestant's signal to a gateman to release stock—either to open the gate for bucking stock to begin a ride, or to a gateman to release a steer or calf to be roped.

Penalty: Refers to penalties in timed events. Common penalties include 10 seconds for breaking the barrier or 5 seconds for a one-hind-leg catch in team roping.

Piggin' string: In tie-down roping, the small rope used to tie a calf's legs together.

Pigtail: A piece of string attached to the barrier in a timed event. If a contestant's horse exits the box too soon, the pigtail will break, resulting in a penalty.

Rank: An adjective of praise and respect used to describe especially challenging roughstock. I.e.: A rank bull.

Rope: In general, rodeo athletes do not use the terms lasso, lariat, or riata.

Roughstock: The bucking horses and bulls used in bareback riding, saddle bronc riding, and bull riding.

Slack: Rodeos might choose to schedule excess entries into a preliminary competition known as the slack. This extra competition is usually held before the rodeo opens to the public.

Standings: Ranking of professional cowboys. Their rank is determined by earnings.

Sweat scraper: An angled tool, usually made of aluminum, used to squeegee excess water from a horse after a bath. Seldom used for sweat.

Timed events: Steer wrestling, team roping, tie-down roping, and steer roping – events in which the contestant(s) who make the fastest qualified runs win.

Thank you for reading. Telling stories is one of our greatest delights and we hope you enjoyed your time in Spencer. Readers like you spark the energy needed to tell these tales.

These Aspen Gold books are independently published by the authors. We thank you for your support, and we take pride in giving you quality books and excellent stories. We're thankful you've chosen to follow us and be part of the AG community.

Again, thank you.

With today's world of vast reading choices, word of mouth is the best advertising. So please let others know about this book. Tell your friends, relatives, acquaintances, the book reading stranger on the bus. By sharing a good book, you may discover a new friend.

Reviews help readers discover and connect with new authors. Every review is important to us and is greatly appreciated. Please consider leaving an honest review of this book at your favorite review sites or at any or all of these places.

Goodreads
Bookbub

NEXT IN THE SERIES

Another Night Alone Aspen Gold Series 15
(Protective Hero Romantic Suspense Small Town Older Man)
~Bernadette Jones

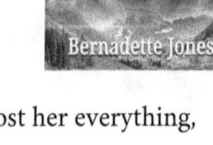

She'd had the courage to save her child. Can she do the same for herself?

Avie Hall's dreams of a better future for herself and her daughter are shattered when the shadows of their past threaten their new life. With their dreams of a second chance on the line once again, Avie knows giving in will cost her everything, but is she strong enough to fight back?

She is the light to his dark....

Deke Ward has witnessed true evil in his life. When he finds the goodness in Avie and her young daughter, he'll do anything to protect them. Their hope starts to heal his lonely heart, and when the evil shadows of their past return to haunt them, he'll go to hell and back to save them.

Even if it means letting them go.

THE ASPEN GOLD SERIES

Once upon a time a group of writer friends got the grandiose idea to create a continuity series. We threw ourselves into developing characters, fashioning families, dynamics and a setting, which evolved from one member's love of all things Colorado. We created character profiles, detailed maps, brainstormed titles and themes. We collected photos and researched. We proposed our idea to a few publishers and got no traction. So, after a time the contracted books came first, members came and went, and the project was set aside.

Years after the initial idea, we rallied again to write the stories, now hoping readers will feel the same intensity and appreciation for this project as we do. We welcome you to join these families, laugh in their good times and cry in their sad times, follow them as they solve mysteries, expose secrets, recover from their pasts, reach for their goals and, most importantly, as the residents of Spencer Colorado fall in love.

Want to know more about Spencer, Colorado, and the Aspen Gold Series? Sign up for our email messages which include the monthly *Rocky Mountain Rumors*, new book announcements, and fun surprises. Your email is safe with us, will never be shared, and you can, of course, unsubscribe at any time. You can find the link on the Aspen Gold Series website www.aspengoldseries.com

Be sure to follow all the Aspen Gold Series updates at:
Aspen Gold: The Series Website
https://www.aspengoldseries.com/

Aspen Gold Twitter
https://twitter.com/@gold_aspen

Aspen Gold: The Series on Facebook
https://www.facebook.com/AspenGoldSeries/

Rocky Mountain Rumors, the newsletter
https://www.subscribepage.com/n9n7p3

The Aspen Gold Authors

THE ASPEN GOLD BOOKS

Dancing In The Dark Aspen Gold Series 1
(Second Chance Small Town Family Saga Romance)
Cheryl St.John
He had everything a man could want--except her forgiveness...

~

Call Me Mandy Aspen Gold Series 2
(Second Chance Small Town Romance)
Debra Hines
The last man she loved took everything from her...

~

Ryder's Heart Aspen Gold Series 3
(Homecoming Forced Proximity Psychic Small Town
Romance)
*lizzie starr
She can't allow secrets to steal love from her...

~

For Keeps Aspen Gold Series 4
(Secret Baby First Love Family Saga Small Town)
Barbara Gwen & *lizzie starr
Hiding the truth is like denying the sun...

~

Second Chances Aspen Gold Series 5
(Second Chance Small Town Single Mom Romance)
Donna Kaye
She tried the fairy tale and the fairy tale didn't work...

~

Sleepin' Alone Aspen Gold Series 6
(Protective Hero Romantic Suspense Small Town Enemies to
Lovers)
Bernadette Jones
Every man is guilty of the good he did not do...

~

Stay A Little Longer Aspen Gold Series 7
(Protective Hero Romantic Suspense Small Town Second
Chance)
Bernadette Jones
Death wasn't frightening. Living scared the hell out of him...

~

Speechless Aspen Gold Series 8
(Small Town Wedding Romance Short Story)
*lizzie starr
How many peonies does it take to get married?

~

Close to the Heart Aspen Gold Series 9
(Friends to Lovers Small Town Seasoned Romance)
Debra Hines
He'd raised her child as his own...

~

Finding Hope Aspen Gold Series 10
(Cowboy Former Military Small Town Romance)
Donna Kaye
Is the peace he's found too good to be true?

~

Fortunate Cookie Aspen Gold Series 11
(Friends to Lovers Small Town Bakery Romance)
*lizzie starr
This woman... wearing frosting... and nothing else...

~

Lonely Eyes Aspen Gold Series 12
(Protective Hero Romantic Suspense Small Town Forced
Proximity Age Gap)
Bernadette Jones
She'd come to the right place. He was the monster hunter.

~

Whisper My Name Aspen Gold Series 13
(Secret Identity Small Town Sheriff Next Door Romance)
Cheryl St.John
She was the girl behind the headlines

~

Gorgeous Scars Aspen Gold Series 14
(Contemporary Romantic Suspense Rodeo Cowboy Heroine
in Peril)
M.A. Jewell
The rodeo never prepared this cowboy for bodyguard duty.

~

Another Night Alone Aspen Gold Series 15
(Protective Hero Romantic Suspense Small Town
Older Man)
Bernadette Jones
*She'd had the courage to save her child. Can she do the same for
herself?*

~

Yesterday's Promise Aspen Gold Series 16
(Anthology Short Stories Romance Collection)
Romantic short stories from the Aspen Gold Authors

~

Maybe I'm the One Aspen Gold Series 17
(Friends to Lovers Second Chance Small Town Deputy
Romance)
Cheryl St.John
While adored by millions, her world has become very small

~

Just My Imagination Aspen Gold Series 18
(Friends to lovers Forced Proximity Family Saga Fantasy
Romance)
*lizzie starr
Will his magic heal her reality?

~

A Better Man Aspen Gold Series 19
(Protective Hero Romantic Suspense Forced Proximity
Bounty Hunter)
Bernadette Jones
*Loving her made him a better man. Can he keep her alive long
enough to tell her?*

~

I Sorta Do Aspen Gold Series 20
(Fake Relationship, Single Dad, Small Town Romance)
Cheryl St.John
Her heart is under lock and key...his knock is irresistible

~

Trust Me Aspen Gold Series 21
Donna Kaye

~

Anything For Love
*lizzie starr

~

Serendipity
Debra Hines
*She didn't realize her happiness was on hold...until a chance
encounter*

~

Right Here Waiting
Bernadette Jones

~

Christmas Promise
Aspen Gold Short Story Anthology

M.A. JEWELL'S ASPEN GOLD BOOKS

Gorgeous Scars Aspen Gold Series 14
   (Contemporary Romantic Suspense
Rodeo Cowboy Heroine in Peril)

*The rodeo never prepared this cowboy for
bodyguard duty.*

Supermodel Harper Inez has it all—
until a bullet to the brain steals her old
life. Worse, the NYPD's top suspect is
her fiancé, and she doesn't dare to trust
a soul. Hiding from the world, she flees to an exclusive
mountain resort located near an equine-assisted therapy
facility. When an engaging cowboy invites her to lunch, she
surprises herself by accepting.

   Professional tie-down roper Landon Macek's horse is
injured, and his dream of a world championship is put on
hold. While his mount recuperates, he takes a temp job
training therapy horses. As a longtime Harper Inez fan, he's
followed her shooting in the news and is stunned to recog-

nize their mysterious VIP patient traveling under heavy security.

Enchanted by the surprisingly kind and vulnerable woman, he can't help but fall in love, patiently waiting until she catches up to the idea. However, it becomes clear that her celebrity lifestyle collides with his modest rodeo roots. Landon would give his life for Harper, but does he love her enough to live in her world?

❦

The Card Game is a short story included in: **Yesterday's Promise** Aspen Gold Series Book 16

A high-stakes poker game, first meets, a dog rescue, loves lost and rekindled, and life-altering choices fill the history of Spencer, Colorado. Discover the challenges faced in these heartwarming stories crafted by the multi-author group who brings you romantic fiction at its finest in The Aspen Gold Series.

This collection includes:
The Card Game~~ M.A.Jewell
Some Days Are Diamonds~~ *lizzie starr
Ah, Venice ~~ Debra Hines
First Chance ~~ Donna Kaye
Racing Hearts~~ Bernadette Jones
Rescue Me ~~ Cheryl St.John

ALSO BY M.A. JEWELL

Jungle Rapture The Jaguar Queens 1

An advocate for endangered species, Kelsi Gorman travels to the Brazilian Amazon to investigate rumors of a mysterious black jaguar the size of a saber-toothed tiger. Instead, the enormous cat finds her knee-deep in mud, blood, and smugglers.

Jaime Salazar, one of a few surviving all-male jaguar shifters, encounters a scent he'd never thought to find–female jag shifter. Jag queens exist only in the elders' stories, but someone's staked out a she-cat like poacher bait.

In a fit of primal instinct, Jaime marks Kelsi as his mate. Now, no other female will arouse him. To avoid a long celibate life, he is forced to woo his reluctant mate to be. But first, he must keep her alive.

Jungle Salvation Jaguar Queens 2

Well-meaning friends drag archaic jaguar shifter Matteo D'Cruz back into the human world. Almost trapped in cat form, the recalcitrant male narrowly dodges execution as a feral. Even so, his final end doesn't concern him overmuch—until he meets the thrill-seeking Dakota Gorman, a latent shifter female.

Matteo helps trigger her first trans-formation into a magnificent jaguar, and in turn, she schools him on the twenty-first-century woman. Hopeful for the first time in decades, Matteo embraces a possible future with the formidable jaguar queen. Tragically, their intimacy nearly forces him back into cat form, which would put him on death row.

Unwilling to selfishly ask Dakota to wait for him, a desolate Matteo resigns himself to torture and watching her mate another. Instead, in a vicious plot to weaponize shifter DNA, a rogue military faction snatches her, carving Matteo's heart from his chest. He will bring her home—but at what cost?

Autumn Renewal

Devastated by her cheating fiancé, operating room nurse Poochie Thibodeaux returns to her not-so-well-loved hometown and runs headlong into her high-school flame. Guarding her soul against new wounds, she resists his seductive charm—with limited success.

Horse trainer Jack Holland, Jr. wagers all—his business and his heart—for a second chance with Poochie, the woman he never got over. Just when he hopes for their future, a friend's treachery costs him his livelihood and, worse, makes him a prime suspect in a criminal investigation.

Only faith in each other will overcome loss and betrayal. Will it be enough?

ABOUT THE AUTHOR

M.A. Jewell started adulting as an oper-
ating room nurse. An avid reader for
many years, she traded in her reading
addiction for a pen to write in her
favorite genre, romance. Now, she can't
stop.

Recently transplanted to Dallas,
Texas, she enjoys her own happily ever
after with her biggest fan and supporter, her husband, Jim.
Their two sons have fledged and married lovely, competent
women. And if you have an extra twenty minutes, go ahead
and ask about her three perfect grandchildren.

Visit her website
https://www.majewell.com/

Sign up for her Precious Gems Newsletter
https://www.majewell.com/talk-to-me

facebook.com/MA-Jewell-120409722014412
twitter.com/MAJewell_author
instagram.com/melodyjewell11
amazon.com/M-A-Jewell/e/B071RN7J45
bookbub.com/authors/m-a-jewell